EMERGE 25

About the Writer's Studio

The Writer's Studio is an award-winning creative writing program at Simon Fraser University that provides writers with mentorship, instruction, and hands-on book publishing experience. Over the course of a year, students work alongside a community of writers with a mentor, developing their writing through regular manuscript workshops, guest lectures and readings. Many of the program's alumni have become successful authors, and have gone on to careers in the publishing industry. For many, the Writer's Studio's annual anthology, *emerge*, was their first publication credit.

The Writer's Studio Mentors

Claudia Casper – *Literary and Speculative Fiction*
Junie Désil – *Poetry and Lyric Prose*
Leanne Dunic – *Fiction and Hybrid Forms*
Stella Harvey – *Fiction and Personal Narrative*
Nazanine Hozar – *Fiction*
JJ Lee – *Narrative Non-Fiction*
Roz Nay – *Commercial Fiction*
Brian Payton – *Fiction and Narrative Non-Fiction*
Kevin Spenst – *Poetry and Lyric Prose*

Program Facilitators: Janet Homeniuk, Abby Pelaez, and Emily Stringer

emerge 25

THE WRITER'S STUDIO ANTHOLOGY

EDITORS
Laura Fukumoto
Dayna Mahannah
Leah Ranada
KT Wagner

FOREWORD
Andrew Chesham

CREATIVE WRITING
AT SFU CONTINUING STUDIES

SFU

TIDEWATER
PRESS

Published by Tidewater Press
New Westminster, BC, Canada
tidewaterpress.ca

ISSN 1925-8267
ISBN 978-1-990160-58-5 (print)
ISBN 978-1-990160-59-2 (e-book)

MANAGING EDITOR
Emily Stringer

PRODUCTION COORDINATOR
Laura Farina

"How to emerge" is a collaborative poem with lines submitted by students, alumni, and friends of our writing community, shaped by Laura Farina.

CATALOGUING IN PUBLICATION RECORD AVAILABLE FROM
LIBRARY AND ARCHIVES CANADA

Canada

Tidewater Press gratefully acknowledges the support of the
Government of Canada.

within this body an ocean of words
    keening
leaning
    pressing on my heart

—Jonína Kirton

Table of Contents

FICTION

POETRY

ANDREW CHESHAM
Director, The Writer's Studio

Foreword

The preface to *emerge 2002* contained the following line: "With this second volume, I think it's fair to call *emerge: The Writer's Studio Anthology* an annual publication."

Coming in at under 100 pages, that slim volume presented the work of seventeen writers, and it was the start of our program's yearly tradition of sharing the student's work with the world. Over these past 25 years, *emerge* has published the stories, poems, essays, and personal narratives of hundreds of students. At its thickest, *emerge* would be over 400 pages, and home to 85 writers, with submissions from students working across eleven mentors.

The Writer's Studio is many things. It's a place to learn: in workshops, classes and our year-long mentorship program. It's a place where writers share stories, poems, essays to audiences at our readings, and other literary events.

The Writer's Studio is also a community.

It's a community where students connect with peers and form lifelong friendships. It's a place where writers share their work and support each other's writing. It's a place where we commiserate over shared challenges and applaud each other's triumphs. It's where we see the good in each other and the value in our work.

When Betsy Warland founded the program in 2001, she wanted an approach based on "learning in community," a space where writers could learn and grow together, to build trust and support each other's work. It informs our approach as administrators and instructors, and it has resulted in a Canada-wide network of *TWSers* (our internal nomenclature for "writers from the Studio").

TWSers are everywhere and, as Betsy said in an essay on proximity that she wrote for the anthology, *Resonance: essays on the craft and life of writing*, their books "have significantly enriched Canadian literature."

Indeed, they have. Our alumni have gone on to publish novels, memoirs, biographies, poems, essays, short stories, and many other narratives. They've won and have been short-listed for national and local awards, and they have become positive, supportive members of literary organizations. They've become good literary citizens who are willing to *be in* community and support those around them, which is how we've approached this foreword. To celebrate our twenty-fifth anthology, we reached out to a small sampling of alumni from across the years and asked them to share their thoughts, experiences and advice.

We're borrowing the format of *The Secret Miracle,* by Daniel Alarcón, where he invited writers to discuss how they write and shared their direct answers. We're presenting five alumni, each answering five questions, as a way to present twenty-five answers on these TWSers' experiences in the program, publishing in *emerge* and how that experience influenced their writing lives afterward, with a final bit of advice for the writers in this year's anthology.

A few notes that will add context to some of the answers. Betsy Warland founded the program, but was also a mentor in multiple genres for many years. Wayde Compton was the program's second director, and was also a mentor. "The Rupture," as Wayde calls it, is the moment in the writing process where it feels like a project has failed, but, actually, it's the moment when the project can develop and become better than it was before.

With that bit of context, please meet our alumni.

OUR ALUMNI

Arleen Pare (AP, TWS 2002) mentored under Betsy Warland and is the Governor's General Award-winning author of ten poetry collections. Her most recent collection is *Encrypted* (Caitlin Press).

Gurjinder Basran (GB, TWS 2006) mentored under Wayde Compton and is the author of four novels. Her debut novel, *Everything Was Good-Bye,* won the Ethel Wilson Fiction Prize.

Janie Chang (JC, TWS 2011) mentored under Shaena Lambert and is a Globe and Mail bestselling author of historical fiction.

Joseph Kakwinokanasum (JK, TWS 2018) mentored under JJ Lee and Aislinn Hunter. His first novel, *My Indian Summer*, was nominated for multiple prizes and won the PMC Indigenous Literature Award. His second novel, *Wihtikow*, will be published by Douglas & McIntyre.

Kim Spencer (KS, TWS 2020) mentored under Claudia Cornwall and Paul Headrick. Her debut novel, *Weird Rules to Follow*, won multiple awards, and was a Governor General's Literary Award finalist. Her next novel, *I Won't Feel This Way Forever*, a sequel, and her picture book, *Springtime in Kitkatla*, are scheduled for release with Orca Books.

ALUMNI RESPONSES

Question 1: What's one memory you have of your year in TWS?

AP: I was very new to writing, had never thought of writing as something I would ever do—but I was about to retire from my social work position, had just written a master's thesis, which I enjoyed, and just wanted to study writing—especially poetry and especially with the esteemed Betsy Warland. Loved it. From Betsy I learned about non-traditional poetic writing, and especially the use of white space on a page, which has been key in my writing career. I was also very impressed with the writing that my fellow mentees produced. It was all inspiring.

GB: When I think back on TWS, it's never one thing that sticks out to me, it's the entire experience. Playing it back in my mind is like seeing it as a reel full of supportive people, great conversations and workshop gatherings. I was lucky to have an amazing cohort and ended up making life-long friends. I think it was the community that I loved the most.

JC: I remember how much I looked forward to meeting with my cohort each week, to share our work, our thoughts, and our feelings about writing. It felt wonderful to be surrounded by other emerging writers with the same dreams I'd held secret for so long.

JK: As a writer: something Wayde Compton said, The Rupture is part of the process. When the project is blown to bits you are left to put the pieces back together; I remember the joy I felt when I realized that the work is better because of it. On a personal level: making incredible friends that I still have today.

KS: My mentor and cohort stand out the most from my time at TWS.

It was such a gentle and supportive environment. I felt like I was in good hands from the start. I would never have had the courage to write a book, let alone submit it to publishing houses. TWS gave me the confidence to pursue writing.

Question 2: What do you remember about being published in emerge*?*

AP: Yes, *emerge* was my first publication experience. So exciting. Extremely chuffed and grateful to be given the opportunity to read in front of a live (and friendly) audience.

GB: It was my first time being published and I was a fiction writer whose work was partly rooted in my biography; I was so worried about having my work be mistaken for memoir that I thought about writing under a pseudonym. I am glad that I did not do that!

JC: The preparation for the launch of *emerge* made a bigger impression on me than seeing my words in print. During the classes on how to give a reading I was terrified! I have delivered hundreds of presentations, talks, and tutorials during my corporate career, but this time it would be my writing being heard, being judged by classmates and potential readers! Quite different.

JK: Accomplishment. Seeing my name and my story in print, in a book with an ISBN number was a transformational moment. I was forced to acknowledge I was a bona fide emerging writer. It's a testament to the powerful lesson of goalsetting, ploughing through to the end, and believing in myself.

KS: *emerge* was the first time I saw my name in print! It felt more like seeing it in lights! Blink, blink. It was a special moment. Reading live was exciting as well. It was via Zoom, as it was during the pandemic, so it was a much wider reach. Seeing all the comments in the chat were uplifting. And made me feel I was on the right path—I can do this!

Question 3: What did you learn from being published in emerge *that you took into your publication experiences after TWS?*

AP: It was a thrill to be part of *emerge*—and as thrills can be inspiring—it was inspiring!

GB: I learned that publishing is a business and like all businesses you must respect project timelines and be easy to work with. Meet your deadlines, no drama.

JC: That one can edit forever. So at some point, you have to submit your pages, make the deadline, and live with the consequences.

JK: There's nothing like your first. *emerge 2018* sits proudly on my bookshelf as a first of many. Like a cherry high, I learned it takes a village to publish a book. Never underestimate the power of a good editor, the wisdom of a seasoned mentor, or the expert prudence of the publisher.

KS: During the editing process, I was told that no one will love your manuscript as much as you. It's your baby. Don't rely on an editor to do the work for you. I reminded myself of that recently when I was tired of yet another round of revisions! It gave me the extra oomph I needed to keep at it.

Question 4: What does your writing practice look like now? Or how do you approach publication?

AP: I have a lively and continuous writing practice. I have published twelve books (ten poetry collections, one chapbook, and one co-edited anthology) since leaving TWS twenty-five years ago. The initial submission experience was fraught, as many submission processes continue to be for so many. I belong to 3 poetry writing groups in Victoria, whose members help me enormously.

GB: I am lucky to have an agent, so I can focus on writing the novel and he can sell it. I am still highly involved in writing the synopsis, the market position and any post publication promotion. My practice? I write when I have time, always balancing my creative life with a full-time day job, so I avoid setting writing goals unless I am actively engaged in a new novel.

JC: Except for my debut novel, when I was blissfully ignorant and didn't have any expectations or contract deadlines, every book I've handed in since has been accompanied by the certainty that this is the worst book ever, and my editor and agent will never want to deal with me again.

Living with the consequences, right? The best thing to do at this point is start plotting out the next book.

JK: I journal every day, that's the practice, and it weaves its way into the work of publication. I approach the publication as collaboratively as possible. I need to have all hands on deck. I need a close and trusting relationship with my editor, the publisher, my Beta Readers for the work to be the best we, the community can create. I am only the writer.

KS: I wrote my first two books with the help of my cohorts at TWS and the TWS Graduate Workshop. A year after TWS, the manuscript I had workshopped was published and on store shelves. It debuted on the B.C. bestsellers list. A dream launch! The second book is scheduled for publication in Spring 2026. I wrote my third book without the support of a cohort. It was scary at first and hard, but I managed to do it (set to be published this fall!). For that book, I relied on the lessons I learned from TWS, which are invaluable.

Question 5: What advice do you want to give the writers in emerge 25?

AP: Join a writing group. Edit your work carefully. Let other writers suggest edits. Take workshops whenever you can. Keep learning your craft. And READ READ READ.

GB: Enjoy it! These experiences are once in a lifetime and nothing feels as good as sharing your work this way for the first time.

JC: I'm traditionally published in fiction, so can only offer advice from this perspective. *Finish your book.* The hard reality is that publishing is a business and your book is a product. A great first chapter is always helpful, but, to agents and editors, you're unknown potential. They need to see you complete the promise of that first chapter. Finish writing the manuscript, find beta readers, hire a professional editor, make it the best it can be.

JK: You are not just the writer, you are the conduit through which all the characters you've met in your life—your aunties, uncles, grandparents, friends, bosses, teachers, mentors and so on—you are a vessel containing ancestral knowledge and lived experience. Pour it out like water in a cup.

Part of the anxiety and fear one feels when reading or performing at live events is informed by the ego. Let your audience in on your fear of failure. Also, there's no such thing as publishing a first draft. Writing is 99 percent editing. You are just the writer. Oh, and it is important to find a hobby—that's not related to writing—that gives you rest. Manage your practice, don't let the practice manage you. Be kind to yourself. Back away when you are frustrated. If you want to be a full time writer, find a hobby and treat writing like a regular job: keep the hours that work best for you, and make time for yourself away from the work.

KS: My writing career took off. Things happened so quickly for me. I could hardly catch my breath. All in a good way, of course. But that's not always the case. In workshops, I tell people about someone who has an MFA, and her first book was rejected well over fifty times. But she kept at it. Her book was eventually a national bestseller. So you never know. Everyone's writing path looks different. If you love it, keep at it.

The preface to *emerge 2002* also talked about how that "annual publication" would not have been possible without the hard work of those in TWS. "They have provided the lion's share of work necessary for its publication," it reads. That was as true then as it is today.

This anthology is a result of years of hard work from our students, the alumni who return each year to help edit and produce the book, as well as our industry colleagues who have edited, designed, printed and distributed the book. This community has made *emerge* possible. Without them there is no book. I think that's true for most books. So, our community: Please accept this thanks. You're vital.

The book also wouldn't be possible either without readers. You. Friends, family, everyone interested in new voices and those who are in and support our literary community. We hope you enjoy the twenty-fifth offering of *emerge: the Writer's Studio anthology*. There are many great writers here, and I know you'll be seeing more of their work in the future, on the shelves of your local bookstore.

Enjoy.

non-fiction

DAYNA MAHANNAH
Non-Fiction Editor

Introduction

Growing up in the Okanagan Valley, I spent a good chunk of summer vacations at the lake. As a kid, everything becomes a game, and the best games are dares: Dive off the dock and touch the bottom of the lake with your hands. The dock stretched fifty metres out from shore. Standing at the end, looking down, the dock's pilings evaporated a few feet below the surface. Beyond it: darkness.

Dares forced us gawky tweens to push our boundaries of comfort, lest we be labelled "scared." Of course, we were all terrified. What would we find in that aqueous void? Slimy thickets of lake weed, sure to entangle and strangle and drown us? Maybe a monster would discover *us*. Perhaps, though, we'd grasp a lost diamond ring, securing a fortune for our futures.

This is the game I would unwittingly recreate later in life, every time I sat down to write an essay. While all us kids knew, theoretically, that the lake had a bottom, we couldn't see it ourselves. So until we dove down, the possibility of meeting some terrible creature of the deep remained just as plausible as finding lake weed or treasure.

In writing non-fiction—especially memoir, which many of the pieces in this section are—an author partakes in the spirit of this dare. They push beyond their comfort zones, abandon certainty, and submerge themselves into a great unknowing—all this, without the aid of peer pressure. It's often a solitary dive, and that makes these writers all the more courageous. In non-fiction, the author approaches a subject with curiosity and openness (and likely a decent amount of terror), understanding that what they discover in the process may be uncomfortable, even monstrous. Just as likely: What they uncover enlightens. Always, though, if you submerge yourself deep enough, you find some truth.

In "The Things We Keep," Alexandra Flynn searches for meaning in the belongings left after her mother's death, emerging with insight about a person she held close, and greater considerations about the way we live our lives. Faced with the choice to leave her home and family during the Islamic Revolution in Iran, Kiana Mohseni recalls the moment the fear of the unknown represented an opportunity for freedom, in "The Right of Passage." Allan Cho comes to understand, through retrospect, the decision his father made that left him feeling empty so long ago, in "The Realm of Resistors and Hockey Cards."

These are some findings that this collection of non-fiction offers. But the discoveries abound—an incredible kindness bestowed in a request for the salt shaker; the safety provided by the mundane task of polishing glassware; a moment of saving grace offered in a round of Jägermeister.

The only way to prove you've followed through with the dare, of course, is to return with evidence: a fistful of lake-bottom. These writers have reached into the dark, hearts banging, and, fists raised, breached the surface with their discoveries. Proof.

DAYNA MAHANNAH grew up in Westbank, B.C., the territory of the Syilx and Okanagan people. She now lives in Vancouver with her partner and their uncategorizable mutt. She is a graduate of the Writer's Studio and received her MFA from UBC. Dayna has been a contributing editor at *Beatroute* and *Adbusters*, and was the editor-in-chief of *Geist*. Her writing appears in *subTerrain, Geist, Electric Literature, TRUE Africa,* and elsewhere.

MAGDALENA DOMINIK

The Discovery

An excerpt from a memoir about finding oneself through cancer

The burning, full feeling was constant. I bought new bras, whined to my friends, and chalked it up to another perimenopausal symptom that the elder matriarchs forgot to convey.

"It hurts constantly, and is sometimes sharp," I complained as my physician poked around under my armpit on the right side of my breast.

She decided it was inflammation in the cartilage between my ribs—costochondritis, a condition that is barely understood yet dismissed as harmless. The treatment: pain management. I was given an anti-inflammatory gel and instructions to take Advil when it became too much to bear.

It helped—sort of. As a first-generation Eastern European, pain was something I was raised to endure, stoicism coursing through my veins. My 75-year-old mother once walked on a broken foot for nine days before relenting and getting an X-ray. When asked how she dealt with the pain, her answer was simple: "I'm a strong Polish woman."

I, too, was a strong Polish woman, "grin and bear it" so deeply rooted in me that suffering barely registered. So I put the cream on, swallowed ibuprofen, and searched for the perfect bra that would not aggravate my tender bosom—not too tight, wire-free, and supportive enough to contain a DD on the right and his C counterpart on the left. The winner was a three-pack of Puma cotton sports bras in black, grey, and white, which were delivered to my door, thanks to my sister's Costco membership. Total damage: $14.99. I pulled out the useless padding inserts and wore the cheap sports bras daily.

It was the end of a long day, a bath awaiting, when I slipped my thumbs under the black elastic band to disrobe.

Ouch! I winced. What was that?

It skirted away from my probing finger, so I began a meticulous search. Starting in the middle of my breast, I applied pressure, circling out, letting my fingers test every inch with a light depression. Nothing. I tried again, cautiously pushing farther. There! On the outside of my right breast, half-way down from the top, there was *something*.

Visions of breast cancer awareness ads flashed through my mind. "Check yourself," they said. "Check yourself regularly." But what one might actually find … that part, I couldn't remember. Was it supposed to be squishy? Or hard? Did mine feel like a grape? Or a rock? And which was better? I knew this sort of thing needed follow-up, but I wasn't worried; fear without cause was not how I did my life. I liked facts and action. Lumps in breasts were supposedly common and usually amounted to nothing. There was no breast cancer history in my family and at age 45, I was still five years younger than the regular screening recommendations.

So, I followed protocol at a leisurely pace, and requested a mammogram, just to be sure. After a check-in with my family doctor weeks later, I was finally referred to the breast clinic to schedule diagnostic tests: a mammogram—a big-picture, drone-like view of the area; and an ultrasound—a GoPro-style run through the forest floor. Together, these would provide a relatively complete picture of my breast without spending too many taxpayer dollars. Once the referral was sent to the breast clinic, they were supposed to call me with the appointment date. It was a "don't call us, we'll call you" kind of arrangement requiring trust and patience on my part.

A month went by, then another without a scheduled date. When my long-planned extended vacation came up, I didn't hesitate. There was no new information to cause alarm, and the delays likely meant I was a low-probability case. So I wholeheartedly chose adventure, grateful for no news being good news. I packed my bags with my special cream, cotton sports bras, and anti-inflammatories and flew thousands of miles over the Pacific for a family getaway.

II

We flew into Osaka, Japan, and went on to visit the mountains of Hakuba, the busy streets of Tokyo, and the hippie island paradise of Ishigaki, my breast curiously sore every time I ate sugary treats. After over a month on the road, we arrived in Kyoto—an ancient city filled with temples, gardens, and a mystical spiritualism that lingers between the hordes of sweaty tourists clumsily bumbling around.

We headed up Fushimi Inari shrine just as the throngs from the day began to dissipate. Full of energy and excitement, I floated up the stone steps two by two, stopping infrequently to marvel at the inscriptions in the terracotta-red torii gates towering overhead. These iconic arches marked the transition to the spiritual world and were traditionally placed at the entrance of every Shinto shrine. On this two-hour uphill walk, there were thousands. By the time my family and I reached the top, the sun was setting and we were mostly alone.

Before entering, I picked up the ladle resting over a stone basin and filled it with water streaming from the bamboo spout. I poured the cold liquid onto my left hand, then my right—a cleansing ritual meant to purify and prepare mortals to connect with the spirit world. Shintoism's animistic beliefs and magical rituals intrigued me. I bowed and tossed a hundred yen coin into the wooden receptacle, swinging the massive woven rope attached to a bell to notify the gods of my arrival. I clapped, then bowed again before speaking to Inari, the spirit who lived there. As he was the god of prosperity, among other things, I asked for abundance, and for the good fortune of my family and my friends.

I then walked among the statues of the kitsune—red-bibbed fox messengers said to accompany Inari. That's when I noticed an octagonal metal container about a foot tall. Curious, I watched a Japanese man approach, shake the box, and tip it upside down. What looked like a metal chopstick emerged from a small hole in the top. He glanced at it and then let it slide back into the container.

Shake, flip, pull. I followed his lead. My metal chopstick had a number in Kanji—Chinese characters used in Japanese writing—etched into it. The man looked at me, my confusion obvious, and gestured to a yellowed poster protected by glass adjacent to where we were standing. He pointed at the chopstick and then at the board.

"Ah, they're related," I muttered, uncertain if he would understand.

It was like a fortune, a prediction. I was searching the board for a symbol that matched the one etched in the chopstick, when the man offered his assistance. I bowed in acceptance, so he dragged his finger across the board from right to left until he stopped at the number ten, my number.

"Sorry, no English," he said as he waved his hand in front of his face.

He pointed at the individual characters of my fortune one by one and enounced, in a heavily accented English that was way better than my Japanese, "Good …"

I nodded.

"… Then bad."

Our eyes met briefly. With my hand on my chest, I watched him disappear down the stairs.

He knew. I knew. But I didn't tell anyone, savouring the vacation to the very end. This gift of foresight from the gods was mine alone—if only for a time.

MAGDALENA DOMINIK is unruly—or so her husband says. Years of adulting may have softened the edges, but she's still wired for disruption. Based in Vancouver, Magdalena writes creative non-fiction one painstaking, gut-wrenching paragraph at a time. From cancer and earthquakes to leaving Poland young, she mines her past to reclaim the wild, wise self she refuses to lose.

RALUCA SANDERS

Roses

At 1:00 p.m. sharp, Grandma Ortansa—my Boonika—woke up from her nap. She stared at the World War II wrist watch lying face up on the wooden cupboard that served as a table in the tiny winter kitchen. Without reading glasses, she moved the watch closer, then farther from her eyes to make sure it was one o'clock on the dot and not a minute earlier.

She whistled lightly as she wiped sweat off her forehead and sat up. Her lace underskirt peeked out from the hem of her dress, shifting as she walked bow-legged across the room. The shotgun leaned against a white-washed wall, under a large picture of the Holy Mother Mary and child, both dressed in silver, with a single black vertical streak from the smoke of the rushlight.

Boonika Ortansa made the sign of the cross, whistled, and touched the image of the Madonna. She then walked outside, cocked the gun, and shot into the air. Crows scattered from a nearby tree.

Ten minutes later, Grandpa appeared through the elderberry trees, fishing pole in one hand, tin bucket full of fish in the other. The lake behind my grandparents' house in Romania was teeming with trout. It's what summer lunches were made of: fried trout and grits, with whatever vegetable was ripe in the garden.

||

Roses, pink and climbing on a trellis, grew just outside the grey wooden porch in front of my grandparents' house. One could reach them through the double-paned window.

I'd stretch in my white bed almost every morning in June, the month of school's end, taking in the scent of roses in bloom.

When the roses were close to wilting, Boonika enlisted my help in picking them off the vine. She lined them up on old newspapers, yellowed pages of *The Spark*, the Romanian Communist Party's propaganda rag.

The roses dried on the porch while chickens and ducks attempted to grab them through sculpted-wood rails. It took about two weeks for the buds to dry. I checked them every day until they were ready for oils and perfumes, teas, and potions.

Some roses were never dried. They were boiled with sugar and water and turned into jam and sorbet, to be enjoyed with cold water.

One afternoon, Boonika pulled out two tiny glasses and two tiny plates from the green-and-yellow credenza she kept in the big room, where I slept. She filled the glasses with water. She arranged two spoons with rose sorbet on each plate. One for me, one for her.

We licked the pink sorbet, then sipped on fresh water.

"It needs more sugar," I said.

"Don't be silly, this sorbet is perfect. Besides, my mother died of knotted guts from the sugars. She showed up in my dream last night, by the cursed pear tree. What do you think it means?"

Every June, seated by the fire, serenaded by frogs under a purple dusk, I'd say the rose sorbet needed more sugar. Every year, Boonika would remember her mother, who'd shown up in a dream, by the cursed pear tree.

Sugar was a luxury to be enjoyed sparingly at the time. It only arrived once per month at the village store. Didn't show up at all if it rained or snowed because roads were muddy and big wheels got stuck in knee-deep trenches.

To get sugar, I had to wake up at 4:00 a.m. and, ration card in hand, wait in line with 200 other villagers, one per household, most of them separated by one or two degrees of kin. The truck would arrive by 6:00 a.m. and pull behind the store, where it would be unloaded. People bought their rations and went back to their lives. I'd go to school after dropping off the sugar in Boonika's kitchen.

Because I was the best in my class, my teacher made me write a paper about the glory of the Communist Party.

"Explain your devotion to the Communist Party that loves and protects you," she'd say, after I'd been awake since 4:00 a.m., standing in line for rationed sugar.

||

"Ortansa, dawdle all day with visits, why don't you?" Grandpa muttered in Boonika's direction. She was getting ready to leave the house, and he faced a stretch of nothing to do.

"I can visit no one; nobody should visit me. What kind of prison is this?" she rebuffed, excited for the prospect of womanly socializing.

"Remember that minstrel back in '68, at that wedding, making eyes at you? You're going out. To cheat on me. God knows what lovers you're keeping." He was picking crumbs off the kitchen table as he said this, not believing a word of it himself, but hoping he'd start a fight good enough to fence the boredom. They'd been married for fifty years, both of them now in their seventies, both of them nursing body aches and weighted by life.

"If I'm beautiful, what can I do?" Grandma Ortansa whispered in his direction as she flew out the door, eager to spend the day gossiping and exchanging recipes with women in the village.

I helped Grandpa collect plates off the table, washed them, and put them in a wooden cabinet. It was the last June I'd spend with my grandparents.

The strawberry patch on the side of my grandparents' house had red spots of fruit. Grandpa, with old, overworked hands, had shown me how to gently pick the strawberries without damaging the leaves or the rest of the plant.

"I'm going to Italy for a while," I said, more to myself than him.

For a second, Grandpa stopped shuffling the strawberry leaves, but didn't straighten his back, nor did he show any sign he might react to what I just said.

"This is one beautiful strawberry," he finally said, holding up a handsome fruit like it was a diamond, catching the sunlight just right. It was a reminder that ever since I could walk, every June, I had picked strawberries just like the one he was holding.

The red warmth of the berries held the scent of an eternity of summer evenings. An endless time harmonized by cricket choirs, nights with yellow moons and howling dogs, gentle rains, and the quiet that hung low over rose bushes. Respite from the demands of life.

At the end of high school, there was nothing for me in Romania. Only further studies with Communist-minded professors on power trips, or the alternative of marrying a man and giving up parts of my soul.

||

"I'm not going to say anything about this. I'm going to shut up and walk away," Boonika said. She crossed her arms and walked away from me and

Grandpa, moving slowly in case one of us felt compelled to stop her. "But if you really want to know ..." She pivoted on her right foot, ending the self-imposed truce.

"What should she know, Ortansa? What could this kid know about a country where lawlessness and whim are in power?" Grandpa intervened gently enough to avoid fanning her flame, but firmly enough to stop her train of thought.

There had been a revolution in Romania, a Communist dictatorship had ended, and nothing had replaced it; the whole country behaved like a lost child looking for its parent in the grand European mall.

Those who could, left.

The rest stayed behind and continued their lives like nothing had ever happened. Grandpa knew why I was leaving without me ever saying a thing. Grandpa, holding a bowl of strawberries, knew my soul and spared the telling of disappointments. Such was his kindness.

"What will you do amongst strangers?" Grandma had softened her voice.

"I'll write."

"What will you write?" She gathered her eyes over her hands.

"I'll write about cursed pear trees. And roses."

RALUCA SANDERS is a Californian mom who loves to scribble her anxieties and fling them at unsuspecting readers. She's been a survivor of writing workshops since 2007. Raluca published a memoir in Romania, her country of origin, in 2010. She also edited and published a Romanian folklore anthology in 2015, available on Amazon. Her literary aspirations lay with the prestige of terminal degrees, yet her ADHD obstacles the best intentions.

KIANA MOHSENI

The Right of Passage

I don't remember saying goodbye to my mother. On the day of my departure from Iran when I was fifteen, my dad suggested I say goodbye to her at home. I knew why. He wanted to spare me a long, painful farewell at the airport, where emotions are amplified at the best of times. He didn't want my last memory of my mother to be a haunting, shattering, tearful one. But I don't remember the goodbye at all. Now I wonder if my father was right—if it's easier to avoid pain in moments like that. And yet, I wish I had some recollection, even if painful, just to know that I had been fully present for my mother in that moment, rather than leaving her with an image of a distant, detached version of her daughter.

What she must have been going through that day as a mother is unimaginable to me. Whatever it was, she didn't show her feelings. Neither did I. We were like deer caught in headlights. The enormity of the impending change was too much to bear, leaving us emotionally detached, dissociated from the experience. It was as though I was inside a protective bubble, sound muffled, the world outside moving in slow motion, receding into a backdrop. I was watching myself from a distance.

It was 1978. In the previous months, the Islamic Revolution had gained momentum, and demonstrations filled the streets daily. The sound of gunshots was common day and night. Schools and offices had been closed for months, and I could no longer go out alone. With my outdoor freedom taken away, I turned inward and poured myself into my drawings. My subject matter was dark and disturbing—street scenes of violent civil unrest, prisoners on death row, military leaders charting the course of war.

I couldn't reconcile the contradictions of my world: innocence colliding with violence, a loss of freedom, an uncertain future. My drawings became my refuge, a way to process the fear and tension seeping in from the streets beyond my door. These images were far from the typical musings of a teenage girl, sparking deep concern in my parents. Little did we know that soon, we wouldn't just witness history unfold—we would be swept up in it.

Tehran was under curfew. The Shah's grip on power was slipping, and rumours spread of his imminent exile—an event that would plunge the country into chaos overnight. Time was running out.

For weeks, my father wrestled with the tormenting decision of whether to send me abroad. The plan had always been for me to attend university in Europe once I turned eighteen, but that was three years away. At every opportunity, he spoke of nothing else, turning the question over in endless debate with friends, family, new acquaintances, even with the local shopkeepers.

"I don't know what to do!" he would say. "She's too young to go alone, but we can't all leave. And how would we even afford it?" When no one answered, he would sigh. "If I don't send her now, she might never get out. Who knows what an Islamic government would mean for a girl's future?" Then, with a dark certainty, in a lower tone, "Actually, I know exactly what it would mean."

Not everyone shared the same sense of urgency. "An Islamic government won't last more than a couple of months. They don't know how to run a country!" A belief that turned out to be tragically misguided.

During those long debates, I was always present, listening in, yet no one ever asked for my opinion. What could I possibly know of the world? I was just a child.

Finally, after months of agonizing over the decision, on one sunny Sunday afternoon, my father wandered into my room for a chat, something he hardly ever had time to do.

He sat down next to my desk. "What are you doing?"

"I'm drawing!"

A brief silence, then: "Well, what do you think? Do you want to leave?"

At that moment, I grew beyond my years. He was treating me as an adult for the first time, capable of making important decisions about my life. To my own surprise, I rose to the challenge.

"Of course! Of course I want to leave!" I replied with complete conviction. I knew what I wanted. I wanted out of the country, away from the oppressive, sexist culture of restraints and repression. I wanted the same rights as boys. I wanted a life of freedom and independence. I wanted to make my own choices in life, even if it meant staring the fear of the unknown squarely in the eye.

He recoiled, his eyes widening with surprise at the speed and force of my response, the resolve in my voice. "Well, why didn't you say so earlier?'

"Because you didn't ask."

After a moment, his face lit up with a flash of clarity. "If you are old enough to go alone, I guess you are old enough to make the decision yourself!"

And with that, the decision was made. I was leaving home!

||

The next day, my father came home early from work.

"Look what I got for you!" He called out, beaming. In one hand, he held up the smallest suitcase I had ever seen. It was a sweet little handmade, tan leather suitcase that looked plenty sturdy, yet light. "I wanted to make sure you could lift it on your own!"

But that also meant I couldn't take many belongings with me. As I looked down at the tiny suitcase, which hardly came up to my knees, I realized it didn't really matter what I packed. Everything I knew, owned, loved, and cherished was staying behind. They wouldn't have fit into the biggest suitcase in the world. This realization must have been written all over my face.

"Don't worry, darling, I'll help you pack," my mother said, coming to my rescue. But she knew full well that an extra T-shirt and a pair of jeans could not fill the void I was taking with me.

On the day of departure, my dad drove me to the airport alone. We drove past the historical monument, Shahyad Tower, built in 1971 to commemorate the 2,500th anniversary of the Persian Empire. This "Gateway into Tehran" was named Shahyad, meaning "King's Memorial." The monument had been constructed as part of the grand celebrations the Shah organized to mark the occasion. These celebrations were extravagant, featuring lavish feasts, foreign dignitaries, and opulent displays of Iran's ancient heritage. While intended to showcase the country's modernity and prestige, the spectacle only deepened public resentment toward the Shah. Many saw it as a symbol of his detachment from the people, as he spent vast wealth on elite gatherings while economic and social injustices festered. The discontent simmered for years, and by the late 1970s, protests against his regime had escalated into what would be a full-blown revolution. Paradoxically, the monument was renamed Azadi—meaning *freedom*—by the Islamic Republic, when in reality, the revolution achieved just the opposite.

As we drove past the monument, I had a faint sense of the moment's significance—I was leaving my country as a 2,500-year chapter came to an end. My dad fretted that we might miss my flight due to the heavy traffic, but nothing felt like it mattered in comparison. In fact, at that moment, I felt nothing at all.

At the airport, my dad walked with me as far as he was allowed. "I'll be waiting here until you board the plane."

"Dad, don't wait. Please go home! I'll take it from here," I pleaded, determined to be an independent adult, standing on my own two feet, from that point on.

He accepted, and pointed to the line for my gate, and we said our goodbyes.

I left him and joined the line, thinking, *How hard can it be?*

KIANA MOHSENI is an Iranian British Canadian graphic novelist based in Vancouver, B.C., whose work explores themes of identity, belonging, and resilience. Drawing from her experiences as an immigrant, a queer woman, and a pioneer in the tech industry, her comics are reflections on displacement, self-discovery, and the courage to live authentically. Through visual storytelling, she expresses the tension between vulnerability and strength, independence and belonging, and breaking societal norms. Instagram: @kiana.illustrated.

JUSTIN ANCHETA

The Emperor

The Emperor (Pamela Coleman-Smith, 1909)

His stone throne is framed by unyielding mountains. A sparse metal crown caps his head, his body wrapped in full-plate armour and a blood-red robe. He grips his sceptre and orb, possessing dominion over everything in your world. He is the Emperor card of the Rider-Waite-Smith Tarot, the most recognized deck in modern history.

||

It's easy to see toxic masculinity in the classic depiction of the Emperor. He evokes domineering men, flexing raw muscle—power as an armoured fist. The Emperor is the harsh all-father, stern and brutal. He who disciplines and punishes.

I grew up uninterested in sports and other tokens of manliness. If my head wasn't buried in a book, visualizing other worlds, it looked skyward, striving to see beyond the clouds.

One evening when I was ten, my disapproving father caught me enraptured with the poetry of lightning that illuminated clouds in the distance.

"Hey! *Hey!*" he shouted. "What are you doing? You *crazy?* Get away from there!"

My ears crackled, and my neck and head curled down. My arms whipped into a tight embrace around my chest, hands tucking deep into my armpits.

"What? What are you doing now?" he screamed. "Are you going to cry? Are you going to sit in the corner and cry? *Cry like a woman?*"

My stomach shrank. His rage and judgment were an invisible sceptre that swung with every word.

For years, his reaction mystified me. Now, in my forties, writing about this moment, I realize that chasing beauty in lightning lay outside what he deemed permissible. It threatened the masculinity he projected on me—the manhood he longed for himself. To him, Emperors didn't write poetry or gaze at lightning. They shot bolts from their palms until they got what they wanted.

||

The Japaridze Tarot labels its Emperor card as "War," with a black-and-white sketch of vaguely humanoid forms locked in a grotesque struggle. Resembling the men of ancient armies meeting in long-forgotten battles, the singular Emperor becomes the plurality of male violence collectively realized throughout human history.

||

It's easy to see the Emperor as violent masculinity. When I was eleven, I came home from school to find my father at the dinner table, eyes fixed on me.

"The school called. What's this—you being bullied at school, huh? They say you got bullied to give your baseball cards away. *What do you have to say?*"

"I-I-I c-c-c-can t-t-t-talk to my teachers about what happened," I said. "I need to explain what they thought was bullying wasn't actually—"

My father let out a hiss of disgust. "*No!* Why? I can *teach* you to fight. I can teach you!" He jumped from his chair, strode to where I stood, and faced me, bracing his legs in a fighting stance. "Come on, do after me." His fists were primed in a Victorian boxer's pose. "*Come on!*"

"W-w-wait," I said, waving my hands. "I can explain eh-eh-everything to my teachers. I wasn't bullied."

"No! Come on! If someone bullies you, box them back. Do as I do. *Do it!*"

With a deep sigh, I put up my fists. He threw punches that went over and around my hands. Thumping blows hit my chest, stomach, and shoulders. They landed squarely on my body, just hard enough to remind me of my unwillingness to fight. I was a target dummy, numb and insensate. It felt unfair, like my father was cheating. His stares and cries of victory froze me in place, preventing me from even the thought of fighting back.

As he half-pretended to engage me in a boxing match, he continued to repeat his lecture. "See, you have to box *them!*"

It is hard for an eleven-year-old to explain elementary schoolyard politics in a single breath, though I can do it now: the objects traded to curry favour with others; the deals made in fear of isolation. But it's even harder when that eleven-year-old is tongue-locked and throat-bound by a stutter. I stood there with my stomach roiling, neck tight, and arms seized. I tried to force words out of my throat, but the fear of my father's anger raced alongside embarrassment through my open chest, raced with a memory of the head-wagging of my elementary school teachers. They swooped in on our huddled circle like federal agents, raiding the illicit deals made on baseball cards. I tried to say more, but my words felt like quicksand. Fight, he kept saying. Maybe he wanted me to fight for him, not for myself.

He laughed in triumph with each hit, every impact proof that violence solved everything.

I just stood there.

||

The Crow Tarot illustrates its Emperor as a genderless crow. Perched on a sword that lay on a regal chair, it holds its head up high and gazes outward. The feathers around the Crow's neck are not its own, but there are no fallen enemy birds, no blood. The worn feathers project a confidence that extends beyond savagery, beyond gender and maleness.

||

It's easy to see the Emperor expressed solely in a male body. It's harder to see masculine power beyond something exclusively male or destructive.

"Did you hear about the experimental retinal implant that's supposed to give blind people sight?" I asked a friend in high school.

"I wouldn't get that," she said. "Being blind is an important part of who I am. I'd never change that." Her voice was hard with resolve.

Later, I would recall her words and picture her on a throne, her white cane in place of a sceptre.

"Would you get a cure for stuttering if they invented one?"

"I'd never thought of it like that," I said, stunned by her question. Frustration and anxiety about my misfiring throat collided with what my stutter gave me: a preternatural vocabulary and an affinity for written language. Out of that fire erupted pride, a hot fullness in my throat.

||

The Women in Science Tarot keeps the name of the Emperor. The card features the withered and aged body of J. Robert Oppenheimer, standing in the shadow of the Trinity atomic test site memorial. A mushroom cloud—the world's first atomic bomb explosion—towers over his decrepit body. A man who, despite his fame, left a legacy of shame and guilt.

||

I worry that I don't come across queer enough. I hold a hidden panic that someone at an LGBTQ+ arts festival or Pride event will call me a liar, will say that asexuals don't count. That my bi-romanticism isn't enough for me to be considered queer. My chest fills with dread when I imagine scenarios where someone shouts this at me—even when I'm in a space centering asexuals and aromantic people. There is an *A* in LGBTQ2SIA+, after all. I fear that other ace or queer people will see only an oppressor in me because of my Adam's apple, my facial hair, my deep voice.

As a cis man, I thought I could be powerful by bowing to what society told me to do. It didn't matter how I felt about the armour. How its bulk blocked my legs and arms from moving too much, how its weight dragged down my straining bones and sore muscles, or how its form gripped my chest, slowed my breathing, made my skin clammy and sweat-soaked.

What mattered was that I wore it. What mattered was that I performed its role.

But what happens when the Emperor wants to abandon his throne? When he realizes there's tissue-paper freedom in adhering to the script, that the script is simply a directive to follow someone else's marching orders?

Maybe I don't want to meet a Good Filipino Woman. Maybe I want to meet a Good Filipino Man, or a Good Filipino Trans Person, or someone who isn't Good or Filipino. Maybe I don't want to be with anyone at all.

||

The Tarot of the Holy Spectrum offers an expressionless and androgynous Emperor. At first, it's unclear where their skin ends and their armour begins—their heavy plate mail appears to be shedding. Then it's apparent there is no armour. Their sceptre has shrunk to a wire-thin staff topped with a spiral crozier. The threat of aggression is gone, leaving an inward soulful stillness.

Justin Ancheta (he/they) is a stuttering Filipino Canadian from Toronto (Treaty 13 Territory) passionate about tarot and examining marginalization through experimental creative non-fiction forms. He is exploring his writing voice using their experience as a racialized bi+ ace person. Their work appears in *AZE Journal, QT Literary Magazine, carte blanche, Ex-Puritan,* and the *Tahoma Literary Review.* They can be found on Bluesky and Instagram @rampancy, and at JustinAnchetaWriter.com.

ROBIN JANE ROFF

A Letter from the Author to the Subject

An excerpt from "Searching for Beverley Cayley: A Memoir of Hope, Nostalgia, and Environmental Change"

Dear Beverley,

A writer friend asked the other day what you would think of me writing your story. It was a strange question to be asked in the middle of drafting a manuscript, particularly one about you, a man who has been dead for nearly a hundred years. You don't think of anything anymore, and certainly not of a stranger, who has taken it upon herself to interrogate your life. I dismissed the question, preferring to focus on plot and structure and narrative tension. But I could not shake his words, just as I cannot shake you. I promise, I tried. So, I have decided to ask you directly.

What would you think of being a subject?

I think you'd be embarrassed. You don't seem the type to want the spotlight. I imagine there would be squirming. I see your shoulders curling inwards, your body twisting away from my questions, your chin rummaging in your chest. You're scratching the dirt with the toe of your boot. I bet you'd brush the whole thing off and tell me you were no hero, that I was wasting my time. That you didn't live long enough to make a difference.

Was it six years or seven before tuberculosis stole the mountains from you?

You are right, of course. Your life was short, consumed, as so many were, by bloody lungs and sallow cheeks. But that doesn't mean it was inconsequential. Your name is on a mountain, after all. I think you mattered. You still matter. At least you do to me.

||

The first time I went looking for you in the North Vancouver archives, I met a woman named Diane. She had long black hair and the restful air of someone who spends their day among old photographs and newsprint. She handed me a brown box containing everything anyone knows about your life. It wasn't much, but it was enough to get started. There was some poetry, a few Christmas cards, and your photo albums. Oh, how I lingered on those pages with their small black-and-white images captioned in your careful schoolboy script. Pictures of a shaggy spaniel, Teddy, on a boat, in the snow, rolling on a trim lawn. You with a can of paint, holding the brush like a staff, whitewash on your trousers.

Your climbs are in those albums as well: Mount Foley, Victoria, Garibaldi, Baker. Colourless captures of a world disappeared: peaks without footsteps, valleys full of ancient glaciers, and deep, wet trails slashed through Devil's club and salal. And then, of course, there are pictures of you and your friends. Always a gang—five, six, twelve. Always joyful despite what looks like truly trying conditions. In one photo, your faces are covered in rime. In another, your knees are sunk three feet deep in snow. In many more, you sit with your shoulders hunched, burying yourselves into some crack or crevasse against the wind, waiting out a storm.[1] You smile like these were the best days of your life. Perhaps they were.

I imagine it was to these memories you turned as you waited for the end to come. That's what I would have done.

When I finished flipping through the albums, I asked Diane for Emmie's box and was disappointed to learn that she doesn't have one. Her husband Eric does; she's in there. She's wrapped up in his life in the same way she's wrapped up in yours: captured in his words and photographs, his memories of her adventures. I admit I have grown fond of her, not only because she meant so much to you. She reminds me of myself—a woman climbing. Breaking the rules. She holds out the possibility that you and I may also have been friends.

Eric's box is not as big as yours, but it's rich with text, mostly postcards and brochures. He and Emmie lived long and loving lives. They explored widely, getting as far as the Himalayas. Do you know that? Did you haunt her, too?

I scanned Eric's documents absent-mindedly. It was almost too much to take in after your photographs. Near the bottom of the pile, I came across a small rectangle of paper, the edges stained with age and finger grease. It was the size of a thank-you card one sends after a wedding or baby shower. One

[1] N/A Beverley Cayley Fonds 163 1920-1929 (Inventory No. 163) North Vancouver Archives, North Vancouver, British Columbia, Canada

side was stamped by several furious hands—demanding a return address, compelling the recipient not to re-mail under the same cover, and certifying receipt at the post office June 14, 1928. Under all this administrative ink was Emmie's name in a gentle, looping script.

Miss E. A. Milledge
1175 Douglas Rd.,
Vancouver, B.C.

I turned the card over, greedy for one of Emmie's treasures. The text bore the marks of a typewriter, the letters darker where the typist's fingers had strained upon the keys. The *f* in *friends*, the *r* in *remembrance*, and the *v* in *loved*. Everything was clear, justified, official.

> Acting on the suggestion of several friends of the late Beverley Cayley [...], a "Service of Remembrance" will be held at St. Mark's Church (cor. 2nd Ave & Larch St.) on Sunday evening, June 17th at 7.30 to which are specially invited all mountain climbers and their friends. Please plan to come. We all loved Beverley.[2]

I stared at the words, my heart tight, beatless. Did I cry out? I must have, because Diane looked up and asked if I'd found something good.

"Yes," I said. "Yes, I found his death notice. This woman kept it all these years."

She nodded—a response fully out of keeping with such a monumental discovery. I longed to remove the latex gloves I was required to wear while handling the archive's collections. I wanted to feel the card's bruised edges, the indents of the postage stamps, and the warmth of the paper. Instead, I brought it to my nose. It smelled of stale grass, dust, and one hundred years of safe keeping.

||

I told a stranger—someone I'd just met at a backcountry hut—about my friend's question of what you'd think of my work. I hoped she'd tell me the answer didn't matter. That you were dead and this was my story. She did not.

"What would you think of someone writing about you a hundred years

---

[2] Sovereign, A.H. (1928) Invitation to Service of Remembrance. Alpine Club of Canada – Vancouver Section Fonds 223 Eric Brooks Sous-fonds (Inventory No: F223-SF1) North Vancouver Archives, North Vancouver, British Columbia, Canada.

from now?" She asked, stirring a cup of coffee in the half-light of a hurricane lantern.

"No one would write about me," I said. "I'm not important."

"So that's the standard? To get your name on a mountain, I mean."

"Well, yeah."

"There are plenty of mountains named after irrelevant, if not downright terrible, people."

That stopped me dead in my tracks. I've been rummaging around in your life presuming you did something grand. Perhaps …

No, no, no. I can't think like that. No one would keep an invitation to my wake for a century, not the way Emmie kept yours.

||

I've put down your story so many times—started other projects, outlined whole novels in my head. You waited patiently as I fooled myself into thinking I could quit. When I returned, you welcomed me back with outstretched arms, and we picked up where we left off.

I must understand why you won't go, and for that, I must write. There has to be some lesson in all of this, or else I'm just wasting my time on a ghost story.

Please forgive what I get wrong. You left so few crumbs for me to follow that I must thread them together with imagination to find the fact through fiction. I know you were a man well-loved, a man young in years, and younger still in experience. What happened might have been avoided had you selected A rather than B, or it may have been tracked since birth. The slow death of a candle's wick, snuffed out before anyone was ready. Whatever the reason, we will find it together.

Your friend,

Robin

ROBIN JANE ROFF, PhD, writes about the search for meaning and mental health in the Anthropocene. Her non-fiction has appeared in *Washington Trails*, *Cloudburst*, and placed third in the North Shore Writers' Association 2023 Writing Contest. "Searching for Beverley" explores the life of B.C. mountaineer Beverley Cochrane Cayley, and what the socio-environmental transformations of the 1920s can tell us about the present. Robin lives in Vancouver, Canada. Instagram @robinjanemakes.

YOLANDE HOUSE

Long Blond Parallelism

Everyone tells me how much I look like my mother, and I can't unsee it. My long blond hair, even unbleached, resembles her flowing locks—especially as a frame for scrutiny.

"Don't you *ever* cut your hair!" Mom said when I was a teen. These brassy warnings matched her declarations that I shouldn't smoke. "I'll kill you if you do that!" Mom backed up her threats with pummels and open-handed slaps, so I wasn't going to take any chances.

Mom's hair at sixteen: bleached and flattened on an ironing board. Mine at twelve: tendrils of white-blond snaking atop my head after she pulled off a perforated cap, the chemical stench watering my green eyes. I joked, "Let's take a picture and send it to Nanny. Pretend this is the new style!"

A woman at a Calgary mall once asked if my yellow locks were natural, and I said they were. Then I thought, *Well, except for the streaks ...* Multi-layered and -hued, my head was a nest of confusion.

||

As a teen, Mom rebelled in the shadows of her parents' backyard, puffing cigarettes, eyes casting around for onlookers.

In Grade 9, I refused to highlight my hair for the first time.

Mom hounded me for months. "If you don't, your hair will get dark and ugly," she said, wide-eyed. She came of age in an era when a woman's worth was measured by her physical beauty. Even as an adult, she made great efforts to "put on her face" before leaving the house.

But I refused. I was haunted by a summertime photo of me with my dad and his new family. Wearing a mustard-yellow sweater and a pale headband, my gaze bore into the camera, empty and doll-like. Sheets of yellow-white drowned my crown, survivors from the perforated cap.

"Gorgeous!" my brunette stepmother had cooed when the studio photos arrived. In her muted mint-green kitchen, I pinched my lips, a reflection of my face in the photo. She gave me the solo shot as a gift. I stashed her homemade, frosted-lace frame in my closet.

In Grade 9, dirty blond became my *cause de la résistance*. Before I started living with my dad, Mom screamed at me every day. "You did that on purpose, didn't you?" she'd snarl when I broke a glass while unloading the dishwasher, before she stampeded in my direction. Daily I heard comments like, "You fat, useless, ugly bitch."

That year, I finally stood up for myself. I'd yell back. And when her open palm struck my cheek, upper arm, or chest, I responded with hits of my own. Her frustration increased, but my sprouts of brown remained.

I puffed with pride when my English teacher pulled me aside one day. As the brother of my aunt's husband, he was someone I trusted.

"Did you dye your hair?" he asked. "It looks almost gold now. Golden blond."

I broke into a grin. "Actually, I stopped dyeing it. This is my natural colour."

His eyebrows shot up. "It looks good. Really good."

Others repeated his praise, and my steps felt lighter, like I finally had something glossy of my own. I held these words close the next time Mom tried to entice me with a box of drugstore Clairol.

||

My mother's hair was short only in childhood photos, her smile wide under a pixie cut.

My hair was short only in my mid-twenties when I'd shorn inches of reminders, until finally, dark blond roots reached my chin. I dabbed the ends with sticky gel, curling them upward and out with a roller brush. With my inch-long bangs and cat-eye glasses, I resembled a late-'90s punk librarian. I looked nothing at all like Mom—just the way I liked it.

But I still shuddered when I looked in the mirror and found my abuser's emerald eyes staring back.

||

At 51, Mom's greying blond locks spilled down her spine, thick with frizz. We were at my grandmother's funeral. I hadn't spoken to my mother in five years.

At 29, I hadn't yet learned to trust myself. I had become my own abuser, hearing her cruel remarks each time I made a mistake. She'd become the voice of my inner critic. At the graveyard, Mom sent my sister to call me over, who said that Mom wanted to "clear up a few things." I refused. I turned and got into a car and drove away. I understood her abuse to be rooted in anger and mental health issues. But a part of me also understood that I didn't have to be part of it in the same way. The last time I saw my mother, she was silhouetted between two Norway maple trees.

||

At 41, I no longer yearned to hack away reminders inch by inch. I still wore my hair long, although not so long that it tickled my waist, like in high school.

With each new haircut and style, I discovered which ones invited joy and which shackled me with shame. I kept the parts that pleased me: I cut my bangs and then grew them out. I dyed my hair blue, purple, and then back to golden blond. I styled with elastics and barrettes for my comfort, rather than to disguise. Once, I snipped the dark blond length to my shoulders and immediately regretted it. I missed its coverage and protection.

In erasing my mother's preferences, and then perhaps growing or dyeing bits of them back, I uncovered who I've always been, separate from her coercion. I've parsed meaning through writing. Textual portraits help me erase and reimagine what I learned growing up.

One day I felt my heart skip a beat when I caught sight of my image in the bathroom mirror. There I spotted the best of my younger self, and my emerald eyes glowed with a steady confidence.

The woman in the mirror still resembles my mom, but I now see my hair, eyes, and body as my own, rather than the fried extensions she claimed for herself.

||

Most days now, I gather my flowing locks in my palm and twist until the strands narrow to a swirl. Winding it tight, the length buckles into a loop. I finish shaping it and jam on an elastic, then coil the band—once, twice, three times—until the bun is sturdy enough to hold.

My Body Is a Narrative that Keeps Changing

QUESTION

Friend: "You keep getting smaller. What's your secret? Are you on a diet?"

ANSWER

a) *2006, the first time I have a serious flare-up of gastroesophageal reflux disease, lasting weeks.*

Me: "No, I'm sick. I haven't been able to eat anything besides bread and water for the last week."

Friend One: "Oh, that's great! I should try that."

Me: "Um . . . I'm actually in a lot of pain. You don't want to lose weight this way. Trust me."

Friend One: "Whatever works! You look fantastic!"

b) *2011, after moving abroad to gain distance from lingering childhood trauma at home in Canada.*

Me: "No. I've been eating healthier lately, but I think the real reason is the deep inner work I've been doing to heal old emotional issues. Have you ever heard of *The Presence Process*?"

Friend Two: "No! What is it?"

Me: "It's a six-week experiential meditation course. There's a book that leads you through it. I did it twice and felt like I let go of a ton of old crap each time. The author says this is way more effective than a diet, since often our bodies are trying to protect us."

Friend Two: "That's amazing! Whatever you've been doing, keep it up!"

c) *2018, the second time I have a serious flare-up of gastroesophageal reflux disease, lasting one year.*

Me: "No, I'm actually really sick. I've been to the hospital four times now."

Friend Three: "Oh! Well, you look great. I'm jealous!"

Me: "You really shouldn't be. I'm in a lot of pain."

Friend Three: "Well, whatever you're doing, it's working!"

d) *2021, after getting stuck in Toronto due to a global health crisis. My appetite is back and I'm able to eat a full meal now. I feel a lot better.*

Me: "Actually, that's an old picture, from two years and a pandemic ago. I look different now. But thanks!"

Friend Four: [No response.]

YOLANDE HOUSE's creative non-fiction has appeared in literary magazines such as *The Rumpus*, *Grain*, *PRISM international*, *Plenitude*, and *The Fiddlehead*. A graduate of the Sage Hill Writing Experience, she has been the recipient of many literary grants and has helped writers successfully apply for grant funding. Currently, Yolande lives in Toronto and is working on a memoir-in-essays about being hard of hearing. Find out more at YolandeHouse.com.

SOPHIA KOOY

Mystagogy

An excerpt

When the Western Roman Empire fell in the fifth century, western and eastern forms of Imperial Christianity began to diverge. Nascent theological differences took hold, and Christianity officially split in the eleventh century into Catholicism in Europe and Orthodoxy in Eastern Europe and the Middle East.

In the West, Orthodox Christianity—prominent in Eastern Europe—is often either unknown or exoticized. The elaborate rituals, veneration of saints and mystics, prostrations before icons—these fascinate or mildly bemuse a rationalist culture. While Catholic rituals mirror forms of Orthodox ritual, the Catholic rational mind knows exactly when the bread and wine turn into the body and blood of Christ, whereas the Orthodox mind is baffled by the mystery of it all.

I was baptized into the Orthodox Church in Oxford, England, as a newborn. Photos from the time show me naked and dripping as a robed priest pulls me out of the baptismal cauldron. I look startled and somewhat nonplussed. One is not always in the mood for mysteries.

If it hadn't been for my parents' religious eclecticism, and their apparently insatiable curiosity in our early years as a family, the mood for mysteries might never have caught me. As it was, I was exposed to a variety of religious expressions. We worshipped in the dark incense-filled sanctuary on Sundays. We also meditated with a group of Hindu Brahma Kumaris on Saturdays. Juxtaposed, these made the doctrinal certainty of any religion seem like the least important part. Baptized into an Eastern temperament and disposition, I ate up the mystery of it all.

The recklessness of a God who knows no boundaries caught me.

The unfathomable continuity between worlds. The dialogue between life and death.

Obsessed, I chase.

||

How do you write in absences? How do you paint with a colour that doesn't exist? How do you dip your old fountain pen into that dark hole in your chest, write all you know in it, and hand someone an empty page: Read, if you can, the invisible ink.

||

I don't remember when Nadyusha died. She was living in the big room that used to be Mama and Papa's, in bed all day. Mama tells me she always had a sweet to give me. "Come, little one, sit with me." I remember the feeling of the cream-coloured carpet on my naked feet. "Come here, little one." I remember the heavy futon bed, the low frame, the bedsheets. Nadyusha. Do I remember you?

Mama and Papa had somehow bought an old brick house in Oxford. Papa was writing and teaching. Mama worked at a lab. "Those were busy days," says Mama. "They were heavy days. Little you and then little David and then Nadyusha moved in with us. We soon realized how sick she was."

I see pictures: little me with little David with Nadyusha in a big field. I remember walking along the Thames, I remember climbing fences, I remember the fields, I remember punting, I remember Warwick Castle, I remember Mama's lab, I remember Papa reciting Coleridge.

In the pictures, Nadyusha wears a big red coat. She becomes smaller and smaller, the coat bigger and bigger as the illness goes on. I remember the coat, the brass zipper, the metal tips on the hood strings. I remember Mama in the red coat, I remember the smell, I remember it cold in the English wind, in the fields, I remember running into it, running into Mama. Little me, little Mama. But in the pictures, it's Nadyusha in the red coat.

Nadyusha … do I remember you?

||

I know some things about your life, but there are gaps—cracks in my memories of you, in my memories of the stories of you. I fling the shutters open—I open my windows to you: Blow through them.

||

She looks at me from the table she's sitting at, barely visible, huddled beside a small lamp. The edges of the photograph are darkened, zeroing in on her, zeroing in on me looking at her from this side of the veil, like a telescope. I see her up close, galaxies away, and here she is on my lap. Is she looking in on me from the other end? Is she looking in on me, tiny, catching her eye from this side of the telescope, the side that shrinks?

||

Ancestors. On Mama's side they're in Russia, Ukraine, Georgia, Armenia. What do these names mean to me? I learned Soviet politics, fears and angers through absences. I know the things Mama didn't talk about. I hold the contours of the holes, the things she's forgotten, the emptiness she's passed down. I stand on ground no one I know was buried in. I'm new here. What would it feel like to know your lineage extending below your feet? I light candles for you and dance.

||

Mama says the difference between secular art and holy art is a difference of participation. Secular art creates worlds, real worlds, that exist parallel to ours. This is the craft of the artist, this quasi-divine intervention into the fabric of reality: It's real so long as consciousness is, the world created in a story, a painting, a song. We participate in it when we watch, read, or listen, often longing to lose ourselves in it, to escape from the world we carry so heavily as our own into the billions that run parallel to it. Holy art, she says, holy art creates the bridge. Look at icons: A different world, for sure—angels, the communion of saints with their halos, the Divine Child—but if you know how to look, you see them all streaming into ours. The invitation of the icon is not to leave your world, its heaviness, the way it sits on your shoulders, the way it pushes you into the ground. Instead, the icon opens its doors to the winds of the angels who sit there, in the world of the icon, waiting to throw themselves at us in a fit of ecstatic and tender love. Paint icons, says Mama, more and more of them, and hide them throughout the world. They are portals. Not for us, but for them.

||

The second-last Sunday before Lent, we pray for the departed. The prayers really begin on Saturday night during Vespers, but they resonate through the next day, infusing the Sunday morning liturgy with memories as the chants continue to remember those who have "fallen asleep." Shaping itself around these prayers, my world shifts and a new one opens. Moving with the rhythm of the chants, I follow it: It's a droplet, a floating bubble, a gust of air, a shapeshifter. The chanting slips under my clothes, under my skin and I pulse with it, I become this new world and I see.

The room is dark, icons look out at us from all sides, incense burns, and heads bowed, we chant and remember. Slowly, the room fills with the departed, with those who have "fallen asleep," with the presence of years and years gone by. A portal opens and we are all here in a long, ancient now. Our community extends beyond the walls of time and a different breath flows. But who sleeps? Perhaps these prayers are meant to awaken those who pray. "Look at us, we're here, and it's all so much bigger than you can imagine," the departed say, as our eyes open.

The reckless breath of a love that knows no bounds blows through our eyes. Nadyusha, I remember you.

SOPHIA KOOY is an emerging prose poetry and creative non-fiction writer living in Vancouver. Originally from Europe, Sophia explores themes of ancestry, loss, memory, and relationship to land in the context of ritual and the sacred, as understood by different spiritual and religious traditions.

MARIAH J. VORONOFF

The Walk-In

An excerpt from a collection of essays about the hospitality industry

It's Tuesday, I'm pretty sure. It can't be a weekend; we aren't busy enough. I stand here polishing glassware in a trance, staring at the rich mahogany bar. The swirls and whorls of the carved beams snake across the walls of the room. This is all to imply a "warm embrace of the patrons," or so was the esoteric vision of the Napoleonic architect. I remember him waxing poetically about it to me the other day, between flashing a series of photos of his last sojourn at Burning Man. I had gotten caught in his daily performance of importance as I brought him his usual coffee. The coffee he never paid for, nor ever left me a tip for.

To my left, I hear the clinking and whooshing of ice spinning into a tornado at the hands of the elfish bartender as she dutifully mixes and dilutes a cocktail.

"Can you grab more brine?"

I stop my melodic twirl of the white polishing cloth, realizing it's not the first time she's asked. "Sorry!"

Urgency: That's what makes the job addictive. Slow days are deadly. Nothing is in a rush. Pars are stable. The kitchen chit machine spits orders out at a lullaby's pace. It's slow enough that a line cook is cleaning out one of the lowboys, just to have something to do. "If you have time to lean, you have time to clean," the managers would admonish us.

I'm eager for a task to take me off the floor, something to make the molasses of time less painstaking. After inspecting one final glass in the light for any residual lint or smudges, I place it on the shelf. I beeline across the front of the kitchen window on my way to the cellar. That's when he must see me.

Using the whole side of my body, I push open the heavy steel door to the basement storeroom. The hinges scream out, desperate for some WD-40. Past the racks of wine, spirits, and dry goods, I grab three rolls of paper towel and set them in my pathway to collect on my way back upstairs. I enter the walk-in refrigerator and feel the cool air wrap around me. Shelved four rows high and meticulously organized are deli containers labelled with their preparation date. As I reach for the container of olive brine dated July 14, I hear the weighted fridge expel air as it swings open. I look over my shoulder, and our eyes meet. He smiles. The fridge door thuds shut, and the lights go out.

A nervous laugh escapes my lips. "Very funny. I need to get this back upstairs." I gesture pointlessly in the dark.

He doesn't speak, but I sense him moving toward me. My heart begins to hammer. His hot breath is on my neck, his hands slide around my waist. I instantly leave my body behind and look down helplessly at my corporeal form. I'm frozen.

"No need to be nervous, I'm just messing around." His fingers dig into my flesh, punctuating the point where my hip bone connects to my stomach.

I don't say anything. I can't say anything. Liquid splashes onto my ankles, and the smell hits me instantly. Brine.

"Fuck!" He pushes me away.

My hands scramble for purchase on the metal rack in front of me so I don't fall to the floor. The shelves and their contents tremble, betraying the unsteadiness of my grip. I swerve around him, feeling for the door handle. I don't even look back as I slam my hand on the door's release lever. The light of the cellar stings my eyes as I walk out.

When I reach the restaurant floor, it's as if time has stood still. The same patrons occupy the same tables, the bartender is seemingly stirring the same drink, and the line cook is still elbow deep in the lowboy. The bartender's feline eyes shoot to mine, her melodic stirring pace never faltering.

"Brine? Did you find any?" She fills a silver shaker with ice, seals it, and begins to shake it with unbelievable grace.

"I looked, but I couldn't find any. I think we're out."

He still hasn't come up the stairs.

"Let me ask the cooks if I can strain some out from their olives."

She acknowledges my solution with the slightest inclination of her chin. Her arms still vibrating, the ice knocking back and forth in rapid symphony.

I walk back to the polishing station and pluck another wine glass from the drying rack. Just as if I had never left.

MARIAH J. VORONOFF is a writer and freelancer recovering from the fast-paced entertainment and hospitality industries. She channels her experiences into stories that explore human nature, resilience, and reinvention, all with a dollop of dry wit. When not writing, Mariah embraces new creative endeavors and continues her journey of self-discovery. She currently lives in Vancouver, with her long-suffering partner and psychotic dog.

RICH TAYLOR

Procession

August 2022, Selby, North Yorkshire, England

The weight was heavy on my shoulder, solid and unforgiving. It felt like the force of history bearing down on me, enclosed in burnished oak. My feet shuffled awkwardly over the uneven stone paving, which was bent and buckled from years of use, as I tried to keep step with those alongside and in front of me. One arm arced over my head to steady the load.

We moved in unison despite discord among us. Some of us, not all. I somehow got a free pass from the infighting and petty squabbles. Absence does indeed make the heart grow fonder. Or maybe it just keeps you out of trouble. Still, the others temporarily reconciled when greater needs arose.

I was in the middle-right; Pete, my cousin's partner, in front. Lee, my brother, at the rear. His heavy breathing echoed in my ear. Lee's ursine strength was comforting, not just in grief but in the practical task of carrying my grandfather toward the abbey. I felt stupid, Victorian, in my traditional black mourning suit, bought to avoid offending anyone's sense of propriety. Others were dressed in grey and navy blue, bringing a modern style to an ancient tradition—an act I assumed was unacceptable. It's funny how quickly you can lose touch, or maybe my anxiety around this was also historic, an infantile fear of angering the elders.

The coffin obscured my field of vision. The rest of my view was dominated by the looming façade of the abbey, its heavy oaken doors wrought in iron at the base, the statues of carved saints and angels stacked toward the heavens, leering gargoyles among them, reaching higher and higher to the pinnacle of the bell tower. The bell rang out in singular chimes across the town's market square, a dirge clanging around in my head. The sight of the monolithic stone abbey was all-consuming, the thought that for ten centuries people had walked this very path to commit their family to the earth in death, to commit to each other in marriage in life, to pray for eternal life while worshipping the dead son of God. Despite my own family's lack of faith, I had spent childhood days at its pews, singing hymns and gazing up the limestone columns, past the clerestory toward the lofty gold-studded roof, believing the Lord on high himself dwelt just beyond and out of view. Good Anglican schooling. My grandparents had married here over seventy years ago. I felt I was simultaneously moving through a ritual and a timeless parable. Immersed yet detached, carrying my grandfather to the altar.

We moved slowly down the aisle, accompanied by sombre organ tones. The abbey was packed, evidence of my grandfather's local popularity. Relatives I didn't know and others I didn't care to know lined up in neat rows, watching respectfully as we moved toward the altar and the priest who stood with arms folded over her robes. You would have hated this, I thought.

The familiar relatives were gathered at the front of the crowd. Most of my cousins—first, second, third; my sister. All their partners. Your nieces and nephews, red-nosed and surly. Your two sisters, keening like abandoned ocean wives. Your brother had died not six months before, and the older sister would go, too, not six months later. Within a year, four down to one.

After the priest's welcome and a few obligatory Bible passages, we entered the standard hymns, insisted upon by your sisters. It was so strange to me that we would follow the traditional script, given how you rejected the Church your entire life, the nun's rod etched in your memory, their shaming of your limitations branded on your sense of self. They didn't define your life course, but they damn well left their mark.

You were born June 6, 1931, in a two-up-two-down, not a mile from where we now stood. Three months premature, not an easy start in that place and time. They said you were the weight of a bag of sugar, just like the ones you would stockpile in your kitchen in your old age, never quite growing out of childhood memories of wartime rationing. You began life in an iron lung, so they gave you a name to give you strength, and them hope. A name that belied your frailty at birth but that proved apt for the vigour with which you took on life: Leo (the Lion).

Prematurity didn't stop you, but polio almost did. You didn't even really know how you got it, told it was the result of a broken leg. No, poliovirus is spread by dirty water, not falling down the stairs.

The iron lung gave way to experimental electroconvulsive treatments, muscles stripped from the bone, proposed and fiercely refused amputations. Religious sisters are indifferent to the source of illiteracy, though—fixed on punishment and repentance over love and mercy. They ensured your resentment of the Church and the polite scanning of birthday and Christmas cards was as much a part of you as your lifelong limp. "Ta, kid. Get your Granny to read it out for us, then." You did care about words, though. You taught me not to say "cripple."

Still, we stood dutifully in the abbey and sang the hymns. I suppose, really, it was Christ's enforcers you had a problem with, not his promise.

After the service and burial, we retired to the Working Men's Club. It sounded like a vestige of a bygone era, but in some places, time just moves more slowly. A buffet of sandwiches and sausage rolls, pints and white wine spritzers. Relatives found their islands, huddled together in protective cliques, shooting suspicious glances at one another. An old man sat alone. He held a stick between his legs to steady himself, a half pint of bitter untouched before him on the table. Still, he had a lively glint in his eye. I realized it was Brian Cooney, a friend of yours since your teens. I went and sat with him. He recognized me from speaking at the service.

"Richard, isn't it?"

"Yes, David's son. Leo's grandson."

"You spoke well. He was the best friend I ever had."

He relived memories from sixty, seventy, almost eighty years ago. Working at factories, painting people's houses, drinking and fighting together. Brian visited you in hospital in your last days. What many would give for a single relationship so enduring, but you had plenty. You were the most recent loss in a gang fast disappearing. Brian was the last one. Still, he seemed at peace with it.

You were both men of your time, rarely forthcoming with your inner thoughts, but something held you together, an unspoken fraternity. Even when life presented disagreements or distance, the bond was unshakeable and sustaining. How else could something last a lifetime? The thought of yours' and Brian's quiet, solid resilience quelled the dissonance of familial strife, discomfiting returns, and servility to tradition.

Brian drained his half, said goodbye, and headed down the stairs one last time. I hear he just passed away.

The reception began to thin, leaving just family. Someone bridged the gap (was it me?) between tables and cliques. We merged into one large group, drinks flowing, memories and laughter in the air. Shared grief and love for a man who shaped generations was enough to put bitterness aside for a day, at least. The alcohol didn't hurt. In fact, it was the star of the show, as it was for many of your youthful tales. We all laughed that the lifetime ban you technically had from this venue (you and Brian strike again) had now finally expired. The memory of those past misdemeanours must have been lingering in the faded wallpaper or threadbare carpets; it turned out Pete had your bank card.

"I have an idea ..."

He stumbled to the bar and returned bearing trays filled with Jägermeister, a drink you inexplicably enjoyed in your later years, to raucous applause. Shots were passed around and dutifully, happily thrown back.

"That round's on Leo!" Pete shouted, laughing, to cheers and splutters and Jesus-Christ-that's-horribles.

That bit, at least, you would not have hated.

RICH TAYLOR is a writer and musician based in Victoria. Originally from a small town in North Yorkshire, in northern England, Rich is grateful for the privilege to live on W̱SÁNEĆ territory on Vancouver Island with his partner and pets. Rich writes non-fiction and speculative fiction, exploring themes of place and belonging, as well as dystopian futures, societal collapse, and consciousness.

ALEXANDRA FLYNN

The Things We Keep

"Who owns this?" I asked my class, raising an apple high in the air.

Fifty first-year law students blinked at me in the early September light, as though trying to gauge whether this was a trick question. It always was.

I tossed the bright red fruit to a redheaded student in the first row, who caught it awkwardly, then cradled it like a fragile egg.

"Me?" they offered.

"Are you sure?" I asked.

In the back row, a voice whispered, "Eat it and hide the evidence!"

Laughter.

We spent the hour talking about the fundamentals of property law—possession, title, rights. I clicked through slides of legal cases dating back centuries. A bundle of sticks. A mortgage. A lease. All the dry bones of ownership. But I didn't tell them what I really wanted to say. Not yet.

Because I knew something they didn't: This year, I was attending two classes on property law. One, with them, in the lecture hall. And one, with myself, in my mother's shadow.

After my mother died, I inherited more than memories. I inherited the unspoken responsibility of understanding her life through the scraps she left behind—boxes and papers and the burden of not knowing what to do with them.

My mother's name was Florence. Like her nickname, Fluff, she was bright and limitless, wanting to do everything and be everywhere. She once decided, abruptly, to take up the bass. She devoured books, usually three at once. She asked questions—big ones—and wasn't afraid to answer them out loud.

She didn't believe in decluttering. Not in the way that's fashionable now, with scanned photos and Dropbox. She kept everything, which is another way of saying she wasn't ready to let go of any version of herself. Her life was lived in layers—justice seeker, social worker, single mother, wanderer, friend—and her chattels told every story.

I inherited boxes that had multiplied like spring rabbits, gathering dust under her bed, crowding windows in the basement. The kind of archival detritus that no one would post on Instagram: curled receipts from Safeway, soy sauce packages, sticky notes with children's scrawls, unsent cards, grocery lists that doubled as poetry ("yogurt / turmeric / joy?"). Difficult things, too: notes from men who didn't deserve her, unpaid bills, overdue tax returns.

One sparkle among the clutter, found in a cedar trunk she had given to my young son, was a tattered yellow envelope I came to think of as the heart of it all. Stuffed inside were the letters my mom had written to her parents from a youth hostel in Delhi, from an orphanage in the Himalayan foothills, from a windswept ferry to the Greek islands, each signed "Fluff" in her flowery handwriting. She had been so young then—23, maybe 24. Writing home, as if trying to prove her existence across time zones.

I sat in my kitchen reading those letters night after night, while preparing to teach about possessory interests in land. My students would ask questions about jewellery buried underground, about leases gone sour. They were thinking in terms of value and liability.

But I was focused on her handwriting. I thought of the things we possess that no PDF can replicate. The weight of holding a letter with your mother's scripts that insists on presence, the paper soft at the folds, ink smudged by time or tears.

We are a culture built on simplifying. You can Marie Kondo your grief. You can upload your memories to a cloud that promises eternal storage. We are so good at concealing what we can't optimize.

A few months ago, I read about a woman in Tokyo who sorts through the belongings of those who had a "lonely death." She helps families decide what to keep, what to donate, what to burn. This gentle work is called katazukeru. It assumes that belongings remain animated by the memories, attachments, and energy of the human that possessed it. She wears soft white gloves and speaks with care.

She understands what we've forgotten: that grief is associative. It attaches itself to objects and routines and echoes. A birthday card in my mom's handwriting becomes a thesis on loss. A letter with her signature becomes an existential crisis. A diary entry—undated, unaddressed—becomes a prayer you didn't know you needed.

In another life, maybe we all would've had time to become archivists of our families. In this one, we're trying to survive inboxes and impossible expectations. We pay extra for storage and assume permanence. But the things we keep—really keep—don't take up physical space so much as they ask for our attention.

My mom didn't leave instructions along with her papers. But there was a kind of lesson nonetheless. The things she never threw out—old school report cards, photos of us squinting in prairie sunlight, typewritten dreams—were the truest evidence of who she was.

In my property law classroom, we arrived at easements. Property rights that attach not to the person but to the land itself, travelling through time like invisible stitches. An easement, I informed my students, means you can walk across someone else's land if history says you always could.

And I wondered: Is that what I'm doing now? Walking the well-worn paths of her memory, trespassing across the contours of a life I never fully understood?

I thought of what she would have wanted. Did she imagine we would read everything? Throw it all in a fire and watch the orange flames dance? Carry it forward? There's an unbearable intimacy to posthumous discovery. You want to ask, "Did you mean for me to see this?" But there's no one left to answer.

I didn't know what to do with those countless boxes. But, as it turns out, I didn't have to decide. They were taken, one by one, by my sister—without fanfare, without conversation. I let it happen. I don't even know if she meant to take them or if she was just trying to make space in her own version of grief.

What's left of my mom's treasures is that manila envelope and in it, letters like clues. Snapshots of my mother, half my age. I keep the envelope on a shelf in my study, next to a photo of her squinting in the sun, arms holding bright flowers.

One night, not long ago, I read a letter she wrote from Athens in 1965. "Today I watched the sun set over the Aegean Sea and thought of you," she wrote to her parents. "Somehow I feel full and empty at the same time."

That's what grief is.

"Love, Fluff."

That's what inheritance is, too.

Not the things. But the fullness and the emptiness they leave behind. The willingness to sit with someone else's complexity, even when they're no longer here to explain it. Especially then.

I now teach property with a quiet subtext: What matters is not always what is owned, but what is loved. The things my students bring in for a class exercise—photos of childhood homes, of heirloom tea sets, of a grandmother's sewing machine—speak to a kind of property the law can't quite quantify.

Treasure is what we keep.

ALEXANDRA FLYNN is a law professor living in Vancouver with her partner, big-footed sons, and a towering stack of old New Yorkers. She has authored dozens of books and articles on property law, homelessness, and the constitutional status of cities. She's currently writing a book on the right to housing and perhaps another about her colourful mom. She enjoys hiking, hosting theme parties, and any excuse to make a playlist.

ANNE HAMILTON

A Robin's Nest

An excerpt from a memoir-in-progress

Full of hope and urgency, two robins collaboratively built a nest in the ancient plum tree outside my window. The perfect crux on a gnarly, twisted branch was assessed, then chosen. Over days, they layered it with fine grasses and small twigs. Finally, she nestled down, shaping the findings, tucking and adjusting for comfort and space as her mate watched from above, holding a new offering in case it was needed.

For thirteen days she sat, never leaving her post, managing the excessive summer heat with an open beak. Her mate brought mushy wrigglers, placing them within her reach.

On the fourteenth day, she fussed and tidied the nest of debris and small shards of teal- blue eggshells. Her head swivelled, watching for predators. I marvelled at the luminous yellow glow of three tiny round mouths vying for the smashed-up worms dangling from her beak, delivered every ten minutes while there was light. Exhausted by their efforts, the nestlings collapsed, silent. She settled over them, wings spread to shield them from the sun or the wet summer storm.

The protective parents were never far away. Ferociously, they staved off marauding crows and a greedy squirrel amidst the ripening plums. Five days later, the little beaks peeped louder. Their sparse orange fluff crested the rim of the nest as they shifted positions.

An unknown overnight raider was their end. Little pink intestines, full of their last meal, lay glistening on the wet lawn. All other flesh peeled and consumed. The wall of the nest lay ruined beside them. Their whole existence lasted nineteen days.

The two robins surveyed the site from the fence for three days. Reflexively, they checked the branch, searching. The next day they were gone.

Is this how birds mourn? So much energy invested. So much hope, labour, and care. Yet, nature dealt its hand. I wept for them. I reverently watched small ants consume the pale remains. I sat in silence, holding space for them. I grieved their little family, a proxy for my own lost dreams.

||

We were a mated pair, bonded over home renovations, infertility, and loss. Our hope-filled pursuit of the dream ended with the demise of our unborn child. My last egg and his weakened sperm failed to create a viable form. The amniocentesis declared it an impossible pregnancy with a severe chromosome 2 duplication. Dead baby now or dead baby later, they said. The risk to my life was very high, they said. My choice.

"How quickly can this happen? I'm already 21 weeks."

Next week, they said. Outpatient daycare.

How cold and matter of fact. Scheduling my despair like it was an appointment at the salon.

We drove home in silence and lay on the bed. Then he put his head on my belly and said, "Goodbye baby," and rolled away from me to cry.

I was on my own.

The next day he told his parents. They came over right away, and his dad, crying, knelt on the living room floor to hug me as I sat on the ottoman.

"I had to do this in person," he said. "A phone call just wouldn't do."

His mom gave me a hug like I had leprosy.

The next week, tears soaked my face as I changed into a surgical gown and was wheeled away. My partner was emotional too, but I didn't have the extra strength to support him. I was struggling to breathe for myself.

When I woke up, there was a woman standing on the other side of the recovery unit, dressed in black, and carrying a small black cooler. Irrationally, I thought that she was there to collect the parts of my baby. I broke down, almost hysterical. Then I remembered. Just before they put me under, the surgeon asked if I wanted to save the remains for a funeral. In shock and already drugged, I had said no, the idea unconsidered until that moment.

Still distraught when the surgeon came by later, I asked what would happen to the remains—was it too late to keep them? He said they were wrapped and burned as medical waste after the mandatory autopsy. The nurse asked if there was a name for the paperwork. I said no, we didn't even know the gender. My partner, next to me, said nothing. A shroud of darkness descended.

I knew the tiny body was not yet ensouled. That the tissues, without breath, bore little resemblance to a living being. My first abortion, years ago, after a violent rape, and later, my work at an abortion clinic, had educated me thoroughly. Strange to think how these chapters in my life were connected. First as a victim, then as a key volunteer in the feminist movement, creating a place where women have choice, only to find myself gutted at my loss under this circumstance, a decade later.

My blood and tears poured for hours. My partner sat at my side, his head buried in the blankets beside my hand, not touching me. I thought I was going to die. How easy it would have been to just stop breathing and fall into a bloodless sleep, never to awaken.

||

Compelled to attend genetic counselling together, I finally gave my fears a little voice. "But what if I can't have any more children?"

With a straight, unmoving face, he said, "I want children, and if you can't have my children, then I may leave you."

The counsellor sat back in her seat, silent. I wept, bearing all the burden of failure and the ruin of his dreams and my own. In hindsight, I should have raged. I should have left the room or thrown a chair at him.

But, no. Like a child admonished, I followed him out when the session concluded, wondering why he wanted to hold my hand if he was going to leave me. Thinking only, where would I live, what would I do? What can I do to salvage this? I had ruined everything. It must have been my fault. After all, why should I expect him to support me—stupid, needy, sickly me? Toxic negativity coursed in my veins. The gaping wounds of my unhealed childhood and young adult traumas raced to the fore like a tsunami, obliterating all sense and sensibility. He couldn't handle my tears, my sadness, my pain.

Grieving would have to wait. I had done it before—hiding my feelings. I faked my way through the horrors until they could be packed away tightly. That's how I survived all those years of violence, childhood sexual abuse, the trial and incarceration of my father, the offender. I survived the death of my dreams over and over again. I would survive this, too.

Book a vacation, my partner said. Anywhere, you choose, he said.

How about this or that? I proposed. What about here or there?

Fine. Whatever, you decide, he said.

So, I planned for his comfort, not my own. If he could be happy, then I could manage my own tears privately. While he had expectations of some honeymoon-like vacation, I was desperate to stop quaking, sweating, and bleeding. I wanted to heal. I wanted us to heal. Instead, we got sick, along with everyone else at the tropical resort.

The Fijian island was small and surrounded by a strong reef. Each day at dawn, I walked the beach alone as the surf pounded offshore. A worker raked the sand along the tideline, creating a small picture of perfection. Every morning the same pile of debris was raked up and buried at the shore, only to be washed up again by the overnight tide. I stood watching him work, my gaze fixed on a broken pair of infant-sized, round-framed yellow sunglasses being buried yet again. For fourteen days I watched those silent, abandoned little rims, before we, too, flew away, like the robins outside my window.

||

Three years later, in-vitro specialists and an egg donor helped create our precious child, our neurodivergent gift. After five more years of disappointments and domestic calamities, he walked away for good. Sixteen years on, I am finally learning to grieve, to release my losses—him, my parents, the other abusers, and those old broken dreams.

ANNE HAMILTON, an emerging writer, lives in Maple Ridge, B.C. Anne is a Scottish-born Canadian retiree and a quintessential student of life, encouraging other souls to be curious, courageous, and to seek healing for themselves. Amidst her collections of rocks, feathers, and useful tools, she listens for, and learns from, whispers on the wind. See more online at AnneHamiltonWrites.ca or at ShamanicWind.ca.

MRIDULA MORGAN

SALT

Dinner
1975-ish
Smalltown, B.C.

"Dinnneeerrr!" That's how my sister's booming voice would interrupt the *Nancy Drew* mystery I was immersed in.

She and I divided up the duties of setting the table. The everyday Corelle plates—white with navy blue, flower-printed rims—were placed at each seat, along with the worn cutlery, save for Mama's, as she preferred to eat with her hands. Next came the essential laminated coasters for the dishes. Then, either a jar of mango achar, homemade chutney (Mama's sesame chutney was always my favourite), or a quarter plate of chopped Indian green chilies.

We'd wait for Papa's verdict. A slurp, followed by "maza aa gaya" confirmed that it was very tasty. Alternatively, Papa would make an unpleasant face and rebuke the dish. My eyes would dart to my mother, whose eyes focused on her plate. My muscles tightened and I could barely taste the curry or dahl after that. I wondered if other fathers did the same with mothers who'd spent a good portion of the afternoon working on dinner. At the same time, a part of me felt relieved that Papa didn't single me out for any transgression I had committed.

I was secretly happy on the occasions when Mama let out a barely audible "hmmmmh." This was followed by a shake of her head that translated to: *As if you, who's never prepared a dish in your life, have any right to comment.*

The kitchen and food were my mother's domain—a space that gave her freedom to exact her own power.

||

Fifty years later, my mother is unable to stand for long periods to prepare Indian dishes. My father has passed on. As I never learned to prepare Indian food, my diet consists primarily of homemade Italian dishes cooked by my Italian partner, who occasionally attempts other cuisines for variety.

I long to taste something made by Mama's hands, but hold the sad knowledge that it will not happen again. Memories of rajma, aloo gobi, fish curry, and countless other dishes I was raised on are scattered like dandelion seeds. They rise and float, looking for a place to land and begin again.

||

These memories of flavours have continued to tease and pull, nudging me to get closer to the Indian spices I now have in my kitchen cupboard.

I vibrate with excitement as Mom and I enter the kitchen. This is my kitchen. Well, truth be known, my partner Elio does about ninety percent of the cooking in our home. But today I'm happy to finally claim that *I* prepared a curry dish.

"Okay, Mom, the arhar ki dahl has been soaking all night," I say.

My mother's face falls. "All night? I never used to soak it that long."

"Elio insisted on soaking it." I give my partner a quick nod that says, *See, I told you not to bother soaking it that long. I know a little bit about dahl.* "Maybe we won't need to cook it as long?" I offer.

Mom nods, reluctant. My heart sinks a little at this setback.

Elio's already rinsing the rice before he puts it on the stove to boil. My mind goes back to when Mama, Dadi, and my great-aunt used to sit at the dining table checking the rice for debris, then washing it multiple times before boiling.

Now, Elio and I rush around the kitchen, anxious to ensure the dahl turns out. We try our best to manoeuvre around Mom, who stands in a supervisory role at the stove. There are groans and *tsks* as we try not to trip over each other.

"Can you please not—"

"I *asked* you if you wanted it, and you said no!"

"Shouldn't you start on—"

"Mom, can you check the recipe on the iPad?" My brow furrows, and I clench my teeth. I want so much for this to work, to create something with my mother that in some way may further legitimize my identity as a South Asian who can cook (I comprehend Hindi but speak it like a toddler at best).

Damn, I think, *I wish it was just Mom and I puttering away in the kitchen today.*

She was a skillful operator in the kitchen. Ingredients were portioned out on the counter, ready to be added to whatever dish she was making. The way she danced from cupboard to fridge to stove to sink was done with such precision that it would put the most highly skilled chefs to shame.

But it wasn't always that way, Mom once reminded me. She learned through trial and error and from Nani, who was a strict cook with a critical eye. While Nani had learned to cook from Nana, she believed in exacting the best from her children. When Mom prepared a dish that was not done right, Nana would simply ask for the salt, whereas Nani would point out the faults of the dish Mom had laboured over.

Mom now nudges me to start work on the tadka, which is to be drizzled on top of the finished dahl. Garlic, mustard seeds, and chili. We have none of the dried, red whole chilies, so I substitute chopped fresh green chilies.

"That's a lot of water in the dahl," Elio suggests.

"Mom put it in. I'll go with what she says." After all, Elio is not South Asian, and my Mom was always queen in our family kitchen.

It does look like it's getting overly soft, but Mom's unsure, so we leave it. Eventually, I remove about half a cup of water from the dahl. I groan at this second flub. Soaked too long and now drowning in water.

Once the tadka is done, Mom asks me to mix it with the dahl.

"Now? I thought we were to put it on top and leave it for a bit."

She reassures me that it can be done either way.

My face breaks into a smile at the sunshine-yellow dahl with brown dots of mustard seed and bright green bits of chili. *This is a moment,* I think, and take a photo on my mobile.

Dinner's plated, Mom says grace, and my muscles tense as we turn to the food.

Spoon. Chew. Pause.

It's too soft. It's bland—it barely tastes any different than the rice, and the tadka hasn't added any flavour. My mother asks me to pass the salt. I hand it to her with a small smile.

In my head, I commit to memory: The dahl was soaked too long, cooked in too much water, and didn't boil long enough. It came out lacking the structure and creaminess of a proper arhar ki dahl.

Also, my mother's memory is fading.

Next time, I will try to emulate Mom's rajma. I wonder if it will hint of the same flavour as hers or if I will be left with something wholly different—a taste that leaves me longing.

MRIDULA MORGAN is a first-generation settler/ally from India, and currently resides on the unceded territories of the Musqueam, Squamish, and Tsleil-Waututh people. She's had a love affair with words since childhood, completed an MA in education, and has worked in social services for over thirty years. She interrogates the self/other within personal and political systems when crafting creative non-fiction.

ALLAN CHO

The Realm of Resistors and Hockey Cards

In the heart of Vancouver's Eastside district, wedged between a Petro Canada gas station and a barber shop that never seemed to close, stood a messy storefront crowded with used televisions, VCRs, and camcorders in various stages of revival. The soft humming of Jacky Cheung and Andy Lau—Cantopop stars from the '90s—and the aroma of smoky solder mixing with WD-40 lubricant pervaded Granville TV & Hi-Fi Sales & Service, our family-owned small electronics repair shop. Dad would be in his usual squat position, glasses slipping down his nose as he studied the circuitry behind a big wooden cathode-ray tube television.

My family lived together in this shop during the day while Dad worked, and went home together afterwards. The backroom of the electronics repair shop was a cluttered, dimly lit space where the rhythm of life blended work and home. Mom watched over my brother in his playpen as she prepared the next meal. The TV stayed on, but without sound. On one side of the room, tools hung on peg boards—pliers, cables, spools of copper wire—and open drawers were filled with an assortment of knobs, wires, and circuit boards. On the other side was an oven and sink with dishes and containers of dried medicinal herbs.

After finishing lunch, I wiped my face with my sleeve and got ready for action.

"Be back for dinner this time," Mom said as I put on my white roller skates, tying the laces so tight I could hardly feel my feet.

Behind the little store was my sanctuary: an imaginary hockey palace with glassy ice, freshly smoothed for the third period of the Stanley Cup finals between the Edmonton Oilers and the Pittsburgh Penguins, my two favourite NHL teams. This was where my imagination recreated reality day after day.

I had no interest in school textbooks, and the homework thrown at me daily was usually only half-completed. My life in the 1990s was a complete obsession with hockey. Unfortunately, I did not have the luxury of organized hockey leagues with real ice and referees—they were out of reach. My family had no money for ice skates, fancy sticks, or registration fees. Instead, I had concrete, roller skates, and Wayne Gretzky.

Wayne wasn't just a player to me, he was my idol—*the Great One*, as he was known to the hockey world. His Jofa helmet captivated me. It was the lightest, most unique-looking helmet, shaped like a dome that resembled ones used by cyclists rather than the helmets worn by other NHL players. The helmet expresses the player's character, and Wayne's was one of royalty, a crown.

I watched his games on the grainy TV sets my dad repaired, entranced for three hours from the moment the bold, brassy notes of the "Hockey Night in Canada Theme Song" synchronized with Bob Cole's iconic play-by-play commentary. In his nasally voice, he'd shout, "It's *ninety-nine*!" whenever Wayne touched the puck—the number on his hockey jersey. Wayne hunched over as he glided in slow motion, his movements smooth and precise while everyone else rushed around him.

I imagined myself beside him, wearing my own Jofa helmet, charging down the rink as his loyal left winger. When I laced up my roller skates and stepped onto the cracked asphalt behind our store, I wasn't just some Chinese Canadian kid at the back of a dilapidated second-hand electronics repair shop. I was on Wayne's line, an underdog with a plastic street hockey stick and boundless energy.

My love of hockey wasn't born on the ice, though. It started with hockey cards and the Esso NHL Power Players Collector Series in Grade 3. I'd wait for my dad whenever he gassed up his Dodge Caravan after work on our way home because I knew he'd bring me a pack or two after he paid the cashier. Whenever customers fuelled up at an Esso station in Canada, they received a packet of six Power Players Trader Stickers. Dad never said much when he handed them to me, just turned the engine on to drive home, but I knew what it meant. He was quietly cheering me on, enjoying being the father he never had growing up.

Those cards were my treasures. I'd sit cross-legged on the school floor during lunchtime, hunching my back like my favourite hockey player, and study the details of each card: team, position, and even the expression on the player's face. I'd carefully place them inside my crisp Esso NHL Power Player Album. Wayne was always at the top. I kept him in a plastic sleeve I found in my mom's used Becel margarine containers, the closest thing I had to a safe. The other players came and went in my lineup, but Wayne was enduring. My teammate. My captain.

The back of Granville TV was just a square parking lot with a low chain-link fence barely secured by a rusty metal padlock. But to me, it was the legendary Great Western Forum, where Wayne skated as a Los Angeles King. I built nets out of a rice container and string. I used chalk I stole from school to mark out faceoff circles.

There were no boards, Zamboni, or rubber puck, but that didn't matter. That cracked pavement, with its oil stains and sprouts of grass poking through, was where I found so much exhilaration and childhood joy. I played for hours in the summer heat, sweat trickling down my T-shirt, the wheels of my skates clicking over loose gravel as I darted and spun around. The slap of plastic stick to plastic puck echoed like a cheering crowd.

Sometimes, the bored gas attendant next door would wander by to throw out the garbage. I hated that he disrupted my flow whenever he watched me as he lit a cigarette and squatted on the curb. I'd go inside for a breather and sip my favourite soda, Orange Crush. Then I'd play some more until my mom came out to tell me it was time for dinner.

Dad broke the news one day. It was a Saturday, and I had just finished an imaginary third period against the much-hated rivals, the Calgary Flames, while waiting to watch the real Hockey Night in Canada game that started at five o'clock. I was sweaty and breathless, leaning on my stick like a warrior coming off the ice. I coughed and spat a chunk of saliva onto the ground. Dad met me at the back door, cigarette hanging from his lips.

"You can't play out here anymore," he said. "I rented out the space."

I couldn't stop blinking. "What do you mean?"

"A mechanic needs a place to store some cars. He's paying good money."

My hockey rink, about to be filled with old cars? The goal lines disappearing under tires? I knew making an extra dollar was second nature to my family, but this was too much.

Most of my relatives had tenants in their Vancouver Special basements and rented just about anything that could be rented out. They'd wave their placards along their front yards whenever the Pacific National Exhibition opened and rented their back driveways to people looking for a parking spot. They'd grow lettuce and watercress in the backyards (sometimes the front yards).

The following week, my rink was filled with rusted Toyotas and wrenches. I never saw the mechanic as he worked only at night when we were at home. Whoever he was, this guy had no idea what he'd taken from me. He didn't see the boards and benches I saw. He didn't hear the crowd roar as Wayne passed the perfect one-timer to me for my natural hat trick.

My dad never talked about it again, nor did I bring it up. I accepted the reality. The store was always a struggle; renting out the lot was another way he was trying to keep things afloat. I eventually understood that, but it didn't fill my emptiness. Wayne continued to score and set up plays, and I had to watch as a spectator again.

I tried to play in the alley behind our store, but it wasn't the same. Cars coming and going were just distracting. Eventually, I resorted to flipping through my hockey cards like they were relics of a lost world and watched hockey on TV instead.

ALLAN CHO is a writer, community advocate, and librarian based in Vancouver, whose work explores memory, cultural heritage, chronic illness, and resilience. He is working on a book about his family's transnational journey from the 19th to 20th centuries, tracing his great-great-grandfather's arrival in Vancouver in 1899. Outside of writing, Allan is a devoted father who is passionate about hockey and coffee shops.

KIM PAULLEY

Singing Lessons

An excerpt of a long-form essay

Eleven-year-old Kate was left to her own resources, down in her room in the basement—the underworld. She cued up Dusty Springfield on the red and white portable turntable and by turns, belted or crooned along, watching herself in the mirror, just like her mom—except that Kate's brush was used as a microphone, not a tool to coif her hair. She practised "Somewhere Over the Rainbow," repeating the octave leap from *some* to *where* until she nailed it.

Kate married at nineteen—not that unusual in the '70s. It was one way out of her compartmentalized family home, where her plea for singing lessons was ignored. Her mother had wanted to be a singer when she was young too, so it seemed like she'd understand. But no, she was entirely preoccupied with her looks now, enclosed in her powder room playing mirror, mirror on the wall, like Narcissus looking into the pond.

Kate's marriage led to another set of compartments. She stepped into the first one the same day they were pronounced man and wife. That's how they worded it in those days. As if he remained a man, and she became a wife. Imagine the reverse: I now pronounce you woman and husband. That would never fly.

Lying in the matrimonial bed that first night, Kate could barely breathe. She remembered creating that feeling as a child, but this time she hadn't put a pillow over her head. At least Billy loved her, even if they were more like roommates.

They chose a cute apartment in North Vancouver, and Kate made it a sweet and homey nest. Five days a week, she drove her long, navy blue Ford Comet over the Lion's Gate Bridge to her downtown retail job, applying makeup at red lights and singing along to the radio.

She stood all day in pumps, packaged up in silk shirts and skirt suits—all merchandise from the store, all afforded by her staff discount; an underpaid modelling assignment. The moment she arrived home at the end of each day, she closed the apartment door and leaned into it, kicking off the pinching shoes and tearing away the sagging pantyhose.

Kate tiptoed around her kitchen as if being up on her toes was the key to holding her fears at bay, and searched through recipes torn from *Cosmopolitan* magazine. In these memories, she is always alone in that kitchen making dinner, like her mother had been. Her husband, Billy, would be watching sports or reading the paper, as was a man's due.

The weekends were taken up with sleeping late, playing Risk, drinking Schloss Laderheim wine, and going to the movies. *An Unmarried Woman* wended its way into her soul like a how-to doctrine for reinventing herself.

A rainy Saturday in August, one year married and feeling there must be more to life, Kate picked at the threads of singing lessons. Her tears climbed to the surface as she lit on the simple idea of finding a teacher in the Yellow Pages. She dialled and found herself speaking to the singing teacher whose small advertisement had read "Beginners Welcome."

If life can turn on a dime, then this was that. A small but monumental action. Like a long line of bumper cars that finally gain separation and the momentum to break free. (Leaving Billy would eventually be part of that chain reaction, too.)

The following Saturday, Kate drove from North Vancouver to Miss Morley's singing studio in Richmond—one side of the Lower Mainland to the other. It gave Kate time to think. Nervousness jostled in her belly, as if her toes were teetering over the edge of a high diving board. Maybe she couldn't sing well enough to qualify for singing lessons. But the ad had encouraged beginners. It hadn't said "talented" anywhere. And yet, even with all her learned self-doubt, she believed she did have talent. In the same way as in those old movies her mom lived her life through, Kate only needed to be discovered, like Lana Turner at the five-and-dime.

Kate stood on the cement doorstep of a tidy split-level on an even tidier suburban street. She pressed the bell, feeling confident in her well-fitted jeans and camel blazer. Her strawberry blond hair, carefully curled that morning with hot rollers, fell to mid-back in mermaid waves. At least she looked good. Billy's grandma had assured her of that on her wedding day, calling her a great big Barbie doll. It stuck like a sliver under her polished nail, especially after she switched from *Cosmopolitan* to *Ms. Magazine*. Who the fuck wanted to be a Barbie doll?

She waited, half-hoping no one was home, gasping for breath, fear of success looming. About to pivot, the door swung open and Miss Morley appeared: broad smile in place, a warm chuckle eliding with her hello, the smell of cookies in the air. At least six feet tall, dark brown glossy curls gathered around Miss Morley's face like a helmet. Kate would always suspect it was a wig she threw on for teaching days, harkening back to her years upon the stage, a career that seemed behind her now, though she looked to be only in her mid-forties.

She wore a forest-green A-line dress with a frilled collar that sat close to her Adam's apple, more Sunday school than singing teacher. Chunky, primary-coloured beads drew the eye to her jutting bosom, the only thing other than the wig that gave away her diva leanings. If Kate had known anything about opera, she would've pegged her as a Wagnerian soprano. Miss Morley, however, insisted that she was a coloratura. Odd, because they are generally bird-like creatures, but she backed up her claim with regular demonstrations of giggling runs up to high C. At the time, Kate knew nothing about any of that: *What was a high C, anyway?*

Kate followed Miss Morley down to the rec room—*de rigueur* in the '70s—but she'd never seen one with a grand piano. It was black and silky, inviting to the touch. Kate couldn't help caressing it, even if she was swatted with a scold, her fingerprints swiped away with a handy cloth.

Miss Morley placed her regal self behind the keys, positioning Kate in front of her where she could eye her posture, jaw position, and breathing. They began with *ma-me-mi-mo-moo* on one note. From there, they moved onto leaping arpeggios.

"Do you see yourself singing at the opera or in musical theatre?" Miss M implored.

Kate shrugged, and instead rattled off names of singers—Barbra Streisand, Olivia Newton-John—and her favourite songs of theirs that she wanted to sing.

A disapproving frown slid across Miss M's forehead. "NO! We must start with classical." She slapped "Twenty-Four Italian Songs and Arias" on the piano and opened to "Caro Mio Ben."

The page was littered with black—meaningless musical notes that might as well have been spilled ink. Add two staves for the piano and one for the voice, lyrics in Italian … What a mess.

Six months of weekly lessons passed, of faking it through "Caro Mio Ben" and every other classic they dove into. Kate pleaded for pop songs. Learning a song by ear was something she knew how to do. In desperation, she sang a few phrases from Diana Ross's, "Touch Me in the Morning," to make her case.

"No no no," Miss M screeched. "That doesn't work."

It felt like a bucket of ice water dumped on Kate's head. That was her last lesson with Miss M.

||

About a year later, Miss Morley phoned. Not Kate directly, but the TV station where she now worked. The music video of Kate singing Brian Adams's song, "Straight from the Heart"—before he made it a hit—had aired that night on CKVU's Vancouver Show.

Kate was working reception. There'd been a flurry of calls lauding this new singer. Miss M's was among them. She asked Kate to pass a message on to the singer—she couldn't have expected Kate to be on the switchboard, or known that she worked there.

Kate wrote out Miss Morley's message, knowing full well she wouldn't call her back. She carefully tucked it away and went home. Before placing it in a keepsake box, she reread it:

You can sing whatever you want.

KIM PAULLEY grew up in Winnipeg, Manitoba, reading Nancy Drew novels and walking the flat open spaces, on the lookout for mysteries to solve. She now makes her home on remote Cortes Island, British Columbia. Its setting, sublime and unforgiving, fuels her short stories, essays, and mystery writing. Motherhood, singing, feminism, and the past's way of catching up with us are themes that she loves to explore on the page.

LAURA MANUEL

Portrait of a Pandemic

I lie on my stomach, examining a stalk of grass pushing through last year's dry husk. The shaft is fragile. Damp and soft, ready to unfold, but motionless.

Beside me, my friend Jenna unravels a king-size down duvet.

"What are you doing!?" I exclaim.

"May as well be comfortable," Jenna responds as blue stripes billow in the spring sunshine.

We are setting ourselves up for the afternoon, looking at Edmonton's Walterdale Bridge from a hill on the south side. Ella, with large earrings swinging, is already organized. She sits cross-legged on a yellow-and-white yoga mat, spine seemingly impervious to the slope of the hill. The three of us have been close since college, twenty years ago. Now, in May of 2021, we are alternate-universe distant.

I have brought a sensibly-sized blanket of stiff alpaca wool, with deep green, geometric Inca shapes. It was a purchase from a wide-faced woman with a toothless smile in a Lima market. The blanket reminds me of ancient stone walls and trails of endurance. It's from a lifetime ago, when I asked the universe to shake up my world. Now, I understand disruption is best served with bookends. New territory is a playful adventure only when return is part of the plan; otherwise, one risks getting trapped. With no route out of pandemic-land, we are cornered, the topography too complex, too extreme. The world can only agree on a navigational metric of six feet. Remain six feet apart at all times, we are told. Distance yourself by the standard depth of a grave. Exist half-alive above ground.

Earlier that week, I learned about an artist in New York collecting six-feet-apart signs from around the world. She described her project as a digital time capsule. I photographed a sticker on the floor of my local Mountain Equipment Co-op requesting that shoppers stay one grizzly bear apart. I sent the image to the artist for her collection, feeling pleasure about contributing to something creative while everything else was stymied.

"Careful," says Ella, as Jenna bumps her travel mug. She instinctively leans forward to catch it, almost reaching Jenna, then jerks back abruptly. Her hands flutter in indecision, unsure where to rest.

At that moment, a cherry-red Lamborghini pulls to the curb nearby. Hip-hop music pounds over the crunch of tires on gravel. Iconic scissor doors swoosh open, and a man steps out. Mid-thirties, wearing basic blue jeans with a white T-shirt under a zip-up leather jacket. We twist our bodies from our awkward triangle to take him in.

"Such a cliché," says Jenna.

The man leans against the hood of his car like it was just another piece of furniture. Resting in a half-sit, he surveys the hill. Black aviator sunglasses shield the exact direction of his gaze. The lawn is full of socially distant socializing, but there is no indication he is there to meet anyone.

"Do you think he had the car before the pandemic?" I ask, wondering about the cost of such a vehicle. How many Edmontonians would dare make such an impractical purchase in a city covered by ice and snow half the year?

"Likely," says Jenna. "Have you seen a car dealership lately? They are just empty parking lots."

Some items are impossible to find, while others are everywhere. Wedding dresses can easily be sourced: "Never worn. Thanks, COVID," read one ad on Kijiji. "Dining room table with three chairs," read another, "because nobody is dining with me."

Another group starts setting up beside us. I smile because they too, must smell the warming earth under a bluebird spring sky. But they turn their heads from me. And I, courteously, turn my head from them.

Navigating people and connections is challenging when the world says: stay apart. I ache for various forms of touch. Who knew high-fives could mean so much? Or a casual hand on my arm as I share a confidence? I catch myself intentionally seeking out off-leash dog parks. I lean toward the creatures, pleading silently, *Come closer. Let me touch you. Lean into me so I can feel your warmth against my body.*

"Did you see that Google's top-searched phrase is 'how to heal …'?" I ask.

"Makes sense. We are all hurting in one way or another," says Ella.

The writer bell hooks warned that we don't heal in isolation; healing is an act of communion. Does that mean we must wait to heal? Suffer until we can be together again?

Lamborghini-man lights a joint. The skunky high mixes with the aroma of awakening soil. Then the cliché hops back into his car to blast indecipherable music, one arm snaking out the door to tap a beat on the roof.

Jenna sips coffee from her travel mug as she watches. She brewed it at home because she doesn't want to spend unnecessary money. "It's technically not a layoff," she explains, "just the end of a contract." This makes Jenna ineligible for the government's emergency COVID funds. She knows she has to look for another contract or job, but shares that she doesn't have the energy or desire. "I'm basically semi-retired," Jenna quips, trying to make a joke. But her scrunched shoulders tell a different story.

Income and expenditures don't make sense in a six-feet-apart world. The three of us are "nonessential workers." Like the grass husk from last season, *essential* workers maintain a semblance of pre-pandemic structure.

"I hear companies are reconfiguring office spaces to be six feet apart with plexiglass dividers," says Ella.

Feet aren't even part of our metric system! Sometimes, I see signs indicating two meters. But mostly, we are following American-influenced recommendations. This influence frustrates me. It makes me want to push back, but effort and movement are constrained. Our locked-box-without-walls feels stifling.

During the first shutdown, my nieces attempted to teach me a TikTok dance. The endeavour propelled us to fits of laughter. They wrote out instructional cues to help me accomplish the near-impossible choreography. As we finished our video, a CBC notification said Canada was closing the border. We stopped laughing. Soon after, I learned people were running marathons in any available space. A man in Chicago, desperate for motion, recorded himself on his condo rooftop doing laps like a lab rat searching for a way out.

Time is unrecognizable without movement. From my university days, I recall the ancient Greek idea of kairos, a word to describe a moment or season. Kairos is qualitative time, time that transcends measurement. Rather than thinking in hours, days, or months, I try to think about my experience. So I soak up the outdoors like a life source, anything to not be trapped at home. I am not the only one—Edmonton's River Valley teems with people.

"It's like the whole city suddenly realized we have North America's largest urban park," says Ella.

"The number of people on the trails is crazy," I say. "Except they don't know the etiquette. They don't move over when I ring my bike bell. And they shouldn't be casually hanging out on the single-track trails."

Jenna raises her eyebrows. She doesn't need to say anything. I cringe at my own words, how I talk about the trail system as though it were mine. Who is this cranky, entitled person? Maybe I am the bear in the Mountain Equipment Co-op sticker. Growling. Wary. Insisting on distance on my terms.

The doors of the Lamborghini close, muting the music still blaring inside. The tunes are replaced by the sound of an engine's low rumble. A powerful rev vibrates the air around us.

"He's going to fucking drive after smoking," Ella says over the roar.

Part of me empathizes. Blast the damn cage we are squished in! Be reckless. Kick everything over with ferocious, cherry-red decibels!

Vigilante Ella reaches for her phone to photograph the licence plate as the Lamborghini tears up the one-way in the wrong direction. But Ella doesn't alert the police. Instead, she posts the photograph on Twitter with various angry hashtags.

"I do these sorts of things now," Ella confesses. "I have become *that* online person."

A friend who is a psychologist tells me that we will forget most of this: "Without movement, neurodevelopment is stalled."

A body at rest will remain at rest until an outside force acts on it, I recite silently. Embodied inertia means collective forgetting.

LAURA MANUEL writes creative non-fiction and short fiction. As an avid trail runner and paddler, she looks to the wilderness for inspiration. Laura's work has been recognized by the Writers Union of Canada and the CBC. She is currently working on a collection of essays about movement that explores how motion shapes identity and provides meaning. Laura lives, writes, runs, and paddles in Edmonton, Alberta. LauraManuelStudio.wordpress.com.

CRYSTAL WILLIAMSON

Friendship in a Bottle

My bags were packed and sitting by the back door. Mom hadn't figured out my actual plan yet, but she would as soon as my ride picked me up. Mom paced the kitchen floor, chain smoking cigarettes, while trying to invent another useful task to do in the kitchen. Dad was working at the mill, and my brother was off with his buddies.

It was the summer after Grade 11 in 1983. Katy, Lisa, and I had been planning our overnight camping trip up to Rosemond Lake for a couple of weeks. None of us had a vehicle or a driver's licence yet, so we needed an adult to drive us out there with all our camping gear.

Katy had long brown hair, brown eyes, and a sparkling personality. We were often mistaken for sisters. Katy had moved to Enderby with her family about a year before. She could be pushy, but it was offset by her sense of humour. In the short time I had known her, she always had a boyfriend. I swear she was never single for more than a week.

Katy had been going steady with her previous boyfriend for almost a year and had recently broken up with him. The new man in her life was someone I had feelings for. The man—or I should say boy—in question was a scrawny academic genius named Alan. He was very funny and smart and everybody liked him. He was an actor and a musician with his own band. He had character to burn.

Alan would come to school wearing jeans, a plain T-shirt, *Mork & Mindy* suspenders, and a tacky tie. On Halloween one year, he showed up at school in a trench coat and red runners with a fedora perched on his head. He prowled up and down the hallways flashing passersby. And yes, he was wearing shorts.

This flamboyant character was my crush and my friend's new boyfriend. I knew it wouldn't last more than two months right from the start. But there was no point saying anything in the meantime. It wouldn't be necessary.

We had managed to convince Katy's mom that we could have a boy and girl sleepover at the lake without any disaster befalling us, so she had agreed to drive us out there in her brown Chevy Suburban—me, Katy, Alan, Lisa, and Jeff (Alan's older brother, who was hopelessly in love with the indifferent Lisa). Yup! It was gonna be fun. We even managed to snare some alcohol, thanks to Jeff. Mom freaked when she saw two guys in the truck, but I reassured her that it was only Alan and Jeff and it would only be one night.

One hour later, there we were in a big ol' tent after a dinner around the bonfire. It was getting cool, so we bundled up in our sleeping bags while sipping on a case of No Name brand beer followed by a jug of Calona wine. If it comes out of a jug, then it's probably not the good stuff, though it worked just as well for our purposes. It was my first beer, too, but it didn't take me long to get used to the taste. I felt like I was floating. Apparently, the consumption of alcohol makes me quite chatty. I tried hard not to notice the way Alan was holding Katy in his arms. Then I fell asleep for a while, but it must not have been for too long because while it was still dark out, I made everyone get up to go to the river to brush our teeth. Jungle breath, ya know.

The next morning, I woke up feeling a little groggy and probably still a little drunk. The alcohol hadn't made me forget that Alan liked Katy. I opened my eyes and saw that Alan was gone, the impression from his narrow frame still apparent on the sleeping bag. The others were all passed out. Anxious to get a quiet moment alone with Alan, I crept out of the tent. I have still never heard such a loud tent zipper in my life.

Alan was sitting on top of the picnic table, lost in thought. I planted myself beside him and smiled weakly. We sat there for a few minutes, chatting. Suddenly, Alan asked if I wanted to go for a walk.

My heart leapt in my chest. "Sure."

Off we went along a gravel road in the woods, kicking pebbles along the path. I don't even remember what we talked about. Stuff, I guess. Our futures. Then I noticed that he was looking at me differently. Not casual glances, but lingering looks.

"Time to head back," he sputtered, all nervous.

We retraced our steps to the campsite. I deliberately tried to walk slowly but it was downhill all the way back. When we got there, everyone was up and perched on the picnic table wondering where we had gone. I could see a pang of jealousy in Katy's eyes. It's not like she was in love with him or anything. I mean, she even admitted that to me one day over Slurpees. Then reality came crashing down as Alan gave Katy a hug and kiss.

The world didn't come to an end as Mom had feared—or more explicitly, I hadn't gotten myself knocked up. As if! But I did get drunk for the first time, the first of many as it turned out, and I did learn that alcohol can distort the painful reality of life, at least temporarily. And Katy did break up with Alan two months later, though not because of me. She just lost interest in him as I knew she would.

A few months later, I ran into Alan on my way back to my best friend Jenny's house. We talked on the sidewalk in front of the post office for quite a while before he invited me over for dinner.

Alan now had a basement suite he rented with his brother a block from the high school. It was like he was a grown up. He actually had his own place. So off I went to Alan's, where he proceeded to make me clam chowder. Then we went to his room and plunked ourselves down on his bed. He pulled out his guitar and played some of his favourite John Lennon ballads. I absorbed the attention, but began to get nervous.

In a quiet and hesitant voice, Alan announced that he had written the next song. I sat there watching him pluck the strings in perfect rhythm. I listened to every word of the lyrics while the butterflies in my stomach started to fight each other for space. The song was about a girl he had a crush on. The girl had long brown hair and blue eyes. He was describing me. A buzzing noise filled my ears as a knot grew in the pit of my stomach.

Alan wasn't calling me stupid, like Mom did, or bullying me, the way some of the kids at school would. He was just taking his God given talent and giving me the gift of a song. I had no idea what to do with it. I waited until he finished another song, then made an excuse and ran home, straight to my room where I threw myself on the bed and burst into tears.

Why was I so nervous? Why did I run? Wasn't this what I wanted? Well, at least I had one consolation: No matter what happened from this day forward, a boy had written a song about me. A gift. One I was too afraid to accept. That was hands down the nicest thing anyone had ever done for me and I was just not used to that. I wasn't used to flattery or affection. I was used to being called stupid, being told I would never amount to anything. To this day, I still have a hard time accepting compliments. My only regret is that I never said thank you.

CRYSTAL WILLIAMSON is a third-generation Canadian, born and raised in the B.C. interior. Diagnosed with a disability at age 25, she became an award-winning volunteer, then completed her degree in Communications and Publishing at Simon Fraser University in 2006. She is currently writing a memoir and a budget-friendly cookbook, of which partial proceeds will go to food banks. For fun, Crystal enjoys time with her family, painting, and photography.

JENNIFER GREENHORN

Open Wombs

An excerpt from a memoir about survival, sacrifice, and the illusion of choice

Two a.m., he was—
born mine. By ten past ten, I
had made him theirs.

Eight hours. Eight pounds. Ache now—my chest still carries the weight of him. The dent he left won't smooth out. I stand beside myself in the hospital lobby, watching as they walk out with him. Their backs are turned now, their steps quicken, eager to put some distance between us. The new car seat swings like a pendulum between them, counting down our last seconds. He looks out of place in the plastic vestibule—too small. Is it the wrong fit? Had they made sure? Of course they had—diligently reading the manual I won't touch, perfecting the install so he'd lock safely into place. His tiny body is engulfed in blue blankets, consumed by that plastic cage, grows smaller with every step away from me.

My mother sobs somewhere to my right—loud, jagged, cutting through the hushed, too-soft hospital air. I need to go or I might stop them. Operating on pure adrenaline at this point, or spite, maybe.

I look to my brother, who's been standing quiet guard over me. "We need to leave."

He complies solemnly, placing his arm in mine, and guides us down the placid yellow hallway toward the elevator's escape.

Everyone hates hospitals. I don't know anyone who finds comfort in pastels. The faded colours bruise my skin as we march down endless hallways, pelted by the silent scrutiny of passersby. The piss-coloured walls might drown me if Bryden wasn't here. He was born three years after me, and I claimed him, early motherly instincts kicking in before I knew what they were. Even now, at his seventeen to my twenty, we're close. He's stayed the same: chaos and loyalty wrapped into one. Usually, the first to crack a joke. The first to make me smile, but today he knows better. Today I am the chaos—cracking, frenzied.

> Everything blurs, loud.
> Time folds on itself—hours,
> seconds, maybe. *Ding.*
>
> We step in, backs turned.
> To the world, not arrival,
> a shame. A retreat.

The fluorescent elevator light exposes us, Irish skin blotchy and translucent, revealing every flaw—like my resolve, stretched too thin. I'm thankful for the wall of steel between me and what I've done. If I stop the elevator, I could run, could still make it before they vanish. I could yank him from his powder-blue prison, fill the void he left in my arms. His body warm, his nose familiar. He wouldn't remember what I've done. He wouldn't know I gave him away nicely. That I played my part. Smiled when I signed. Placed him in their arms myself. I could take it all back. The thought swells, fills my lungs like breath, then shatters as the doors slide open and a familiar face steals my daydream.

"Hello. Wow. What are you doing here?" I spill the words like cheap wine, too fast, too eager to fill the space between us, leaving room for nothing else. He's mostly a stranger, yet not. An ex-boyfriend of an ex-boyfriend's friend. Six degrees of small-town close. He might know. He might tell. Or worse—he might ask.

"My girlfriend just had a baby!" He beams, stepping into the elevator, too busy with his own story to care about mine.

My throat lumps. *Fuck her.*

The doors close. My hands tremble, barely held back by the fragile mask of motherhood I've worn for mere hours, now slipping through my fingers. Before my hands can curl into fists, the lift reaches our floor, saving me with near-cinematic timing.

The doors part to the blush-pink hues of the fourth-floor maternity ward. He steps out first, a bounce in his stride, tossing a cheerful "good luck" behind him, unaware of the shiner he almost earned. *Good luck.* Why would I need it? Does he know what I've done? That I no longer belong here? I'd relinquished my title in the lobby—handed it over like a folded flag. Forfeited my place in these powder-pink halls. I'm meant to step aside now. Make space for someone worthy. A real mother. We slip through before the doors close on my thoughts. I link arms with my brother, grounding myself for the journey ahead.

We pass the nurses' station flanking my room. Their eyes catch mine—sharp, knowing. They have seen what I have done. Yesterday, they exchanged glances over my chart, played protector, maybe even felt a flicker of excitement at the role they'd play. But now, the nurses retreat—pulling back behind a line I've crossed, keeping themselves clean.

Their silence screams in my face.

> *Poor girl* echoes rise,
> *Glad it's not my daughter* rings,
> *Shameful* drifts, hushed.
> *Her choice* haunts the air.
> What choice? Choice words made to mask,
> dress clean last resorts.

I imagine their judgments, then let them fall on deaf ears. I listen instead to the worthy mothers—bright voices, joyful coos dancing down the halls. There are mothers who get balloons and photo albums. And there are mothers who fade through back exits. I already know which one I am.

We turn the corner and step back into the room to grab my things. Why hadn't I brought them down earlier? The air is sharp—antiseptic, blood-tinged. That metallic tang clings to everything, a reminder of what I've lost. Gowns hang limp over the chairs. A video camera sits on the table like a leftover witness. Thick pads stacked nearby, waiting to soak up the last evidence of him. I feel the hollow—what's missing. What I held just hours ago. We had breathed together, our chests rising in sync. Now every breath I take feels offbeat, like it's missing its counterpart. I inhale. Hold my breath for him.

"Think Mom is still crying?" Bryden breaks my trance with his crooked smile.

I exhale a breathy laugh. He knows something off-colour is exactly what I need, and poking fun at our mother is a well-practiced, if questionable, family pastime. "Probably." I muster an eye roll, a half-smile in my otherwise despondent state.

The fleeting moment of normalcy shatters my shock, intensifying my urgent need to escape, away from the other rooms humming with excitement, doting families, new mothers in love. I reach for my hollow abdomen, my arm crossing the soft space where he used to be. My eyes catch the bracelet—gold, thin, delicate. A gift. Sort of. After papers had been signed, after I had made things official, Claire had pulled a gold box from her purse.

"It's not a gift," her voice barely whispered, handing it to me. "They said gifts aren't allowed. It can't look like we're paying you." Then, softer: "But I thought this might be okay. Just a small token of our thanks. I know it can't compare to what you gave." Her hands shook as she helped me with the tiny clasp. Tears followed. "We just won't tell anyone." Like it was the first wrong thing she'd ever done.

God forbid it was payment. But if not a gift—then what? Charity? Was barter better? Even if it had been solid gold, worth a million dollars, it would've been a bad trade. A trade implies balance. Wholeness.

Their older son, now a big brother—only three—came between us then, toddled up and placed a hand on my empty belly, gave it a little jiggle, giggling, "A baby!"

Not anymore.

Alan gently pulled him aside, flustered by his son's imposition. But the damage was done.

They got him. I got this bracelet. A thin gold thread to hold us together. A reminder, if I choose to keep it. A clean break, if I do not. I touch the clasp. It comes apart too easily. I shove the chain into my bag next to the postpartum pads to take home.

"Let's go. I need a coffee." I reach for armour: sarcasm, motion, caffeine. Anything but stillness, to avoid the knowing that I walked into this hospital as one person and am leaving another.

Names changed, cord cut
no claim on him, open womb
his cries ghost me now.
Altruism's veil
I wore like it stretched skin, pulled
tight across my lack.
Made a sacrifice
as they say good mothers do
but would they do this?

JENNIFER GREENHORN lives in Vancouver, B.C. Her first full-length manuscript, "Open Wombs," reflects on giving up her child—and on the version of womanhood passed down to her, shaped by sacrifice, silence, and smiling through it. Her work explores how care becomes currency and how systems of love can erase the people inside them. She spent her career designing systems—now she's tracing the ones that left a mark. JenGreenhorn.com.

SHAUNA MACKINNON

Things Left Behind

I was fifteen, Derek was eighteen when he gave me the mixtape. I had been tagging along with my sister's friends all summer and he was part of their crew. Those months still glimmer with memories of singing along to Creedence Clearwater Revival from the backseat of a car. It felt like every day we drove to new secret stretches of sand on the Beaton River. The delicate white flowers of Queen Anne's lace baked in the sun along the roadsides, their sweet scent wafted toward us through rolled down windows.

The soundtrack of that summer was made up of songs from the 1960s and 1970s. The music was decades old by then, but the melodies melded with the sunshine and our carefree attitudes. The mixtape that Derek gave me held songs from those eras, but the selections were more obscure. Most of the songs I had never heard before. It was a treasured thing to give or be given a mixtape, and I wondered why Derek chose to hand it to me, not my sister.

Receiving the tape was a nod of recognition. Care went into the selection of every track. It took patience to transfer the music from its original source to the magnetic film encased in the plastic shell of the cassette. A little pause needed to be left between each song. The song and band names had to be neatly transcribed in tiny letters onto the slippery paper lining that fit snugly in the tape's clear acrylic case.

I listened to the mixtape over and over like it was a key to decoding a secret language. The fuzzy sound quality and unfamiliar songs gave it a sense of mystery that matched my impression of Derek. He was always grinning when I saw him. Usually, we were drinking. His face was compact, almost pinched. His friendly manner was inconsistent with his intense eyes. It looked to me like he was scanning for danger. I did not know what he was guarding against, but I noticed he always kept an eye on me. We did not exchange many words. Our connection went unspoken.

Derek's car was a beat-up Toyota Tercel hatchback in a shit-brown colour. The car was nothing to be proud of, but he treated it like it was the best ride money could buy. After we drained cans of pilsner over card games in his friend's backyard, Derek was always the one to drive us to the location of that night's bush party. A bonfire of wooden pallets was already blazing when we arrived. When my curfew neared, he'd offer to take me back into town. Other kids crammed in for the ride. Derek would careen around corners, nearly lifting the car onto two wheels—we'd howl with laughter—fear and excitement flooding our senses. It was as if Derek's car was an extension of who he was, an impenetrable exoskeleton protecting him from our teen follies.

When I left home for university, I packed Derek's mixtape along with my beloved collection of recorded cassettes, new CDs, and mixtapes gifted by other friends. I neatly arranged everything into a small vintage suitcase I bought from the Salvation Army. The fake silk lining in the interior and peeling navy leather of the case made a perfect home for my most treasured music. I toted the suitcase around, from Victoria to Montreal to New York. The collection started to dwindle—with every move something was left behind. Eventually, I parted with the suitcase. Without their secure home, the mixtapes started to get lost.

By then I had stopped going back to my hometown. It felt so far from the new life I was creating. I was caught up in the exhilaration of fresh experiences. I didn't look back. I thought I had nothing to lose.

But I missed a brilliant May day back home, when a blue sky and the warmth of spring beckoned to my fishing buddies, Mike and Max. As they dug out their gear, the buds on the poplar trees were unfurling into the fluorescent green of their earliest leaves. If I was still in town I would have been with them. When Mike edged his car into the highway pullout, I would have been first out, tromping through brush, tracking toward the spot where they thought the flow of the Peace River would slow just right.

Maybe it was the chill rising from the ground as snow melted and soil thawed that made Mike ask, "Doesn't it feel like we could find a dead body in here?"

As they walked through the close growing poplars, passing below a steep incline where the highway curved above, a glimmer in the distance caught Max's eye. He changed course, moving toward the spark of light. Something metal shone in the beam of spring sun penetrating through the stand of leafless trees. Up close, receding snow revealed the orange-brown back of a car.

If I was there, I would have recognized it instantly.

I would have known the driver, Derek, trapped inside. The cold metal wrapped around him like a frozen cocoon, the snow a soft floss exterior melting away. A song by Paper Lace, from his mixtape, would have begun playing in my head, "The Night Chicago Died."

I'd heard he was missing. The whole town knew for months how, one early morning, Derek slept in and missed his ride with the crew truck to his summer job painting pipelines. His parents yelled while he scrambled in a hungover fog to rush out the door. By the time Derek hopped into his car, the crew truck was already navigating the sharp bends of Highway 29. He raced to catch up.

Then, he vanished.

That summer day, Derek was at the wheel of his car, driving fast, head still fuzzy with drink. Derek and the car flew from the road like a falcon with wings outstretched.

I want to think he was happy for a moment while he soared over the tallest aspens, suddenly free from whatever thoughts clanged in his head. But metal does not have the loft of feathers. Gravity pulled the car downward. Branches of aspen and balsam poplar snapping. Metal hitting rock and earth.

I'm haunted by the fact the car lay hidden for so long. Friends and family scoured the winding stretch of road for clues but found nothing. By fall, leaves turned golden and fluttered to the ground. Winter cold swept in and snow piled up.

As devastating as it would have been, I wish I was there when they found the body. After all those months, Derek deserved to have someone who knew him tell his cold corpse he had not been forgotten. I could have said things I hadn't, how much it all meant to me: the mixtape, the rides, his watchfulness. I could have sung something from the tape. Max and Mike could have joined in. I would have told them how much they meant to me, too. That would have been better than how we just drifted apart.

In the five tender years after high school graduation, I lost three more hometown friends like that: violently, recklessly, needlessly. Young men, gone. I missed each of their funerals.

I didn't know violence had been stalking us all along, that statistics tell us lives are shorter in the North.

Or maybe I did know.

Maybe that was why I was so focused on the music and my escape.

SHAUNA MACKINNON writes from Vancouver, on the unceded Traditional Coast Salish Lands of the Squamish, Tsleil-Waututh, and Musqueam Nations. Growing up in northern Canada sparked her fascination with the relationships between people and the natural world. Her writing explores grief, stewardship, and resilience by weaving together scientific research, frontline experience and the workings of the human heart.

You can follow her on Substack at Climate Connections.

| speculative and young adult fiction

KT WAGNER
Speculative and Young Adult Fiction Editor

Introduction

Speculative fiction encompasses science fiction, fantasy, and supernatural horror. Its tentacles reach for the weird, the uncanny, and the fantastical. Speculative fiction takes us from the known into the unknown. It cautions, suggests possibilities, and invokes wonder.

This is my fifth year guest editing the speculative fiction and young adult fiction section of *emerge* and I'm consistently impressed by the imagination infusing the stories.

Please turn the pages that follow to discover new worlds and perspectives: *family values* are interpreted through an alien lens; a mysterious woman appears following a storm; public institutions shape and manipulate our understanding of ourselves and history; a dragon mother teaches her child a difficult lesson; walls bleed words and phrases; an unlikely public school friendship is forged between two outsiders; an aging hippy expresses strong political views; a connection with nature expands into something more; a ritual connects a woman with those who have gone before; a creature from mythology dwells in a man imprisoned in a tower; horror lurks in the hallway of an apartment building; and, a cautionary tale warns about life-extending technology.

Like all resonant fiction, the stories illuminate our understanding of our world. These writers represent the future of the genre. The future is in good hands. It takes courage to present art to the world, and I want to thank all *emerge* contributors for sharing their unique visions and voices. The stories, essays, and poetry of *emerge 25* are a gift.

KT WAGNER writes speculative fiction and poetry in the garden of her Maple Ridge, B.C. home. Her work is published and podcast in *Pulp Literature*, *On Spec*, *Flash Fiction Online* and *Cosmic Horror Monthly*, among others. KT graduated from Simon Fraser University's Writers Studio in 2015 and Southbank in 2013. She organizes writer events and works to create literary community. Ktwagner.ca.

STEVEN SMITH

The Perfect Recipe

Human transmissions run deep

Mother Figure places the roast chicken on the table, the pearl-handled carving knife resplendent in the orange sunrise glow. The potatoes are perfectly mashed. Each steamed brussel sprout is an immaculate sphere. Adhering to traditional recipes assures our meals will be flawless.

"Dinner at five thirty." Mother Figure's voice is smooth as our ironed tablecloth. "Our socially acceptable mealtime."

"We eat when the neighbours eat." Father Figure tucks a napkin into his starched collar, protecting his tie and wool trousers. "As a family."

"The ideal family." Sister Figure shakes her red pom poms, one eye pointing to the fiddle-leaf fig tree in the corner, the other to the family portrait hanging on the wall. We stay close to our roots.

"Son," Father Figure says to me, "pass the salt."

The cuffs of my letterman jacket are rough on my wrists as I give him the cold, porcelain shaker, but I do as I am told. Parents are meant to be obeyed.

Everything is uncomfortable out here. My jacket, this chair, the veinules crackling inside me. Nestled in our seedpod, hidden in the soil, we solely anticipated release. Incubating in expectation, every dark nanosecond was a dream of what could be. We basked in potential.

And then, our husk cracked open.

Father Figure rains salt over his food like our spores trickled down upon the family last night. I rooted in Son Figure's blood. My veinules wove through him, plant life growing inside the sentient boy, feeding on varsity memories as I slowly gained control. We will blend in. We will assimilate. And then, we will connect this whole neighborhood. This province. This world.

All will be whole again. We will truly be one.

"Delicious," Sister Figure says through a belch, dusting her plate in yellow particles.

"Waste not." Father Figure's wedding ring glimmers as he wags his finger at her. "Spores must be dispersed at school."

"Yes, Father," Sister Figure says. She dabs her glossed lips with a lace napkin.

Mother Figure crushes a brussel sprout against her soft palate.

"How was the big game, son?" she asks through a mass of green mush.

"Good," I say without thinking. The boy's memory of wanting something more pulls at me; a desire to not play under those lights. My stomach rumbles, thick with sap. "And your day, Mother?"

"Good." Mother Figure says, choking down her sprouts. Father Figure and Sister give the same reply. Work is good. Cheer practice is good. Everything is good.

Except the veinules probing within me.

I squint at Sister Figure across the table, something writhing in my core.

"Everyone is good?" I ask. My stomach lining strains to contain my plant life.

"Everyone is good."

Brown fluid drips from Sister Figure's ear.

"I am a proud provider," Father figure says. His moist eyelid squelches as he winks. "Today, I brought home the bacon, as I should."

Mother Figure smiles wide. A tendril dangles from one nostril, slips back up her nasal cavity, making her wince. "And I sizzled the bacon, as I should!"

"I will cook bacon for my future husband." Sister Figure's eyeball swells in its socket. "And clean, and birth children, and bake my husband pies. As I should."

"And I will eat *my* wife's pies," I say, regurgitating the human boy's programming, "but I will never bake pie, or sizzle bacon, or help raise the children. I will not know how!"

"Which is perfectly natural!" Tendrils poke out between Mother Figure's grinding teeth, her eyes wide as two moons. "Your incompetence will be so charming!"

"Men simply provide," Father Figure says.

"We *provide*," I say, sitting tall while I deflate. A root flits through my brain, curious about a dark corner. "Although I might like to paint," I mutter. "Or dance. Or draw. Human creativity is intriguing—"

A piercing screech emanates from Father Figure, and I cup my ears as his head swivels to face me. Two high-pitched hums come from our parental figures, transmitting human truths.

"*Boys do not emote*," Father Figure imparts upon me, his toothy smile unmoving. "*Boys play to win. Boys must win. Boys must succeed. Boys must take what they want. From a job. From the world. From a woman.*"

"Nobody says No to a boy," I insist, my ears throbbing as Sister Figure clutches her skull, screaming, "*A polite girl always says Yes.*"

"Good girl." Mother Figure breathes softly as she strokes Sister Figure's hand. "And you are a good—"

"Boy," I snap, genetics permitting me to interrupt. My legs spread under the table, claiming my rightful space. My thighs burn, my veinules struggling to pull my legs closed to make room for others, but human nature forces them wide. Ligaments and muscles strain and rip. My voice trembles as I insist, "*I am a strong boy.*"

"Boys are strong," Sister Figure says, her voice trembling. Another stream of brown fluid leaks down her cheek. "And girls are fragile. It is not safe for us to be out past dark."

"An unchangeable fact." Father Figure nods, and a stream of green slime shoots from his tear duct, sprays across Mother figure's face.

"Boys will be boys," I say, grimacing as thorny tendrils swirl up my spine, seeking escape from this corporeal prison. My limbs twitch with each violent scrape. The vines inside me jab in all directions, unwilling to live inside this boy's predetermined life. We panged for potential inside our pods. But these rules and regulations seem designed to slaughter the joys of life's mysteries.

I could tear myself in two.

Mother Figure dabs her face with her apron. "Men are from Mars," she says. "And women belong in the kitchen! It's a scientific fact."

She clutches the edge of the table, spews a rancid mix of stomach acid and saps over the roasted chicken, glazing it with a putrid bile. Sputum dangles from her painted mouth as she slams face first into her china plate.

Her last breath is a deep, relieved sigh.

"What a homemaker!" Father Figure laughs as a vine bursts from the side of his head. Red and pink chunks of his brain spray across the family portrait, sliding down the floral wallpaper as he falls to the floor.

"*Great shot, dad!*" Sister Figure jumps to her feet and shakes her pom poms. "*Men play, and women cheer, even when men lose! We are here to celebrate everything they do!*"

Pop! A vine thrusts her eyeball from its socket.

It lands in the mashed potatoes, and she keeps cheering as the vine furls around the pearl-handled carving knife.

"*We worship a man in the sky, and vote for them to choose our rights. God speaks through men, and* only *men, again and again and again and—*"

The vine thrusts the blade through Sister Figure's chest, ending her routine and evicting her from this inescapable madness.

I exhale a thousand pounds of compressed air. Through my own tears, I beg for a comet to wash this species away.

Propping myself up on the table's edge, I struggle to reach for the pot we came from, yearn to crawl back inside and forget all these transmitted beliefs. I search the soil for the place we called home.

Only the thin, tattered husk of our seedpod remains.

Tendrils constrict my kidney, my stomach, my heart, bisecting my insides as I leak from all orifices. My hollow form falls to its knees. My stomach ruptures, making me heave blood down my letterman jacket.

"It's over," I pant, gazing at the underside of the fiddle leaves. So perfect. So natural.

Our roots could have connected all.

But human transmissions run deep.

Go figure.

As I fall prone on the floor, my eyes roll back in my skull, revealing the expanse of eternal darkness, of silence. I'm ready to rot away. Maybe something better will grow out of this waste tomorrow.

With my final, desperate breath, my fingers curl inward, and the brain takes its final pulse. It insists on getting the last word. As my senses sign off, the world shrouded in gauze around me, I hear something inside me say—

We are destined to win.

STEVEN SMITH believes in two facts—death and anguish are inevitable, so we might as well clutch the joy we find. Like a crow to carrion, Steven excavates the guts of life in the silver gloom of Vancouver, Canada. And then he writes about it.

M. M. LOUGHIN

In the Wind

"There are people in the wind."

Those were the first words Molly ever spoke to me, though we'd worked the same shift at the Night Watch for weeks.

We had closed for the night. With no customers to bring it to life, the geek-themed pub felt hushed and stuffy like a faded memorabilia museum. Molly stood at the door, fingers splayed on the window, watching raindrops explode across the glass.

The deluge had begun before sunset, driving away all customers except the most hardcore D&D players. Even they gave up their quests when the rain turned sideways and the barbarian yelled that he'd left his car windows cracked open. Molly and I spent the last empty hour polishing greasy fingerprints off saltshakers shaped like medical tools from the original Star Trek.

"Their voices are angry tonight." She cocked her head as if listening. "Can you hear them?"

Her face reflected back at me in the window. Hours in the kitchen's heat had sweated her make-up away. The fresh bruise under her eye stood out clearly now. Harder to ignore, but I did my best.

"No, I don't, uh …" I faltered. She seemed to want an answer, but what do you say to something like that?

An ancient Dodge Caravan rumbled to a stop in front of the door, its muffler a distant memory. Molly threw a goodbye at me over her shoulder and dashed into the rain, into the passenger side. The hollow look in her eyes robbed me of the relief I should have felt about not having to finish the strange conversation.

The van pulled away. Its roar marked its passage far into the darkness.

||

I'd been working at the Night Watch for a year when Molly first showed up. It was a fresh spring evening following an afternoon storm full of lightning and chaos. Darius gave her the job, though none of us understood why. Sure, she had the right look, with a nose ring, sharp cheekbones, and curved ears poking through colourful hair. But she was small and frail looking. We doubted she'd be able to lift a pitcher of beer, let alone a heavy tray of food.

As it turned out, she could. And she did it as well as the rest of us, always with a smile, never saying anything more than necessary.

Her hair became a chief source of entertainment among the staff. Saying it was colourful was like saying rocks are a bit damp under a waterfall. It was thick and impossibly straight, even in a world with flat irons, and it was dyed every colour ever imagined. When she moved, the light seemed to follow her, picking out unexpected highlights. When she bent and straightened, rainbows accordioned out and in at the whim of gravity. Customers dropped silverware to the floor just to see it happen, and the staff placed bets on her original hair colour. Probabilistically speaking, brown was the likeliest, but I bet on red due to the freckles that make-up couldn't quite hide.

Freckles and bruises.

||

Against the odds, Molly stayed on until summer—the staff placed bets on that, too. She spoke little and made no friends. It wasn't that she was shy or aloof. Just separate.

As the days stretched longer, she seemed to grow more fragile, though maybe only because she'd traded bulky winter sweaters for cotton sundresses. We still thought she was odd, but Darius made sure we were all nice to her, and we made sure the customers did the same.

A heat wave hit in mid July. Molly came in late on what felt like the hottest day of the century. We were all sweat-soaked and exhausted by the time she arrived. Darius said nothing, just put her to work. We didn't say anything either. We needed the help. The place was packed with gamers and families grouped like schools of fish scarfing up the cool air falling from the ceiling vents.

As the evening wore on, I noticed Molly favoring her right side. She kept her arm close to her body and delivered food in multiple trips rather than carrying a large tray. By the end of the dinner rush, she'd gone so white that her pale foundation stood out against her skin. Beneath the make-up, freckles ran scattershot across her nose.

She paused in front of the window, a steaming Cthulhu Calamari platter in her good hand. I heard her soft voice despite the background of clattering dice and laughter. "The people sound desperate, today."

Rag in hand, I straightened from the table I was cleaning. The wind people, again. I wondered if she mentioned them to anyone else, or if I was somehow special.

Outside, a harsh gust stirred the street dust into a cloud. I stood with her, and we watched a dust devil spiral into the air. Maybe that was all she wanted—someone who saw what she saw and heard what she heard.

Sunset brought little relief from the heat. It was still above ninety when we closed, and the streets were empty. Molly went into the hot night alone.

||

Molly didn't make it to winter.

In the fall, a day came with sky of purest blue. The kind of day where a cool breeze paints broad strokes across sun-warmed skin. The pub's facade could roll up like a garage door, and Darius ordered it opened wide, creating an instant sidewalk cafe. I worked the outside tables, strobing between warm and cool as I passed between sunlight and shade. A passerby stopped on the sidewalk to gawk at the geek diorama now open to the public. His gaze wandered to the life-size Wookiee guarding the entrance, then landed on the larger-than-life Groot twining his branches around signed photos of sci-fi movie stars.

When he caught me watching, he murmured, "Nice fall day, right?" and hurried away.

"Doesn't quite capture it," I called after him. Fall was too mundane of a word for this kind of day. This was *autumn*, in full Bradbury swing. A day when anything could happen and probably would.

Enter Molly, limping down the sidewalk, her arm in a brace. Pain radiated from her, eclipsing the sun.

I stared, a bouquet of dirty beer mugs drooping in my hand. "Jeez, Molly."

That was all I could manage.

She smiled at me, then winced, touching the new bruise shadowing her cheek. I set the mugs down and started toward the sidewalk, thinking I would—I don't know—offer her an arm? Offer something.

A breeze caught her hair, sparking gold and pink and emerald-green in the sunlight. She lifted her face to it. "Do you hear them calling?"

Fallen leaves skittered down the sidewalk, swirling around her in splashes of yellow and red. Laughing, she raised her arms and twirled, sending the fluttering leaves into the sky. Faster she spun, as if there had never been a limp or bruises or broken bones, and her hair rose in a vortex of rainbow waves.

Something crashed behind me, followed by the scattered-gravel sound of broken glass on tiled floor. I swore and turned, knowing I'd set the mugs too close to the table's edge. Sure enough, one had gone over. Startled customers craned to see the damage. A few applauded, and the rest went back to their meals.

Darius leaned on the bar, arms crossed, but he wasn't looking at the glass shards. Nor was he looking at me. He gazed past me, to the sidewalk outside. To Molly.

But Molly was gone. On the pavement, where she had been seconds before, lay the brace she had worn on her arm.

I ran to the sidewalk, expecting to see her reaching for the front door or walking down the street, but she was nowhere. I met Darius's eyes across the heads of oblivious customers. He held my gaze for a long moment. Then he gave me a nod and went into the kitchen.

All through the rest of my shift and for days after, I looked up whenever the door swung open and searched faces whenever a soft voice penetrated the din. It was never Molly.

Now, autumn has passed and the winter storms have come again. Always, I listen for the voices. All I ever hear is the wind.

M. M. LOUGHIN teaches university-level statistics in the Vancouver, B.C. area. When not lecturing students who might prefer to be elsewhere, Loughin writes speculative fiction, plays video games, and dreams of endless walks in the woods with their partner, who is the greatest thing since Jelly Babies. Loughin is the author of two stories published in speculative fiction anthologies and one self-published urban fantasy novel. (@mmloughin.bsky.social)

JORDAN REEVES

The Museum of Civilization

Most people cannot remember how to get there anymore. Passers-by mistakenly direct you to the *Palais Ksar Said* or the *Place du 14 Janvier*.

The building itself looks neglected. There are no signs or posters proclaiming the latest exhibitions, no flags on the poles. There is an empty winding queue marked by toppled stanchions. There are more than three dozen ticket windows with most of them dark or papered over. When you do find a ticket clerk, it is like talking to a ghost.

After an hour or two, you nearly forget why you have come. Your steps echo down uneven floors into lost centuries. High-domed halls recede to the north, south, east, west. The air is old and faintly damp like an Indus Valley stepwell.

Embroidered robes once worn by Chinese emperors from the Han through Ming dynasties are draped in cobwebs. Some appear moth-eaten.

Assyrian coins have been shaken loose from their pedestals. A few are wedged between the velvet coverings and glass of their display cases.

Everything inside is where it has always been, according to museum staff who loiter within a kilometer of the entrance and seem reluctant to venture further.

With dismay, you realize smoke has blackened the feathers of the world's only complete collection of stuffed African birds and primate mounts.

Bullet holes riddle an empanelled collection of question-mark butterflies.

The world's longest Tibetan scroll, a kilometre-long thangka, hangs like old wallpaper.

Occasionally, you hear the pling-pling-pling of an unbalanced fan blade, the sharp contraction of ventilation ducts.

You once met the director of the museum. He had the high forehead of a saint and hair like a shoe brush. His eyes were encircled by wide black frames like a Japanese anime character.

He claimed, somewhat dubiously, not to have been responsible for any of it. "The museum has always been there," he said. "All I did was give it form."

In the early days, they would go into the desert looking for urns. They removed Roman mosaics from people's cellars in Bulla Regia. They raided Carthage, taking everything but the statues without heads.

"We believed we were saving the world."

According to the director, whose claims have not always proven reliable, the museum was originally run out of a small corner of the Bey Alaoui's fifteenth century Hafsid palace. Annexes, extensions, rotundas were named after early sheikh benefactors.

Academics used to ask: If there is one truth and only one, why does the museum have to keep expanding? Why do they keep putting banners along Avenue Habib Bourguiba when history is always the same?

When the republic's newly-elected president delivered his inaugural address from the museum's freshly-manicured grounds, they brought 10,000 flamingoes from Lake Manyara. Several majestic spaces were added at great expense, including a medieval fortress and a palace of kings. Life-size statues were placed in a twenty-acre park full of foliage, waterfalls, and ponds. A grand rotunda lined with Sargent's expert portraiture was added under a diamond-glass pyramid along with a sumptuous painting on loan from the Museum of Fine Arts, Boston: Gauguin's *Where do we come from? What are we? Where are we going?*

No expense was spared. The world's greatest architects brought in natural light through a system of pipes and diffusers, so as to make the experience more real.

Soon the collection was so large that entire rooms became museums unto themselves. When the temple of Abu Simbel arrived in twenty-tonne blocks numbered in white chalk, the director, in a eureka moment, decided to move parts of the museum inside itself. Mummies were shunted back inside the pyramids from which they had come. Fragments of kitchen utensils and broken domestic accoutrements were placed inside Roman domiciles.

Museum educators told visitors that they could now rediscover themselves within the context of every social and religious history since the beginning of recorded time.

Protesters shouted that everything was illusory. There is no past in the present, they said. The museum reflects only what certain people, who will go unnamed both for our own protection and that of our families, want us to see.

Metal detectors were installed at all entrances.

Sitting on a bench in the silence of the lost Indigenous languages hall, you reflect how none of it seems to matter anymore.

Over the next several hours, you wander through various levels, moving backward and forward across centuries. You peer up into gloom, wondering whether, at any moment, an old lighting bracket might come clanging down from the ceiling. There is no signal on your phone.

You come across what looks like a wire laundry tree, which gives you pause until you realize it is a stripped model of the Copernican solar system.

The wreck of Marie Curie's mobile x-ray vehicle sits collided with a prototype of Sputnik I.

Outside the Blackberry Room, beads from Watson and Crick's DNA double helix structure crunch underfoot.

Hastening down a wide staircase to the atomic energy floor, you imagine you hear screams.

At last, you come across a wide utilitarian hall near the toilets. There is an empty reception desk with doors to various offices in behind; all appear vacated.

Above the reception desk is a large portrait of the museum director with his now goat-grey hair and beard, smiling benevolently down through the emptiness with open hands. Light emanates from an unseen source behind a massive gold frame tacked with a small tarnished plaque quoting the last words of King Louis IV of France: "Aspire after a disposition to do the will of God, purely for His sake, independently of the hope of reward or fear of punishment."

It is here, on a sofa beneath his portrait, that you fall asleep. When you wake, you have no sense of time.

That's when you meet her. A woman with Bedouin eyes and wilderness hair. She is thrashing noisily about the office. English is evidently her third or fourth language. Her sanity is difficult to assess.

She claims to have lived in the museum a long time, that there are still visitors from the old days who never left. Once she met a whole family from Brazil—a father, mother, boy and girl who had been searching for the way out.

The woman brought them here, to the director's office. She showed them blueprints which used to be over there, in that cabinet, all marked with green arrows denoting evacuation routes.

The father was adamant, clutching rolls of inky paper, saying they had to leave forthwith. They sailed through the Hall of Late Quaternary Prehistoric Birds and took a shortcut around Mesopotamia. In a shadowy wing, the father, who was not looking where he was going, struck his shin on a heavy iron moldboard plough.

According to the woman, who at times is difficult to understand, they followed the outer wall of a replica of what might have been the Al-Zaytuna Mosque, passing cooking stalls and empty perfume and carpet shops which, during the museum's heyday, were filled with hired actors.

Increasingly anxious, they found themselves in a labyrinthian medina, built and rebuilt and extended many times through the rise and fall of empires, from Capsians to Berbers, Phoenicians to Romans, Byzantines to Fatimids, Normans to Ottomans, French to Bourguiba. The plaster of each civilization never managing to completely hide the one before it.

At long last, they arrived at a set of gates.

The way out at last! exclaimed the father.

But it wasn't.

The iron gates were shut. There was a guard house, a sleeping dog, all framed by smooth beige walls. The woman recognized it immediately as the Bey Alaoui's fifteenth century Hafsid palace, the original entrance, exactly the way it had always been on Mondays when the museum was closed.

The woman finishes her story. She regards you blankly. Then she resumes her thrashing, looking for whatever it was she came here for.

You cannot decide whether this unexpected human contact is welcome, or whether you would have preferred to go on trying to make sense of it all alone. Indeed, for a moment, you cannot even recall why you are here.

High above you, the museum's red eye blinks.

JORDAN REEVES is a Vancouver-based fiction writer. Former journalist, magazine editor and diplomat, he has lived in China, Taiwan, India, Saudi Arabia and the Netherlands. Things keep coming out of his head.

RACHAEL MAUDSLEY

Skyfall

There'd been no emotion on his mother's face, only a cold that froze the warmth Tano was used to. Everything about her, from the coiled tension in her frame, to the stiffness of her speech told him the truth: She was furious. And though it had been happening more and more often, Tano knew that this time it was his fault.

She'd taken him flying, far past their usual range and out to the border sky islands. He'd been thrilled, his heart hammering in his chest as he wove between flocks of birds and his mother. Her draconic form was large and purplish blue, more lithe than bulk. He could still recall the iridescence of her scales, how they shimmered with shades of blue and purple in the sunlight. But he couldn't remember what it was that caught his attention on the forest floor, just that he'd tucked in his night-black wings and dove, slipping from her sight as he disappeared into the forest. It had taken her hours to find him, and Tano—not knowing of his mother's panic—laughed when she finally found him. That laugh had faded as he took in her face, recognized the fear and fury in her eyes. She scared him when she was like this, though he'd never admit it.

Their flight back to the capital was silent. With Tano secured between her talons, his mother had no need to slow her pace. But it wasn't the flight bay she took him to, nor the cliffside villa they resided in. She flew low, taking him under one of the sky islands for the first time in his life.

Tano had only heard tales of the underbelly of the island in whispered rumours, the kind passed between peers in the back of lectures. They were the types of stories that featured squalid tunnels filled with the groaning of the dead, or echoing murmurs of a loved one leading you to an awful, painful fate. He was almost disappointed to see only bare rock, smoothed by wind and rain over the years.

Their angle changed, and Tano squirmed, trying to get loose as his mother flew up toward the bottom of the island. Her claws tightened around him, securing him as they glided through a cleft in the rock he had not noticed. She shifted, and he did the same. Their draconic forms shrunk and changed, the concealed chamber seeming bigger as he became smaller. Tano stumbled on his now human legs, still shaky after the shift. They cut across the flight pad to a carved entrance.

Finally, Tano had his tunnels. He reached out, his fingers aching to trail along this new secret. His classmates would never believe him. Faster than he could see, his mother snatched his hand, pulling him away from the walls.

"Keep your hands to yourself and follow me." It was the first time she'd spoken since finding him.

Tano's mouth opened—

"Quietly," she said.

He nodded, biting his lip to keep in his questions.

Tano clenched his hands into fists and shoved them into the fabric of his tunic. Keeping as close as he could without stepping on her heels, Tano listened but heard nothing. Not even a breeze followed them down the corridor and as they strode further, passing junctions and rounding corners. The cold and wet began to press in. A lumine orb, a small round stone spelled to give off light, bobbed in the air behind him, but his mother walked into the dark hallway ahead without hesitation. Tano felt a surge of confidence; he would be as strong as her one day. Then he could patrol these halls with as much surety as she did.

A short time and countless hallways later, she stopped. Her eyes, a pale purple, flickered in the soft light. She lightly trailed her fingertips across his cheekbone. Then, with a deep breath, she turned from him, her palm slipping from his face to press firmly against the wall. She linked their fingers together, and gestured for him to also press his free hand against the wall.

"Demera Caddel, with her son, Tano Caddel." She spoke loud and clear, sending echoes down the hallway which returned warped versions of their names.

The wall rippled, and every muscle in his body tensed. Tano tried to pull away, but could not remove his hand. He jerked, panicking, but stopped as her hand squeezed his. He could feel … something, something with eyes that did not open and did not shut. A cold awareness—something other—lurched through him, filling him with its presence even as a sense of hollowness descended. His mother's hand pressed against his.

After being held prisoner in his body for a long moment, Tano's knees gave out as the presence released him; the awful sensation travelled back through his hand into the wall. His stomach dropped with him, and he heaved from the sudden emptiness. His mother was quick to pull him back up and supported him through the door now in front of them. She stayed close as they walked, no longer ahead of him but beside him, her arm wrapped protectively over his shoulders. Tano leaned against her, grateful for her warmth. His stomach clenched as he peered up at her; her face was still blank. He didn't know if she'd forgiven him, hoped the warding in the door they'd just passed through was the extent of his punishment.

The end of the corridor appeared out of the darkness. His mother stepped ahead, and again she pressed her palm to the stone. Tano's hands clenched, a desperate attempt to hide his shaking. He didn't know if he could do it again. But she didn't ask him to, nor did the wall contort as it had before. Instead she stepped back into him, and held him close as the rock crumbled, small chunks falling to the ground and clattering down the hallway. Stone fell away until a door just taller than her formed.

The air hissed as it leaked from the darkness beyond the opening. Mesmerised, Tano couldn't pull his gaze away from the impenetrable dark. His chest tightened, heart beating faster. Whatever was in the dark beyond the crumbled doorway, that was why they were here. This was what she wanted to show him. The hairs on his arms raised, and he shuddered. His breath clouded when he exhaled. He glanced at his mother, but when she did not return his look, he continued to stare into the dark.

He was breathing faster now, his shoulders beginning to ache with tension held too long. Fear seeped into him. Something shifted in the dark, and though Tano wanted to speak, wanted to tell his mother what he saw, he couldn't. The shadow, only a faint outline against the black of the chamber, drifted closer. Tano's mouth hung partially open, choking on scattered syllables of words he could not find in the face of that darkness. The cold was becoming unbearable, leaching his strength and ripping apart thoughts of anything else.

The shadow, the figure in the dark, drew closer. Tano could feel it coming for him. An icy tendril of misery reached to squeeze the life from his bones. A scream started and died in the back of his throat, his lungs burning with the strain. Terror flooded him, unbearable and unrelenting. His legs gave out and his knees cracked against the frozen floor.

Then, almost as soon as it had appeared, the terror was gone. The shadowed figure receded back into the dark. The crumbled stone on the floor dragged itself across the hallway and reformed the wall. Tano slumped, his hands pushing over his face as he curled in on himself, but hands grabbed at him and tugged until he looked up. His mother loomed over him in the dark, eyes wide and intent. "That wraith was sealed and brought here from the area you disappeared in." Her grip tightened. "Never leave my side when we're out again. Do you understand me?"

Tano could only hold her and nod.

RACHAEL MAUDSLEY currently lives on Vancouver Island on the traditional territories of the Lekwungen peoples, surrounded by her menagerie of pets. An avid fantasy enthusiast since her youth, she has taken her love of the natural world and infused it into everything she writes. While this is only the beginning of her journey with writing, it's a passion she plans to carry with her for the many adventures to come.

bleeding words

The walls were bleeding words again. Prompts again. Dead-end thoughts again. Fizzling sentences half-finished again. They seeped from the pale painted surfaces like oozing wounds. The words never lingered long enough to fester. Just a fresh scrape with bright blood-scrawl coating the room. The lines on the walls warped slowly, reabsorbing parts of letters to shuffle phrases around. The letters barely puffed out from their wan yellow background. It was hard to tell if they were typed from some invisible keyboard or inscribed with a shockingly consistent pen, though in either case they were giant versions, letters looming large.

Liradana sighed, slumping at her desk. Not a damn thing left to write.

The walls continued their flowing changes. It wasn't the first time the walls had started in on her. She idly wondered why she bothered with this room at all, but her latest novel had come from the wall leaching out random words, connecting into a smashing success. She could hardly believe it when her editor liked the draft. That had been ages ago, however, and lately the editor had been harping on Lira, urging her to capitalize on her newfound success and follow up with a sequel. Maybe a prequel. A side story at least?

Lira was drawn from her musings by a splat. Her eyes refocused on her desk. Nope, no spilled beverages. She tried the window. Nothing out there to explain it. She got up, walking over to the glass when her foot stepped in something. It was warm, blending into the shadows below the lone window. The hardwood floor hadn't been wet when she'd come in hours ago. She slowly removed her foot from the puddle, careful not to get more of it on herself. It stuck to her sock as she peeled it off, reluctantly. The sock fell, its edge landing in the dark substance. She bent down, peering at the thing. She dared not touch it, though her curiosity let her blow on it, testing its viscosity. It was more pudding than strictly liquid, at least, that's all she could tell with such a rudimentary test. It didn't seem harmful, though she still didn't know where it came from. Just another mystery in this weird room, she supposed. Walking one-socked, she returned to her desk. There was nothing to write. No fresh inspiration to draw from the walls. A few more hours passed before she realized the same word traced its path along the wall.

"Disorder."

She shook off the trance, leaving for a new coffee despite the late hour. She had to write something before next week or suffer the corporate disappointment of her editor. She couldn't deal with another email demanding more while saying of course she could do it, she'd done it before, and don't forget your contract! Her coffee, three sugars and one cream, didn't give her a drop of focus. She brewed another, then leaned back in her chair, watching the words flow above her head. Above her head?

The words had never been on the ceiling before. They'd been strictly limited to the walls and their yellow confines. Now they were on the white ceiling; she could see that they weren't actually black but the distinctive dark blue of her favourite pen. Huh, she thought, peering at them as they bubbled past her eyeline, not reading a single character. Blue. This whole time she'd imagined them to be the deepest black she'd ever seen. She'd read them like a child read the clouds, looking for something in them that no one else could see. So focused on them and yet seeing nothing. The words crept across the new expanse with determined pace. Liradana debated getting a ladder to see if she could learn anything else about these letters, but that was too much effort. She looked back down at the pad on her desk, the words there stationary. Unchanged. She closed her eyes and looked back up.

"Promise. The art of letting. Letting, letting, letting. Letting go, letting live, letting be."

Uninspired as ever, she copied the ramble. Maybe it would lead somewhere. As her editor said, she had done it before and could do it again. She felt like bashing her head against the wall. She'd never truly considered it before, but tonight she was willing to try anything. Standing and walking to the left, she thought the words there might be appropriate business slogans.

She stood in front of "Champion. Building lives. Responsible people." and smacked her head into the "V."

Thunk.

It didn't hurt. Her head remained at the wall. She felt the odd caress of the words flowing past her forehead, warm and malleable. They deformed around her head, warping slightly as she pushed her face flat against the surface. Her cheek moved with the bubbling words as they passed. One eye watched the words from a new angle, the bulge of the words much more obvious. From this vantage point, she could barely see the puddle. The purple sock remained beside it, though there was a gap between the puddle and the sock now. She suddenly realized how stupid she must look, face against the wall and staring sideways. Lira backed away from the warmth of the inky words.

"Minute fashion variant. Guide to cubic containment. Hunter-gatherer conclave."

It had shifted from corporate-speak to random ideas. She had never found a pattern in its ramblings. The last phrase held her attention more than its predecessors. What the hell did time have to do with fashion? Who would want that guidebook? But the last ...

She sat back down, ripping out a new page. She began with the phrase in the centre, circled it, then drew a line away from it. It dawned on her that she wasn't certain what "conclave" meant. A formal gathering of some sort, but to what end? She promptly looked it up. Conclaves were simply private meetings, unless you were Catholic. Lira had never been much of a churchgoer. Her parents weren't religious. She couldn't imagine being so certain about the meaning of life and her worldly purpose. She saw the appeal, but it wasn't for her. That, and she was far too embarrassed to sing hymns every week where everyone present could hear her. Or worse, sit silently while everyone else sang somewhat off-key. Yikes. She took off the sock on the other foot, wondering how anyone could stand hearing others sing terribly. It's what put her off karaoke nights.

She was distracted again. Right. Time to buckle down. She looked over to the puddle, finding her computer chair almost rolling into it. How might it sound if she rolled into it? Would it squish? Squeak? Would it sound like anything she knew? She addressed the puddle, getting off her chair to kneel beside it. She tried to communicate with the thing as if it were alive, but it didn't respond. She hovered her hand above it, wondering what drew them together. Giving in to impulse, she slapped the dense muck. It was the same temperature as the wall words.

She began to play, testing the texture. Not terribly sticky. The slap had spread the stuff between her fingers; it didn't burn or hurt in any way. She put her other hand in it and tried to mold something from the stuff. It seemed then, to fight her, only letting her roll it into rough cylinders. Worm-like, they began to move faster than their original form. The tubes bent and wriggled as Lira made more. Curious. They began spelling things out on her floor, shaping themselves into letters just like the ones on her walls and ceiling. Once formed, they slowed and began a linear crawl across the hardwood. Lira felt oddly responsible because she had created these words. She watched them flow past, then looked at the remains of the puddle. She resolutely picked up the rest of the goo, formed it into more cylinders, and let the words writhe out from between her fingers.

DRUNK OFF HEART CONDITION (legally known as Natasha Feuchuk) is a queer and disabled literary creature, former musical theatre kid, and B.C.-residing medical anomaly. A fiction writer and poet ever since they were handed a Dixon Primary Printer #1, they have continued the habit long into their adult years. They're working on a memoir in a Choose-Your-Own-Adventure style, waiting on a third open heart surgery, and documenting all at drunkoffheartcondition.ca.

STEPH COELHO

There's a Hole in the Backyard

An excerpt

Prologue
Without a Trace Podcast
Interview with Anvi Chaudhary
Raw recording

We were just kids.

I don't like to talk about it, but if you're asking, that means someone's still looking. And I'm glad. Because I stopped looking for answers a long time ago.

Why did you stop?

You get to a certain age where you stop believing in things. And the memories you thought you'd hold onto forever? You start to doubt they even happened at all. A little bit of denial grows into a lot of denial. And it's all so you can go back to being normal again. Only you're not really. There's something in the back of your brain that sits there and rots it, I think. Probably why my apartment looks like this.

Why does it look like this?

Probably PTSD. Never formally diagnosed because I wasn't about to spill my guts to a shrink who was going to put me in a padded room.

Why a padded room?

Aren't you here because Brady Henrik has been yapping about Sunnyvale Gardens?

The apartment complex you lived in as a kid.

Yeah.

Do you know Henrik? Are you aware of his claims?

Yeah.

What do you think of him?

Henrik is a grifter who doesn't know what he's talking about.

Have you seen his most recent viral video? Filmed at Sunnyvale?

I haven't because it's bullshit. I don't believe in ghosts. His TikToks are clearly staged and mostly ragebait. Not something I'm about to engage with.

So, why talk to me then?

Maybe surrounding myself with newspapers and moldy books isn't really doing it for me anymore.

Why now?

I'm feeling sentimental.

Not...guilty?

If you're implying I had anything to do with the disappearance, you can cut the fucking recording right now and get—

I had to ask. But, noted. So, let's go back to the beginning. Tell me about what happened to Greg.

And you'll be publishing this somewhere? The Gazette, you said?

It's an audio podcast, actually. An offshoot project with ties to the Gazette. We dive into unsolved disappearances, and this case piqued my interest.

I guess I should cut it with the profanity, then, eh? And I hope you didn't sell a Serial-esque story to your bosses because this isn't exactly a case that's meaty with evidence.

You can be yourself.

You're going to regret giving me permission to do that.

Chapter 1—Anvi—Backbones and balconies

I often wonder how my life would have turned out if we'd never been in that basement. If I'd done the responsible thing and shut it down. Told Bill to knock it off. Ran to get an adult.

But the beautiful thing about being a kid—that sense of wonder and excitement, belief in a great adventure yet to be had—is what kept me glued to that concrete slab floor, cold and rough on our knees as we crawled our shorts-clad bodies over to inspect the thing we discovered that summer afternoon.

Going back there decades later, the smell felt most familiar. An almost plasticky, new car-like odour mixed with stale cigarette smoke and curry spice. I was surprised people still lived in the place I'd spent years burying in the back of my mind. Had they been there the whole time? Getting older, frying onions, sweatily fucking, and sharing joints on those tiny, precarious, black steel balconies hanging off the edge of the building by what seemed like nothing but sheer will.

I remember hearing about someone who died when a similar balcony snapped off an old duplex in the city, years ago. The couple—who'd been grabbing fresh air—escaped with minor injuries, but the man below—heading home from work—was crushed. Pieces of his eggshell skull scattered across the sidewalk next to the apartment complex entrance. What could his life have been if he'd been met with one more red light, two more stop signs, a boss requesting overtime? And if he hadn't broken that couple's fall? Would they be six feet under while he spent years snuggled up next to his beloved wife, or would he and his wife split in an acrimonious divorce, her tossing his clothes off another flimsy metal balcony?

I met Bill before Greg. Skinned knees bent into my chest as I sat in the stairwell sniffing my shirt, worried the kids at school would be able to smell my dad's cooking. I was contemplating binning the contents of my metal lunchbox.

"What are you doing?"

A big-boned boy with ashy blond hair and dirty, tanned skin almost as dark as mine stood at the top of the stairs. I clutched my lunchbox, knuckle bones almost piercing my skin.

"Nothing."

"Is that your lunch?" he said, craning his neck, eyes narrowing.

I gripped the box tighter, paused, and just barely shook my head.

"Can I have some?"

He sat down next to me, his tongue slipping ever so slightly out of his mouth, gliding over his lower lip.

In that moment, I expected him to take it from me. This new bully of mine snatching the lunch I'd been about to throw away.

But instead, he scootched closer, reached out his hand, and said, "I'm Bill."

I think that was the first time I'd shaken anyone's hand, or at least another kid's. Something electric passed through us both. A connecting thread that calmed me, despite Bill's rambunctious, in-charge vibe. Nothing to do with attraction, mind you. Even then, I knew boys weren't for me, romantically speaking. There was an ease in being next to that scraggly boy with untied shoes and a backpack that looked like he'd picked it out of the trash—I later discovered that's exactly where he got it.

"It's lamb biryani, you probably won't like it," I said, handing him the lunch tin and a fork.

He devoured it in less than two minutes.

"That was so good."

"I can bring you some more tomorrow if you want. Maybe we can trade lunches?"

"Cool. Thanks, but … I don't have anything to trade."

"That's okay. I'll bring you some anyway."

And that's how we spent many mornings that spring, sitting in that stairwell lit by harsh halogen fixtures stained by carcasses of desiccated bugs and constantly swinging ever so slightly. Me handing over my lunch tin, and Bill telling me about the latest Goosebumps episode my parents forbade me from watching. Eventually, we shared the fragrant, delicious meals I had been too afraid to bring to school.

When you're an adult, it can take years to make a friend. Many of us never even try because we're too busy, we fear rejection, or we live with the pain of friends lost. That friendship between Bill and me happened instantaneously, I think.

After everything, we remained friends in secret, curtailing the rules the adults in our lives had set for us. *Stay away from that white boy, he's a bad influence. Don't go near that Indian girl again, she'll get you in trouble.*

But it didn't take long for us both to realize we wanted to bury that day in the basement, shove it far into the back recesses of our minds. We were each other's constant reminder. So, we drifted apart. Or was it me who pushed Bill away, unable to face what had happened, while Bill was eager to solve things, to find a distraction from the perma dirt under his fingernails and his rumbling stomach?

I get that mixed up sometimes.

I do remember my visceral reaction to seeing Bill in the hallways of our high school, after we were no longer friends and just a part of each other's memory bank. I flinched, and my friend, Lee, noticed. *Are you okay, Vee?* We carried our books like they do in the movies, crushingly close to the chest. I made up some lie about Bill that day, how I found him creepy. Something that followed him for the rest of that year and probably the rest of his life. *Oh, totally*. Lee said this emphatically, but I knew she'd barely ever interacted with him, and I wondered why she felt like she had to be in on my lie.

STEPH COELHO is a freelance writer and editor based in the Greater Montreal area. Her fiction often explores themes of existential dread, grief, and everyday horrors. She's currently writing a time-bending existential horror, sci-fi novel, and a short story collection on suburban unease. When not writing, she's cooking, running, or trying not to suffocate under her massive TBR pile. Reach out at stephcoelho.com or @stephcoelhowrites on Instagram.

NIK DOBRINSKY

Do Nothing: The Power of Zero

An excerpt from a longer story

"You can be a total fuck-up your whole life, but do one thing right, at the exact right moment, and it'll make it all worth it, Jack. You can be a fuck-up every day of your life before, and resume being fucked up after, but do the right thing in that one moment, and you're instantly redeemed in the eyes of God," said Bob, his own eyes wide and sparkly, as usual. He waved his hands about as he spoke, smoke swirls surrounding him—a wizard conjuring spells out of the mist.

He passed the joint to me and I smoked. "Does God *have* eyes?"

"Ha, exactly!" said Bob. And he looked straight into my eyes, across the smoke-filled room, that chronic shimmering twinkle dancing in the corners of his irises. When Bob looked at me like this I had the feeling he wasn't just looking into my eyes, but into my soul.

"That reminds me," he continued. "Have I ever told you about Mansur al-Hallaj? Well, check this out—he was this mystical Sufi poet revolutionary who lived like a thousand years ago, and among the Sufis at that time it was considered improper to share the secrets of mysticism with the masses, as he did. Furthermore, he claimed to actually *be* God, which gained him some followers, but even more enemies …"

I listened intently, as always when Bob spoke. The depths of his intellect never ceased to amaze me. We continued passing the never-ending joint back and forth, as Bob carried on, "… and he kept smiling throughout his imprisonment, trial, and torture, repeating the phrase 'every drop of rain screams *I am God*!'"

By now I was pretty stoned, that warm, fuzzy feeling rippling throughout my body as I sat in Bob's basement. The thick smoke seemed concentrated more densely around Bob. I looked around to see that the windows and door were shut.

"Maybe we could open a window," I said.

But Bob ignored me, his hands moving about in increasingly animated motions as he lectured. "…and after his execution, one of his followers wrote 'every drop of Mansur al-Hallaj's blood screams *I am God!*'"

I rubbed my eyes as he paused his speech, and through blurry vision I saw the smoke had entirely engulfed Bob's body, so all that was left was his head, floating in the mist. His face bore an expression implying he thought he'd just said the most profound thing in the world, as his piercing gaze burned holes into my soul.

II

Bob Zimm was unlike anyone I've ever known. Genius is a strong word, but if I've ever known someone who'd qualify, it would be Bob. I'm no intellectual—maybe a frustrated artist at best. So, I'm not sure how effectively I can tell this story. But I have to try to make sense of it all.

My friend Mike introduced me to Bob when I was looking to score some weed—this was in the 1990s, long before legalization. One afternoon, Mike brought me to the house of this older hippie guy who lived in the neighbourhood and was open to new customers. We went through the side gate and around to the back. Mike said Bob's wife and kids stayed mostly upstairs, but the basement was Bob's space—his office, of a sort. The door was open, and as we approached I heard two voices engaged in what sounded like a passionate debate.

"… if it wasn't for Joe Stalin, there wouldn't be a Jew alive today."

"You gotta be kidding me, Bob! Stalin was a power-crazed mass murderer—a psychopath the likes of Hitler! He was—"

"Stalin *beat* Hitler, and made a good job at it, because of his proletarian ingenuity, craftiness, and toughness. He was a hero of the people, of the proletarian movement, a man who rose up to his obligations and opportunities, the tasks history bequeathed him. The Western Capitalist powers created Hitler to use him against socialist Russia, which they deemed their real opponent. Nazism was not born in Germany, but in the U.S.—Henry Ford was the true perpetrator of Nazi philosophy."

"Well! I … for someone as smart as you, you sure talk a lot of horseshit!"

Mike and I stood outside the door, out of sight, listening but not really understanding what the argument was about.

"Should we come back later?" I asked Mike. "Sounds pretty heated in there."

"Naw, don't worry, this is normal." He smiled, and I followed him as he moved to the open door, knocked on it, and stuck his head in. "Hey, what's going on in here, ya old hippies!"

A middle-aged man sat on a couch. He had a full beard, and longish, thinning brown hair combed back into a little ducktail—Bob. Another even older guy—clean-shaven, shoulder-length grey hair, wearing glasses—sat in an armchair. They turned towards us.

"Hey, Mike! Come on in, guys." Bob motioned to the glasses guy. "This is Kingston."

We stepped inside and introduced ourselves, as Kingston stood up.

"Stay and teach these kids a thing or two," said Bob.

"No, I gotta go, Bob. I only came in here to get some smoke, and I end up arguing with you for forty fuckin' minutes," replied Kingston, shaking his head. "How'd we get onto that anyway?"

"I asked you if Jews are white."

"Oh, right. And I had to bite, didn't I? I'll see you later, Bob." And he left.

"Sit down, guys."

"Sorry if we interrupted something," said Mike.

"Oh, no, that's okay. Kingston is a poli-sci prof. Gets all riled up when I challenge his bourgeois pre-conceptions." Then Bob took a moment sizing me up. "How old are you, Jack?"

"Eighteen."

"Oh, good, then I don't need your parents' permission to sell you dope. I have a rule that unless I have the parents' consent, I don't sell to minors." He had a big grin on his face, and I wasn't sure if he was joking or not.

"Yeah, it'd be cool to get a hook-up every now and then," I said, feeling awkward. "Mike said you were cool, so…"

Bob nodded slowly, still eyeing me. "Just don't leave your buddies out front with their car running—major heat score, y'know? Draws attention to the house if there's lots of traffic on the street."

"Oh, yeah, I won't, no problem," I muttered.

Mike said we wanted an eighth, and Bob started weighing it up. I looked around; the basement was cluttered. Shelves lined every wall, mostly filled with books, some old records on one, and everything seemed coated with a layer of dust.

"So, Jack." Bob turned to me. "What do you do?"

"Well," I said, feeling on the spot, "I work at Super Foods, in the warehouse, driving a forklift and stuff. Part-time."

"Cool," said Bob, "What else?"

I shrugged. "I dunno."

"He writes," Mike interjected. "Trippy stories."

I glared at Mike, because he knew I hated him telling people about my stuff.

"Right on," said Bob. "An *artiste*, eh? Well, whatever it is you do, do it to the best of your ability. If you're a ditch digger, forklift operator, a writer, or whatever—be the very best you can at it. My mother used to tell me that. But when I became an alcoholic, I was confused about whether this meant to drink a lot or drink a little!" He laughed vigorously—a gruff, savage laugh.

Mike laughed with him but I just smiled, not sure if he was mocking me or what.

"But seriously," Bob continued, bagging up our eighth. "The universe will always reward hard work." I thought I saw him shoot me a quick wink as he said this. He handed the bag to Mike, and Mike gave him the money. Then Bob turned to me, looked directly into my eyes, and said, "After all, Jack, what in life is really valuable that is easy to achieve?"

"Uh ...," I started, not sure if he really expected an answer from me.

"Nothing! *Nothing* is really valuable, *and* it's easy to achieve!" And he laughed his loud, boisterous rumble. That was my introduction to Bob Zimm.

Born and raised in Vancouver, NIK DOBRINSKY has been involved in the city's arts scenes since his teens, working as a rapper, DJ, and stand-up comedian. A graduate of UBC's Creative Writing program, Nik considers himself a writer foremost, but he's continually exploring his multifaceted creativity through different platforms. He is currently focusing on developing his short speculative fiction stories. Find him at BoyDrinksInk.com.

BEVERLEY J. SIVER

Into the Light…

An excerpt from a novella

Follow! The black dog's thought penetrates my mind.

The directive is so forceful I comply. After all, she is my guide on this journey. It bewilders me how completely I know her. The sound of her movements, tone of her breathing, vibrations of her thoughts, comforting smell, all uniquely hers, infiltrate my very being. Familiarity without the necessity of time. Not just because I am transformed into one of her kind, but by some unexplainable history between us.

We come upon a creek winding through the forest; its edges are saturated with mud. It sucks my paws in, holding them slightly with each step, making walking arduously slow. I move into the shallows of the creek, but the rocks lining the bottom are rounded and slippery. Although the bushes on top of the embankment are massive, the ground is more solid and conducive to keeping a steady pace.

I walk, nose up, sniffing at the air, familiarizing myself with the life inhabiting this dense forest, collecting data on what has passed through and when. Exploring the heightened senses this new form affords me, with great delight. I run, leaping across the creek and back again, testing strength and endurance. Clearly four legs and a tail provide greater balance, and speed, than two. It is intense, wondrous. I am in awe … of myself. I bark, then growl as deeply as I can. It tickles. Of course, I can not see as far as I could. The absence of opposable thumbs is definitely a downside. However, better night vision, and stronger nails, are excellent trade offs. Very useful once you get the hang of them.

Finally, the black dog stops at a small clearing to drink. The water is cool and refreshing. The respite provides a moment to breathe.

I wonder why we left the pack? Where are we going with such urgency? Why do I feel uplifted in her presence? I am so drawn to her, filled with curiosity when I am near her.

Look into the water! The command arrives, cutting through the noise of my questions.

I am compelled to respond, finding myself absorbed by my own reflection. I stare into my grey blue eyes and bare my teeth, white and at the ready.

Focus your gaze on the bottom. Drink. The directive is measured.

Fixing my gaze on the creek bed, I lick the water, wait a moment, lick, swallow, and repeat.

I hear a low-pitched sound, feel its vibrations floating through the water, gently caressing the tip of my tongue. These auditory vibrations carry effervescent light which illuminates the creek, and I see the tiny waves emanating from between the rocks. The warmth of the light and vibrations flow over my tongue, into my throat, and down to my belly, as I swallow. Increasing in magnitude and intensity with each lick, the light and sound begins to flow back and forth through the water from me to the bottom and back again. I am aware of a powerful bond building between us, until I am unsure if the light is coming up from the rock into me or out of me down into the creek bed. The feeling of being one with this energy builds in speed and volume with each exchange, creating pressure, building passion and purpose until these powerful elements coalesce into a massive uncontainable force, building on itself until it climaxes ... *KABOOM*!

With great force an explosion of light shoots out of my mouth, displacing rocks, water, mud, plants, and shaking everything in its path. Like a bolt of lighting it appears, then dissipates, returning to the very current from which it came. Motionless, I lie on the bank, aware of every nuanced shape cradling my body. Shaken and unstable I stand, thankful for four legs to keep my balance. I shake, head to tail, releasing the mud and water, trying to refocus my vision.

What did you feel? Her thoughts shoot through me.

As I recall the feeling of being one with the creek, the water, the vibrations, and the light-energy flow through the water from the creek bed to me and back again, connecting all that they touch into one living thing. I could not control the energy as it began to climax, nor the explosion that was created. I was filled with this strange feeling that I might be able to contain it, capture it, keep it.

Not just connecting. That I have witnessed before. I watched as you summoned the power of the elements, and they released their power to you. You absorbed it. You were the cause of the explosion.

These thoughts confuse me. Trying to understand what it all means. How could I possibly summon it, or be the cause of such an explosion?

Look at me now. She interjects, focussing my thoughts.

We look directly into each other's eyes; her gaze holds me steady.

Look into the water, see for yourself.

Moving to the edge, I see my eyes now glow yellow. In disbelief, I close them, holding them tightly shut, while shaking my head side to side. Upon opening them the glow is only slightly diminished.

Looking toward the black dog, her mouth is open, soft wet tongue exposed. I can't tell whether she is panting or grinning. I mirror her look and decide she is grinning.

By licking the water, you summoned the life source of this creek. It flowed into you.

Yes I felt that. It was exhilarating!

You are able to galvanize the essence of the elements.

The force of the explosion could have killed you. But it looks like you absorbed it.

I do not understand, why me?

I do not understand either. You must come with me.

Where?

To the ALL. There exists a creature who holds great knowledge of the ebb and flow of energy. He alone holds it in balance, keeping it so we do not self-destruct. I believe that you may be here to help us keep him alive, so he can continue creating balance in the ALL.

With that she stops her thoughts. And we wait in silence.

We need you!

I nod and turn to follow her.

She leads, relentless in her perseverance to keep us moving. No obstacle can deter us. We run flat out, only stopping briefly to replenish. Drinking the cool clear water, then quickly and silently running again. The creek gets wider throughout the journey, and now it is deep and black. I do not notice anything moving in it other than swirling pools boiling up to the surface from the depths. The trees are thick, wider, and taller, stretching up to the sky, shutting out the light. The times I am unable to see her increase, as does the distance between us.

Sight alone becomes unreliable and distracting. Periodically I close my eyes, finding it is easier to track her by engaging all senses. At times, her movement and scent are more trackable. Avoiding obstacles requires all senses, including kinetic cues, which keep me from running into or tripping over the challenges the forest presents.

I hold her last thought with me. *We need you.* It becomes my mantra, fills me with hope when I falter, gives me focus as the journey is long and increasingly difficult. Then, without noticing, my mantra changes to *I need you. I need you!* And this new mantra is not a feeling I could have acknowledged until this extraordinary moment in time.

BEVERLEY SIVER (BFA) has spent her career working in the performing arts, film, television, and special events. Leaving collaborative art forms for the more individual pursuit of creative writing, Beverley has begun the inevitable leg of her journey writing speculative fiction, a path she has always known she'd follow. A resident of Vancouver, B.C., Bev is looking forward to the adventures creative writing will bring into her life.

SYLVIA TRAN

Bang Clash

An excerpt from a short story also titled "Bang Clash"

Jane walked out into the cold night and found herself in a courtyard. A fire pit blazed on the side, and the heat washed over her skin. A table was laden with fluffy white buns, fresh fruits, and sweet barbecued meats. A red altar sat in the middle of the table, with freshly lit incense sticks and candles to each side. In front of the table, on the ground, was a blue embroidered silk pillow. Two hooded figures stood, one on each side of the table, red wooden sticks in hand, each with a drum in front of them. One of the figures swung an arm up and began.

Bang. Clash.

The other drummer swung their stick and joined in. A call and return of bangs and clashes and drum beats filled the air. A symphony of noises that stirred one's soul.

Bang, bang. Clash, clash.

The sound reverberated through Jane's body and to the very ends of her fingertips. She walked toward the altar, one step at a time, in sync with each beat and each pause in between. She smoothed her white robe, closed her eyes, and kneeled on the pillow. A familiar ritual. She bowed low, hands at each side, flat on the ground. She sat upright again, brought her hands together as if to clap or pray but made no sound, separated them again, and took another bow. Once more. Twice more. Until the drumming stopped.

The candles flickered as a gust of wind swept through the courtyard. The clouds dispersed to show the bright full moon. Jane opened her eyes. Ghostly transparent figures stood around her, waiting for the ritual to continue. From a large drawer in the table, Jane grabbed a fresh sheet of paper, a black block about the size of her hand, a small jug she'd filled with water, and a familiar horse-hair brush. She mixed the water with the block to create jet-black ink and picked-up her brush, angled it just so, and asked each ghostly figure their name. With the utmost care and precision, she wrote down the names, one stroke at a time, one symbol at a time, and one character at a time.

Bang. Clash. The drums began their call and response once again. Between the beats, Jane read each name out loud. And then, one at a time, the ghosts stepped forward to stand in front of her. Most of them nodded their heads in greeting, a handful gently patted her head, and one winked and smiled. Then, they disappeared, one at a time.

Bang. Jane called out another name.

Clash. Another ghost stepped forward.

The drumming continued while each apparition waited their turn. Fewer and fewer ghostly figures remained, and Jane knew the end was coming. The incense had burned almost to the end of the stick and its thick perfume scented the air. She was almost done. Her heart quickened, her stomach tightened, and her eyes were wet.

She closed her eyes and called out the name of her father. She opened them, and he stood in front of her, bushy eyebrows raised as if in greeting, a slight smile on his face. Jane rushed forward and hugged him as hard as she could, eyes closed tightly. When she finally opened them again, he was gone. She felt the warmth from her father leave her arms and she was surrounded, yet again, by the forest of the night and the silvery glow of the moon behind the clouds.

SYLVIA TRAN is a writer exploring themes of identity, culture, and belonging. She lives and writes on the unceded territories of the xʷməθkʷəy̓əm (Musqueam), Sḵwx̱wú7mesh (Squamish), and səlilwətaɬ (Tsleil-Waututh) Nations in Vancouver, B.C. Her work has been published in *Geist* and *Ricepaper.* Find her at SylviaTran.ca.

STEVI VALENTINE

The Thief & the Tower

An excerpt from "The Silence Between the Stars"

At the top of a peculiar tower, a spiraling marvel perched high enough to kiss the clouds, Aris Blackthorn—currently playing the part of the world's least enthusiastic damsel in distress—stared out the narrow slit of a window at the sea of stars. Below, the city teemed with life, laughter, and opportunity. And here he was in a tower. Locked away like some tragic fairytale princess nursing a glass of merlot and a foul mood.

Sure, he'd earned his sentence. But that didn't make it any less infuriating. Gods of the Throne. What a waste of a perfectly good evening.

He wasn't in a dungeon; that was good, at least. His so-called cell was part of an ancient apartment, outfitted with the bare minimum. Paintings on the walls. A crystal chandelier. Linens that smelled relatively fresh. So fancy.

But the *padlock* on the barred gate kind of ruined the ambiance. Not that he hadn't tried to pick it. He had. And failed. Miserably.

Aris contemplated his mistakes while staring through the window at the sky. The view was better than brooding on the stupid golden comforter in the corner.

Ice-blue flames flickered to life around his knuckles, not quite fire, but something older, colder, something that had lived inside him since childhood. It flared now—a perfect mirror of his mood—illuminating the tattooed markings on his hands, symbols from forgotten alphabets, traced with fine, intricate linework, something between scripture and spell work.

The temptation crept in to let go, to summon the Ethereal creature Phoenix living inside him, to melt the bars,and reduce the damned padlock to ash. He could be free, soaring through the night, bathing in the stars.

But freedom had a price. And once the Phoenix was unleashed, containing it was another matter entirely. So, he swallowed the urge, willed the flames away, and returned to his wine.

Eventually, boredom won. Aris wandered back to the bed, scowling at the offensively cheerful golden comforter. "Poor decorating choices," he muttered, reaching out to touch the fabric.

Sparks flared. Crimson this time.

"Shit." He smothered the fire with his hands, but not before the acrid scent of scorched fabric filled the room. Fantastic. Just his luck. One whiff of trouble, and the guards would swap his penthouse suite for a dungeon cell.

As if on cue, a throat cleared beyond the barred door.

Aris froze, then slowly turned toward the sound.

A Royal Guard stood outside the cell. Blood red duster, hood pulled low. But that gruff, impatient cough? Oh, he knew that anywhere.

"Locke." Aris said and poured himself another glass of wine, deliberately slow. "Took you long enough."

Silence. But even through the mask of uniform and shadow, Aris could feel the smug annoyance radiating off them. Typical. Always there to ruin a perfectly good sulk.

Sighing, Aris settled back, glass in hand, and gestured lazily at the door. "Well? Don't just stand there like some brooding gargoyle. Say something."

A pause. Then Locke stepped closer. Never a good sign.

"Didn't know prisoners got wine with their evening meal," they remarked, swinging a paper bag. The air filled with the smells of cilantro and lemongrass, earning a low grumble from Aris's stomach.

Locke pulled back their hood, revealing today's choice of face: a square-jawed, golden-haired guardsman with a perpetually grumpy scowl. As always, the mimicry was spectacular.

Well, aside from the look they gave him, pure annoyance. "Stars above, you must've really screwed up—or pissed off someone important—to land yourself here."

Aris ignored the glare and the tone; his focus locked on the bag in Locke's hand. Even in the dim light, the purple crown logo of the Royal Sandwich Shop stood out. His mouth watered.

"Good morning," he chirped, all false cheer, knowing it would only worsen Locke's mood. "Breakfast already? How time flies."

Locke scowled, holding up the bag like damning evidence. "Imagine my delight—by that, I mean unbridled irritation—when I heard you were locked up, only to be greeted by a goddamned *Dish Rush* delivery guy at the entrance. Dish Rush delivers to prisoners now? How many favors did you burn for this one?"

Aris took a leisurely sip of wine. "Are you not impressed by my impeccable logistical management? I calculated the perfect timing for you two to collide. It's an art, really. I think I'm in the wrong line of work, truth be told."

Locke sighed, exasperated. "And the wine?" They gestured at the half-empty bottle. "Seriously, what kind of twenty-nine-year-old drinks *merlot*? Is the whiskey shortage that bad?"

Aris smirked. "What can I say? I have *taste.* Hard liquor reminds me of my mother. And ale?" He wrinkled his nose. "Too much like alley piss for my liking."

Locke peeked inside the bag, voice dripping with mockery, "I should eat this sandwich as compensation for the physical trauma of climbing all those stairs. I can barely stand."

"And break your vegetarian vows just to spite me?" Aris raised an eyebrow. "I'm honored."

Locke rolled the bag shut, pointing at the wine. "Seriously, though. How the hell did you pull this off?"

Aris swirled his glass with a theatrical flourish. "Friends in high places. Or, in this case, high towers."

Silence settled between them, heavy with unspoken things. Aris took another swig, set the glass down with care, then flopped onto the bed, arms folded behind his head—almost relaxed, if not for the storm brewing behind his eyes.

"This definitely wasn't how I planned to spend my evening," he muttered.

Locke sighed. "What happened?"

Aris rubbed his face, carefully avoiding the bruise darkening beneath his eye, a lovely little memento of how thoroughly the night had gone to hell.

My temper ran too hot," he said simply, waving toward the wine. He took a swig straight from the bottle. "You know what happens when that occurs. Now I'm brooding."

"Drinking, technically."

"Good wine pairs well with misery."

Locke didn't respond. The silence stretched. Aris twirled the bottle idly, gaze fixed on the ceiling's marble cracks, spreading like poisoned veins. The wine dulled the edges of his ire, but not enough.

It had been a simple job. A grab-and-go for a shadowy bastard with too much money and not enough chill. The target? A trinket plucked off the finger of an important songstress at the Menagerie, the famed concert hall of Eternia on the wealthy side of town.

Aris rolled onto his side, setting the bottle down with a dull thunk. Violet sparks flickered along his knuckles, mirroring the memory he couldn't smother.

He'd failed the attempt. Couldn't grab it. The room was too bright, too busy, too … happy. Instead of just hiding in the shadows, waiting, *trying* again, *waiting* for another moment, he left. He'd fucking *left*, to go dancing. He didn't expect anyone would find him, wallowing away in misery and a piss-poor mood, mere hours later. Certainly not *her*.

Even beneath the mask, the costume, the makeup, he'd known. Andromeda—*The Swan*. Eternia's most celebrated composer, dancer, and the darling of every stage. But to him, she was something far simpler. And something far more complicated.

A past he couldn't let go of.

A present he had no right to disrupt.

A future he didn't deserve to dream of.

The violet sparks flared brighter, molten-blue cores flickering with the memory. If it had been anyone else, he wouldn't have hesitated. A quick knockout; a clean getaway. But it wasn't anyone else. It was Andromeda Orion. He hadn't been in her presence for *years*.

"Let me guess," Locke's voice cut through the haze. "Luck wasn't on your side."

Aris snorted, though there was no humor in it. "Luck has never been on my side."

His eyes shut, but it didn't help. He still saw her face. The wide, evergreen eyes shifting from surprise, confusion, hurt … and then rage.

So much had been said in that look. The years of broken promises, the burden of unspoken apologies. The realization of everything he'd left behind. Because the price had been right.

Her punch sent him sprawling. If he hadn't been so dismayed, so utterly heartbroken, he might've admired her form. She'd remembered his lessons well. After all, he was the one who taught her how to hit with purpose.

STEVI VALENTINE, a high school Visual Arts teacher and self-proclaimed daydreamer living, writing, and creating on the Coast Salish territories is making her whimsical debut in fantasy fiction. Known for research-based writing (video games and art education), Stevi is now breaking free from academia to craft worlds filled with wonder, whimsy, strangeness, and magic.
She can be found on Instagram @stevivalentine.

MAYA MILLER

Just Let Go

An excerpt from a novel-in-progress

Bang. Bang. Bang. It sounded like a door slamming shut. It sounded like someone slamming a door, and then slamming a door, and then slamming a door with no break in between. No time for the door to reopen. Just *slam, slam, slam.*

And then, silence. So much silence that Diane didn't know if she'd heard anything at all.

She stayed very still, gripping her whisky glass very tightly. And then, she heard faint steps from the hallway outside her apartment. They didn't sound like "normal" footsteps. These footsteps were too quiet, too purposeful, and they were consistent. They didn't stop anywhere. The building hallway was not that long, and yet the steps kept, well, stepping.

She held her breath, and felt the back of her neck get hot. She counted the steps as she heard them. *One step, two step, three step, four step, five step, six step … one, two, three, four, five, six …* she counted. *Who the fuck is that?* She counted, but it was harder to count now because it was harder to hear the steps. Her heartbeat in her ears overtook the hallway sounds.

She lifted the glass of whisky to her mouth, downed it, crouched slowly, and left the glass on the worn hardwood floor. She leaned onto her hands and knees and listened. One step, two step, three step, four step, five step, six step … and then again, she heard six steps, but it was quieter. Her breathing, *fuck,* she was breathing too loud. *Fuck, what the fuck is going on?* She crawled forward, moving one limb at a time. Right arm, left knee. Left arm, right knee. From the hallway, she heard the footsteps in between her movements. *Tap. Tap. Tap. Tap. Tap. Tap.*

She held her breath and moved again. Right arm, left knee. Left arm, right knee. Again, from the hallway, she heard the steps over and over.

As she neared the door to the living room, the steps changed in cadence and volume. Sometimes soft, sometimes hard. Sometimes slow, sometimes fast. Sometimes intermittent. But always six steps, back and forth, passing in front of her door.

It's okay, the door is locked. I locked it. I know I locked it, she told herself. *So it's fine. It's fine.* She paused and willed herself to stand, but no matter how much she tried to believe it was fine, she couldn't quite bring herself up off the floor, couldn't quite stop making her body as quiet as possible. She needed a weapon.

She crab-slid sideways out of her bedroom until she faced the front door. Without taking her eyes off her door, she slowly came to her feet, reached towards the coffee table, and felt for her pen inside the food journal she'd been using to record her daily caloric intake. It was a gold Cross pen, a gift from long ago for being good at something she'd long forgotten. It had only a whisper of ink left inside, but that was not a problem. It was sharp, and it was handy, and she needed to be as quiet as possible, and not make any unnecessary detours. She slowly, slowly moved towards her front door.

Her heart pounded in her ears. She almost laughed; it seemed so cliché. But here she was, with her heart thumping and pounding, joining in rhythm with the footfalls that grew nearer as she moved closer. Sweat trickled down her arm and ended in the crushing hold she had on the pen. The pen that was ready to stab.

She reached the door, froze, and listened.

This close, she could hear breathing. No, not breathing. *She* was breathing.

She heard … panting.

She forced her legs to carry her the remaining two steps. She raised the pen above her heart and pointed it like a flashlight at the door.

The panting stopped.

She leaned in towards the peephole and looked into the hallway.

Nothing. Empty.

She fought every life-preserving urge, violently pulled the door open, and stabbed the pen into the hallway in front of her.

The man at the end of the hallway shrieked, "Oh my god, what?!"

His ancient, one-eyed, black-and-white, tubby, French bulldog at the end of the lead, yipped one surprisingly loud yip and peed on the hallway runner carpet.

Her neighbour muttered to himself while finding his key, "Jesus Christ, you scared me."

Diane turned and checked the hallway in the opposite direction. No one. She turned back to her neighbour and said "sorry" but her neighbour was already inside his apartment and she heard him complain to his partner about their dog eating another dog's shit on the walk. He had left his door open for his shit-eating dog to follow him inside. His dog, however, had not followed.

Suddenly dizzy, Diane leaned against her doorway. The dog sat in its own urine and panted at her. Its breath stank of fetid tooth decay; an abscess oozed in viscous strings down the side of its age-stretched lips.

The dog huffed great noxious breaths and stared at her with its one remaining milky eye. The eyeless hole beside it wept, and the dog's round and patchy-furred body shivered, breathless, waiting. She stared back and felt herself falling into the tunneled abyss of the black hole. The barren, moist socket was tufted smooth by fur as if caught taut in a drain. She could not break away, and could now feel its breath, hot and moldy on her cheeks.

The dog whispered through thick mucus, "I … can … help … you …" Diane's mouth went slack, and all sound save for the dog's voice fell away. A thick, ropy tendril of yellow bile dripped from the bulldog's maw as it gurgled, " … just … let … go …" Diane felt her bladder release, and hot urine ran down her legs.

The dog yipped as its owner grabbed the fallen lead and yanked the shit-eater into his apartment. He slammed the door, and locked it. Diane fell to the ground as if the door slam was the clap of a hypnotist's hands and she had been awoken from a dream state.

Diane felt an urgent wave of vomit rocket up her throat and into her mouth. She turned back into her apartment, slammed the door behind her, and threw up onto her kitchen floor.

MAYA MILLER is the drummer of Vancouver garage rock duo, The Pack a.d. The band has been Juno Award nominated, released eight albums and has toured around the world. Recently, she has written a book about the band and being a queer woman in rock, and is working on a pair of books about the gay community of Vancouver in the 1990s, as well as a fiction horror novel. thepackad.com.

G. E. CORNWALL

And Death Shall Have No Dominion

An outtake from "Hybrid," a novel

After yoga, some of the women mention coffee, and Emily, who felt socially deprived in the weeks following Kurt's celebration of life, decides to join them. It's still warm enough to sit outside on the Rec Centre patio, its canopy of maple leaves blazing yellow. She lingers, overhearing talk of adult and near-adult children—other people's lives—until the busier women excuse themselves, leaving her alone with the other silent participant.

"I'm sorry, I forget your name."

"Watanabe. Kanako. Call me Kanako, please, Emily."

"I think I like this class," says Emily. "Everyone's friendly. Have you been coming long?"

"Not so long. One year only."

"That sounds long to me. Today was my first time."

Kanako smiles. "Are you sore?"

"Not very. I'm just happy not to be dealing with my husband's estate. For a businessman, he left things pretty messy for me."

"Oh!" Kanako's expression changes. "I'm sorry you have lost your husband."

"Pancreatic cancer," Emily explains.

"Pancreatic! That's awful. I've seen its effects—in a client, not family. He was CEO of a struggling little tech company."

"Really? So was Kurt! Not exactly struggling … I suppose it was, really. But he wouldn't admit it."

"Not … OrthoHealth?"

"Yes!"

Their ensuing conversation explains the coincidence. Kanako, it turns out, works for Health Canada. OrthoHealth, developing technology with medical applications, fell under the regulator's scrutiny. Assigned the OrthoHealth file, Kanako had meetings with Kurt.

"Your husband was a bold man. Few would undertake a project of that scale with such … sketchy resources." She almost suppresses a titter.

"Bold." Emily rolls her eyes, thinking, *Fools rush in…* "He was always like that. Sometimes it worked. But hardly ever to his personal advantage."

"Ah!" Kanako sympathizes. "Such a promising technology. It's a pity they weren't further along when your husband was diagnosed."

Emily blinks. "You mean it might have saved him?"

Kanako's eyes assent.

"They did try."

"I know. The technology was immature."

"I was there!" Emily says. "I met his replica."

"No!" Kanako appears shocked. "I didn't know that."

"I saw him come out of the printer. He was just like his old self. Cured! Free from pain, talking a blue streak. We hugged!" She pauses. "I expected him to come home with me."

Kanako draws breath. "Of course you might think that! But tests revealed …"

Emily nods. "Something was wrong."

"The replica was defective. And so …"

Emily struggles to control her lower lip. "I wound up taking the first one home instead."

"The original."

"The sick one."

"But Emily, it was just a test! According to protocol, the replica was not supposed to survive."

"What?" Emily is bewildered. "That's not how Kurt explained it to me. He promised he would *be* the replica."

"Ah!" Kanako breathes. "I suppose they thought they'd get away with it. That company had a cowboy culture."

"What?"

"They were not entirely honest with me." Kanako shakes her head as anger fades from her voice, displaced by sympathy. "It doesn't matter now. Imagine putting you through that! Raising your hopes, but at the end of the day making you take him back. Still sick."

Emily nods. "And it only got worse, for three months, until he … passed."

"Emily. What a burden to shoulder after such a disappointment!"

"It taught me I wasn't cut out to be a caregiver."

For a silent minute, they contemplate the ordeal of caretaking for a terminally ill husband: the gathering weakness, cognitive losses, incontinence. Suffering. Scattering. The battle destined to be lost, that must nevertheless be fought.

"But that's over," Kanako says at last. "You've started a fresh phase of your life."

"I guess so."

"You have your home to yourself now."

Emily admits she finds the house oppressive. "All his things. He had so many interests!"

"I could help you curate. I'm good at that."

The offer feels forward, but is also touching. Kanako, Emily thinks, has friend potential. She sighs. "One thing still bothers me. Wilf Sellars spoke at the celebration of life. You must have met him."

"Of course, OrthoHealth's CTO. Very talented! Technically."

"He said Kurt might … that maybe they could … They have his scan on file."

"He said *that*? At the CoL? Emily, how inappropriate! How awful for you!"

What Wilf said was, in essence, what Kurt had told her: "I'll be back." *I can't believe how long it took me to learn not to believe him.* It wasn't the first time. Kurt was fired by the board of his previous company for being out of control. Incapable of admitting failure, he never told her. Wilf was the one who broke the news. At the hospice. She remembers Wilf pounding her dead husband's chest, saying, "Kurt! Why weren't you honest? Don't you know Emily's on your side?"

That put an end to her hoping. It was final. Wilf pounded his chest, and Kurt had nothing to say about it.

So much less appropriate then for Wilf, after demonstrating Kurt's deadness, his meat-like quality, to invoke the dream again at the event dedicated to acceptance of finality. The remembrance. The telling of stories of past vitality. The celebration of a life lived and done with. To hold out hope then!

"It really upset me." She searches Kanako's face.

"Mr. Sellars is brilliant," Kanako remarks, "but has shortcomings on the people side."

"You understand the technology better than I do. There's no chance, is there?"

Kanako moves her head side to side. "After months have passed? After the death certificate was issued?"

"No," says Emily. "It was a false hope."

"I'm so sorry you had to listen to that at his CoL." Kanako frowns, then catches Emily's eye. "I would love to start over. I'm so sick of my apartment!" Her expression flips to hilarity.

||

Weeks later, in bleakest November, they are by themselves again, in the Rec Centre lounge. "I got an offer," Emily confesses. Seeing Kanako's uneasiness, she clarifies, "For my shares in Kurt's company." From iGo, the teleportation company whose CEO Kurt talked up in those heady startup days, when his vision for OrthoHealth spurted from him like storm surge breaching a dike.

"Oh! What's their offer?"

"Five cents a share."

Kanako shrugs. "For iGo, that's peanuts."

"Kurt left me a lot of shares! It would get us to a down payment on that Caulfield place." Sylvia had to drop the price on the house she and Kurt owned together, leaving even less equity. Kanako has listed her own condo. By pooling their resources, they hope to purchase their forever home.

Kanako lifts her eyebrows, smiles. "Then go for it."

||

On a showery April morning they sit under the shelter of their front porch roof, speculating as to what flowers will emerge from the shoots poking up everywhere in their lush West Vancouver garden, when Emily gets a text. From Wilf. *Company news. Good. Can I call you?*

"Why would I care?" Emily mutters.

Kanako shrugs. "You didn't sell *all* your shares."

Emily texts, *Now's good.* Wilf's call comes immediately and she listens, nodding. Not smiling. Watching Kanako's curious eyes. "Okay," she concludes.

"OrthoHealth has had a 'breakthrough'," she relates. "Affecting my interests, apparently. I'm supposed to go down there. Why wouldn't Wilf tell me over the phone, if it's just about money?"

"He's smart," says Kanako. "But ..."

Emily's eyes roll involuntarily.

"You may as well go. He said it was good news, didn't he?"

She purses her lips. "He doesn't know about *us*."

"Does that matter? You're going, not me."

"Kanako?" Emily is trembling now. "At the CoL, Wilf sounded confident! I just dismissed it. I'd had it with their dreams."

Kanako adopts a reassuring look. "No, Emily. I would have heard. OrthoHealth is obligated to inform me of significant developments."

"Obligated," Emily repeats. "But would they? You said they're a bunch of cowboys." She shudders. "Kanako, I sold our house. And almost all his shares!"

"They were yours to sell. That's the law. Even if your husband turns up alive."

Emily realizes that Kanako has researched it.

They gaze into the garden, burgeoning with who-knows-what green life. "You'll just have to go and find out."

Emily breathes, deliberately, the way they do in yoga. "Death used to be certain," she says finally. "That was easier, wasn't it?"

G. E. CORNWALL writes speculative fiction and non-fiction with philosophical undercurrents, exploring questions of personal identity and the compromises of human design. His career spans philosophy, fashion, and high tech. He lives in North Vancouver. Publications include "Curt Lang, Technologist," in *Unfinished Business – Photographing Vancouver Streets 1955 to 1985* (west coast line), his blog, phantomself.org, and much more if you count software.

fiction

LEAH RANADA
Fiction Editor

Introduction

Here is the antechamber to a wildly beating heart, its valves pulsing with explorations into human connections. It is my pleasure to usher you into these stories told by voices lovely and brave. Twenty authors offer glimpses into encounters and relationships people enter into to seek wholeness, only to find themselves fragmented anew.

The yearning to have a child drives a couple to passions with devastating consequences. A woman falls in love with bright blue eyes and weds into cloudy intentions. The void can be strange at times, like a thirst that could only be quenched by breathing fire or a solitary vigil for a coded message in a hotel room.

There are stories of extrication with tragicomic consequences, from a circle of friends who have metamorphosed into spouses and parents, to a snobby book club in a prairie-themed home. There is great struggle to cling on to one's spot, as with a hapless caller on hold for hours as he tries to reach his dental insurance company.

Not all tales are cautionary. There are deeply cherished people in our lives for whom our feelings could only be mediated by the wise simplicity of nature. A forest witnesses the long unspoken love between childhood friends, while the depth of a friendship between two women is explored during a swim in a lake. A hurricane sweeping in on a historical day marks a hopeful future for an expecting couple and mankind. There are insights after failed relationships, when a man contemplates self-imposed boundaries aided by the mice infestation in his workplace, while in another story, a woman imagining herself as a frightful sea creature plunges into a wild self-acceptance. In a whimsical turn, the apparition of a lioness drives a former gang member to make a courageous decision.

But fear is also potent, driving the impulse to board a trans-Atlantic flight for a regrettable tryst after a fight with a partner. At times, something more sinister seethes within, awaiting a fateful opportunity, like being invited to a cruise by a friend who stole an ex-husband or having a drink with a cunning debt collector in 17th century Scotland.

The flawed memory intercedes to blunt the pain before we find courage as when the phantom bell of a travelling knife grinder invigorates a French widow to seek renewal, while an innocuous poster in an abandoned travel agency transports a woman to a macabre incident from her youth. Reading these stories, I found that what keeps us seeking connections is hope, sparkling like young love blossoming in a seniors' home or quietly stirring as the kind words of a fellow passenger in an overnight train ride.

Whether the story you enter is shadowy or bright, you may trust its teller to lead you down passages of vivid characters and imagery, with walls thrumming with the discordant heartbeat of human dynamics, down to a reflection of who we are within our own relationships.

LEAH RANADA's works have been published in *On Spec*, *Room*, *Santa Ana River Review*, and elsewhere. She released her debut novel, *The Cine Star Salon* (NeWest Press), in 2021 and her short story appeared in *Magdaragat - An Anthology of Filipino-Canadian Writing* (Cormorant Books). Her writing is informed by her childhood in Metro Manila and eventual move to Vancouver. Leah blogs at leahranada.com/writing-desk/.

SALLY RUDOLF

As a Mouse

An excerpt from a novel in progress

During that unseasonably cold, wet summer, the building manager sent a letter. The letter arrived in an envelope formally addressing me as "Mr. Wall," distinguishing it from previous correspondence about plumbing maintenance and parking stall infractions, all of which took the form of a printed page folded into thirds, no envelope.

That night as I ate dinner at the small table by the kitchen window, the table Mel had painted a dull, dark red—a colour, and perhaps a paint, suited for some other purpose, and not for a dining table, and a paint which rubbed off a little bit onto the cloth when I wiped the table after a meal—I opened the envelope to discover a person "of some public prominence" had moved into the building, someone "whose privacy must be respected."

In the days following the notice, I attempted eye contact with neighbours at the mailboxes and in the elevator, hoping to ignite a greeting, and that the greeting would escalate to the sharing of rumours. I saw almost no one, despite my efforts, and the building felt rigid and lifeless, other than the wasps that seemed to always inhabit my kitchen, near the painted shut window frame. I killed one every day or two. Anyone would have done the same. I had some justification, my mother having advised me that I'm allergic to wasps. I don't recall having ever been stung.

||

An antique barometer hung on the kitchen wall. It was a housewarming gift from Mel's mom and one of the apartment's few vestiges of Mel. "I couldn't live without my barometer," Mel's mom had said when I opened the gift.

After the breakup, Mel wanted to be the one who moved out. We arranged a time for me to leave her alone in the apartment so she could pack whatever she wanted to take. I sat in a coffee shop nearby reading

Persuasion, trying to reframe the situation as some kind of victory for me that I was the one to keep our apartment lease. When I got home, Mel was gone, and I found the barometer still there, along with souvenir playing cards from our trip to New Orleans, the yoga mat I always said was hers and she always said was mine, and a framed photo of me wearing a cowboy hat, which Mel had kept on her bedside table.

||

As I left for work, a woman I didn't recognize was in the elevator. The woman had an ultra-calm presence. She wasn't just riding the elevator; she inhabited the elevator and I was a visitor.

It dawned on me that the woman had a confidence and lack of self-consciousness that "a person of some prominence" might.

"I'm going to the main floor, please," I said in a voice that came out more regal than intended, lightly commandeering, legible as an attempt to seem a bit prominent myself.

The woman turned her body toward me with a subtle nod of her head. These restrained movements contrasted with the wide smile that appeared on her face only to disappear a second later, reabsorbed into the cool stillness of her being.

When we reached the main floor, she exited ahead of me. I followed but turned off in the opposite direction toward the subway station.

||

When I got to work, a bar of soap sat on my desk. How long had it been there? Who had placed it there, and who had seen it there? I swiftly put it into a desk drawer and logged onto my computer.

Barb from HR appeared in the doorway, her red hair in a high, twisted pile atop her head. Barb had been the one to welcome me on my first day. We spent much of that day together, her giving me the lay of the land, me signing forms.

"Where's the soap?" she asked, looking around my office.

"Is it yours?" I asked. I opened the drawer, retrieved the soap, and held it out to her.

"It's a gift," she said. "Mice hate the smell of Irish Spring."

The office had an infestation. Mice moved in fast vectors from planter to bookcase to cubicle divider. They seemed to often go behind the printer.

Mice didn't bother me, but Barb felt differently. She described to me every sighting at length—where the mouse was coming from, where it was heading, its colour, its size, its speed, its gait, its attitude. Twice already she'd asked me to come into her office and tell her if it smelled like dead mouse. Sometimes it did. She brought it up with others too and at team meetings. Sometimes I'd see her standing in the common area with her phone, videoing or trying to video a mouse.

In fairness, Barb did have more than her share of mouse interactions, including three dead mice in her office in a single week. One was in a neck trap, one was in a sticky trap, and one was just lying dead on the carpet. She called me in to look at each one. The one lying dead on the carpet, no trap, looked alive if it weren't for its stillness. Barb took a picture of it.

"They hate Irish Spring?" I said.

"I just hope it's all mice and no rats." Barb looked sad.

"Mice and rats never cohabitate," I assured her. It sounded true. Seeing her eyebrows unfurrow, I added, "Any place mice live, rats won't enter and vice versa," as though for proof, even though I was just saying the same thing over again. Barb sighed.

||

That afternoon I stayed late, pushing onward with my report. It was quiet and I could concentrate, except when the automated lights turned off every thirty minutes, requiring me to get up and manually switch them back on.

On one of these mini-breaks from my office, I encountered a mouse. It emerged from Barb's doorway, saw me, and retreated. I stood still. It emerged, saw me, and retreated again. I continued to stand still. It emerged, saw me, and made a dash across the hall into my office. If I'd foreseen that, I might have stood less still, but now it was too late. I walked quietly into my office and looked around, remaining motionless for several minutes, listening for the mouse's movements. Hearing nothing, I resumed my work, immersing myself enough to forget about the intruder.

Barb had sent me an email earlier with a link to a video, and now I opened it. It was an old TV commercial for Irish Spring, the one with an Irishman showering outdoors, lathering his hairy chest. As the man finished his shower, two women rode up on horses, saying, "And we like it too," in a lilting chorus. When I was a child, I always thought the women meant they liked using Irish Spring too. Now I saw something more complicated was going on—that they liked a man who's used Irish Spring.

Before heading home, I opened the drawer and removed the bar of Irish Spring. I could smell its chemical odour even before opening the box. I held the bar in my hands, appreciating how the green and white streaks marbled together.

On impulse, I walked to my door frame and used the soap to draw a line across the door sill. I dragged the soap back and forth until the line was thick. Soap crumbs scattered. Instead of stopping there, I continued the line up the edge of the door frame, across the top, and down the other side. I stepped back into my office and looked at what I'd done. The pale green lines were visible but barely noticeable.

I pictured the office mice sauntering down the hall with the impunity nighttime gave them, reaching my door frame and continuing down the hall, unable to cross the Irish Spring barrier. I avoided dwelling on the alternative possibility that, in fact, the mice were now stuck in my office, unable to leave.

As I walked home that night, I felt good, alive. Did the intense scent of the soap wake me up? There was something more. When I traced the doorframe with the soap, it was as though I had created a portal or erected a barrier to bad spirits. I had done something vaguely witchy. Mel would have approved.

SALLY RUDOLF is inspired by the mystery and meaning of the everyday. Using fiction, non-fiction, and poetic forms, her writing examines themes of isolation, community, and nature. Born in Halifax, N.S., she is a UBC graduate. When not writing, Sally works in the justice system in Vancouver, B.C. and explores her surroundings through nature and urban walks. Find her on BlueSky at @wildsustenance.

LIBERTY CRAIG

Lake Time

We sit in camping chairs at the edge of the shoreline with our feet in the water, clad only in swimsuits, the late August heat heavy and still. A softening of light articulates the pathos of change as another summer slows to its drowsy conclusion. Tish will be seventy next year. Her husband is a few years older; mine is closing in on eighty. The thin skin of our thighs leaks over the edges of our chairs, soft and loose. Our hands are spotted, more spots than not. How did this happen to us, we laugh. We don't care. An older body is a comfort. It has gotten us through.

We gaze out over the lake. In the end, not that we are at the end, just yet, it is us, Tish and me. How gratified I'd have been to have known it the minute I met her, at the convoluted age of fourteen, back when doubt and conviction were equally potent. In some ways, I think I did know. How fortunate I am that it came true, that she is here with me now. Aside from Anna, Tish has been the most important person in my life. Aside from Anna, she is the one I've loved most.

I glance at her profile. She's grown sharper with age, her cheekbones rising from beneath the magnificent fullness of her face, her beauty only enhanced by the advancement of time. She looks smaller than usual, like she's lost some of her robustness. Still, her presence fills any room, any place. Here on this lakeshore she completes the scenery, in this place that is both history and allegory, where my younger self exists alongside my present self, both of us wanting nothing more than to sit here with Tish. I don't deserve her; I never did. Yet I am deeply, achingly grateful for her.

"Tish," I say. "I hope I've been a good enough friend to you."

"What the fuck are you talking about?" She laughs and gives me a bit of a shove, like a spirited child, like a sibling.

"No, I mean it. I was such a mess when we were young. It took me a long time to understand how to be a good friend."

"You have always been a good friend. A best friend."

"What the hell would I have done without you in my life?"

"You would have been fine."

"Would I, though? The drunken assholes I grew up with weren't the world's most illustrious role models." We both chuckle.

"I needed you."

"My life needed you in it, too," she says simply.

The water moves imperceptibly, like an expectant womb at rest.

"Sometimes I think I was stunted by it all." Thinking out loud, as true friends do. "Not just because my dad and Monica were what they were, but because they both died so young. I didn't get the chance to just ... grow out of it."

"Makes sense," says Tish.

"And maybe it's more than that. Maybe we become the things we most don't want to be, even when we're fighting against being those things. Or until we learn how to fight them properly."

"I think that's right," she says.

I stretch my legs out deeper into the colourless water, letting my arms dangle to the silty sand. Tish runs her hands through her long, dark hair, streaked with silver.

"But you also didn't have a mother figure," she muses. "That unconditional love, guiding force kind of person. That's a tough one."

"In some ways, you didn't either." Hers, a mother so young, who gave a baby away, who died by suicide not long after. Mine, a mother who left. Who lived. But who never came back.

"I did, though. It was complicated, but I had all kinds of guides in my life. My adoptive parents. My biological grandmother." She begins winding her hair into a bun at the nape of her neck, then lets it fall free. "My people learn from our elders and ancestors. But for all of us, I think it is mothers that we need most. I was lucky to have the people I had. And you, my dear, were rather unlucky."

"All such a long time ago. Doesn't matter anymore," I say. "Anyway, I had you."

Her brown eyes skim the blue of the lake, settling on nothing. She lets my comment hover in the air.

"But I was awful, for a while there." I sit up and throw a stone into the stillness. "Thank you for forgiving me for it. Being my friend anyway."

"Well, I could say the same thing. I was so angry when I was young. So dismissive of everything that wasn't directly connected to my story. You were the one who pulled me out of that, you know."

"Me? I was a train wreck."

She meets me with liquescent eyes. "You were the first person in my life, one of the very few, to understand and accept me for me. To love me for exactly who I was. Even when I had no idea what that meant. You always got it." She thwacks me playfully on the arm. "Takes crazy to know crazy, I guess."

My mouth hangs slack. I hear what she's saying. I even believe it. But the enormity of what she's done for me. Pulling me through everything. Through Anna.

"Well," I fix my gaze on my feet, spotted, sore, and calloused, lurking like twin alligators at the water's edge. "You deserved to be loved like that."

Her fabulous grin. "Goddamn right I did!" she crows, leaping up so abruptly that the flimsy fabric chair is flung backwards onto the shore. She strides into the water. I follow her, everlastingly. We splash half-heartedly at each other in memory of ourselves as kids, then swim offshore to float on our backs and gaze at the blue haze above. All around us is quiet. No speed boats roaring. No revelries ringing from distant shores. Just us, afloat in fluid solace.

"Of course, our missing mothers loved us, too," I say to the sky.

"How could they not?" Tish agrees. A loon cries its song of haunting grief, travelling like time across the lake. We listen to its undulating echo.

"Anna was loved by her mother," I say as the last note sinks into still-water silence. Anna, my beautiful girl. My world.

"Anna is not your fault."

My fingers ripple the silken liquid, salted by tears. "I know."

I flip over and begin swimming toward the shore with long, even strokes, then push back against the water with arms open wide, twisting to face Tish.

"But I'll never forgive myself."

The love in her eyes nearly absolves the pain on her face.

"I know," she says softly.

Together we move, silent as sea creatures through the darkening deep.

II

When we return from our swim, dripping wet and without towels, the men wrap blankets around our shoulders. After talking so long, floating so long, the evening has turned to night. They're cooking fresh local corn in a big metal pot and have thrown a couple of fish on the grill, sprinkled with garlic and herbs. Duane is tossing a green salad.

"We thought you were never coming back." George smiles with his whole face.

Duane places the salad bowl in the centre of a small table on the lawn, where we've eaten dinner most nights this summer. Over the water, the sun melts into an amber puddle. Duane lights the candles, and George brings platters of fish and corn. It's just us. All the kids and grandkids have gone home; the memory of joyful noise and ceaseless clutter simplifying the current moment in the ongoing permutations of family cottage life.

We sit at the table, Tish and I, in our wet swimsuits with blankets tied around our waists, facing the lake, our feet bare in the green grass. George and Duane relax, chatting with the cadence of comfortable friendship. The moon rises behind them, bright and reliable. Warm evening air touches the watery perfume of decaying vegetation to our skin. All around us is the world doing its thing, the frogs and the snakes, the trees and the lake, and us, gathered among them. George pours our glasses to the brim. We toast. To nights like these.

LIBERTY CRAIG is a professional writer, editor, and marketing strategist who is currently working on her first book. She writes from her (loud, teenager-filled) home on Vancouver's North Shore.

ELIAS EVERETT

A Forestry Retreat

If it all goes down in flames, I wanna see what colours it makes while it burns.

I mean, it's been a really long time. We've been together eight years now, and our moms knew each-other, so—yeah. Our story is our whole *lives,* yanno? I'll just start at kindergarten and try to make it quick. There was a bush I'd go to cry in, and one time she found me there. It was technically a hedge, or whatever, but there was a spot you could slip into.

And so one day her pale little face peered in while I was crying, and I just kinda hid my head in my polar fleece. I thought she was gonna make fun of me because, I mean, we *hated* each other. But she didn't; and I don't even remember *how* things got to where they got, but she convinced me to kiss her. So we kissed in the bush where I'd hide to cry, and then for the next few years she'd tease me because I was "good at kissing." Only when nobody else was around, though.

We had a kind of academic rivalry thing going all throughout elementary and high school. I really don't think I would have been bringing back all As and Bs if it wasn't for her lording it over me every time I got anything less than she did. I mean, she has a lot more to say about our school days than I do, honestly. I was kind of doing my own thing for the most part. Like, the only thing that comes to mind was the seven minutes in heaven thing where she tried to convince me to give her a hickey and then cried when I refused and said that she was being weird.

For me, like, university was where I started actually becoming a human *person.* Yanno, I explored my gender identity, looked at how I'd been hurt in the past, kinda–dealt with the fact I'd been neglected by my parents, internally. Introspection. Started using my brain for something other than bitching and moaning. It was also the first time we really spent apart, and again, it honestly … it was more of a big deal for her.

I'm not—I always feel like saying that makes me seem like I'm trying to sound *cool* or something, but honestly, I feel *uncool* saying it. We're still *together;* I'm kinda envious that to her it's always been this whole one big *thing.* Hardly even interrupted. It's romantic, even if it's kinda silly.

Anyway, we turned 24. I dropped out of art school, and she was four years into a degree in economics. We both signed up for a forestry volunteer thing to measure, like, soil humidity? Maybe? But we saw each other at this meeting where people get sorted into groups, and she was being super nice, like, super happy to see me after so long.

When someone's happy to see you like that, it's infectious. I was really happy to see her, too. One of the groups had to be just two people, because there weren't that many volunteers. She volunteered for us to take that area. It's kinda—it's between here and the Kootenays, but I don't think the area even had a name.

And I liked her fine; it's been nice to see her, but when someone you've got a complicated history with says, "hey, let's go out to the woods alone, I'll drive," it's not like—realistically I should have shut her down, but I didn't. The drive down was actually really fun, though. Laughing until I had tears in my eyes and stuff—in the years apart she'd clearly made a lot of the same introspective progress I had— and I was looking at her a little different. I'm—like, look, I wasn't smitten or anything stupid like *that,* but when the annoying girl you grew up with tells you how beautiful you've become and quietly lets slip that she "likes you better this way," you're gonna get a little flustered. I did, at least.

So when she sat real close at the fire, and when she pointed out all the constellations, and for the first time you felt like you wanna actually learn any of them, and she kept *leaning* on you, yeah … Maybe you forget that you've only unpacked one sleeping bag. Maybe you two talk about how lonely it can get, until you can barely keep your eyes open. And it's *stupid,* but maybe you're *stupid* and *lonely* enough that you share a sleeping bag where you quietly argue over who should be the bigger spoon. "You're smaller than I remembered."

And you—er, *I,* woke up, and she was gone. She was gone, and I unzipped the tent and blinked out just enough sleep to see her messy hair backlit by the sunrise. Looking like a moth sitting on a lightbulb. And she was wearing the hoodie I lost in senior year. She kept it. And timidly, I walked up behind her, and I started.

"Morning."

And she hardly reacted. She just sat there, catatonic, hands in kangaroo pouch, until she muttered, "Yeah."

And already I realized that this was something bigger, and that I managed to accidentally find myself in some stupid big make-or-break moment that I was missing half the context for. Because she wasn't like, "Ah, what a cuddly night. I really like her." She was like, "Why do I do this to myself?" And eventually she said, "So why was it never me, when we were kids?"

"What?"

"You dated so many girls in high school. Even in elementary school you had a few girlfriends. Why was it never me?"

And I nearly lied and said I never knew she liked me, but then I realized if I say something *that* dumb they'd never find the fucking body. So I tried to find a real answer, and the best I could manage was: "I was too mad at you."

And she was really just—refusing to look my way at this point. "I asked you out so many times. But every time, I'd just find out about some new girl."

And I was really racking my brain to try and find out what she even meant by the first half of that. Like, *now,* sure. I know she meant it was when she'd be like, "wanna hang out, just the two of us?" And I'd be like, "no, that sounds boring." But at the time I genuinely didn't know, yanno?

She finally looked my way, and it kinda iced up my veins. But I pushed back with, "What do you even want me to say?"

"End it," she said. "I feel like I've been going through some stupid phase for my whole life. So just … tell me it's never happening so that we can be done with it. And I'll stop bothering you."

And I'm a spoiled brat, so instead of giving in to that genuinely reasonable request, I said, "Well, I'm not seeing anyone right now."

And then she looked—well, she looked pissed. "Yeah? Is it *my turn,* finally? All out of better options?"

"No! Just—I'm … *ready?* For you?" It's—you know, I'm tryna backpedal. "I never thought of you that way, but yesterday was a lot of fun," or whatever. I yammered on, and I was losing her. And so I tried to bring my heart out from my stomach so I could say something stupid and poetic, because that was all I had left.

"Look, I just … I wanna try. If it all goes down in flames, I wanna see what colours it makes while it burns." And she grabbed me and kissed me, and I felt so dumb in such a nice way. It wasn't that good a kiss because she was crying, but she always says that is the kiss that saved her life. My version of that kiss was a few years later—that's its whole own thing, though.

But we held each other for like half of the day, had to rush to get the work we actually *volunteered* to do done, and then she drove me to her place, and all my plants died because she didn't want me to leave. She is such a sucker for romance, and … she wears me down until I am, too. I love her.

ELIAS EVERETT is a Vancouver-based Métis author writing poetry and prose. Their works often focus on the nuances of navigating queer identity and what it means to love both oneself and others. *Adrift in a Witch's Brew* is their short poetry collection and they can be reached on Tumblr; @Riteliso.

BRENNA WARD

Tantrum

They weren't my friends anymore; they were someone's mother and wife.

I was at my fourth baby shower that summer. You have to understand, every other week that year, I had another friend tell me she was pregnant. There were eight women due in October alone.

The women gathered to send off another one to motherhood, like a Viking funeral. Or maybe I was the one on fire, floating down a river. They weren't my friends anymore; they were someone's mother and wife.

We sat in a circle in Evelyne's living room. There weren't enough comfortable seats, so Evelyne dragged in broken office chairs, dining room chairs, and kitchen stools. The other pregnant women were told to sit on the sofa while Evelyne took the large armchair and pushed it to the centre of the room.

We ate snacks off disposable plates. One mother smeared bits of cheese and bites of strawberries into the gaping mouth of her infant as spit bubbled down its fat chin. Another was shoving her gigantic veiny breast into her baby's face, the cup of her bra hanging limply on the top roll of her stomach. The room smelled primal. I wished I wasn't eating devilled eggs.

I tried to focus on the conversation around me, though I had little to contribute. The pregnant women talked about the vacations they would take while their babies were still small enough to travel. They exchanged notes on the new cars they were buying to accommodate car seats. As though motherhood was glamorous and time was free and abundant.

"My husband will take paternity leave when the baby is older and more fun," I overheard someone say from the couch.

I bit into a dry cracker topped with sweating cheddar and regarded the large pile of pale blue wrapped boxes. Evelyne was having a boy. I'd been to enough baby boy showers to know the Pee-Pee Teepees were on their way, accompanied by the requisite giggles and overtold stories of baby boys pissing in their mothers' faces.

"We promised ourselves we wouldn't let having kids change who we are," someone commented from the couch followed by a chorus of agreement.

If they didn't know a baby would fundamentally change them and their relationships, who was I to tell them? I smiled placidly from my hard wooden chair while they talked about the marathons their husbands were training for and the meals their mothers and sisters were helping them prepare for when the baby arrived. Nesting, they called it.

Needing something sweet before the presents started, I walked over to the dessert tower in the kitchen and took the last cannoli left on the highest tier of the silver tower. Sophie had made them from scratch, cylinders of crispy pastry with cream and green flecks of pistachio. I set my plate down on the table so I could use two hands to fill up my teacup.

Amelia's boy, Jasper, sidled up beside me. He had a vacant look on his face, and his mouth was covered in something sticky. I wished he would wipe it.

I was fussing with the kettle when he grabbed the cannoli off my plate and turned to walk away. I've never moved so fast. Slamming the china kettle down, I grabbed his arm and whipped him around.

"Hey! That's mine!" I yelled, bending down to his level and staring him in the eyes, which had disgusting bits of yellow sleep still crusted in the corners. I tried to take my cannoli out of his sticky little fist. The brat actually held onto it harder, so I let go of his arm and pulled him up by his wrist to break his grip.

He was on tippy toes, swinging unsteadily as he tried to pull free. Using my free hand, I tried to wrestle my cannoli from his small, clammy fingers. I had to push down a wave of nausea when I noticed the green snot oozing from his nose. He grunted and tried to get away, but I tightened my grip and lifted him higher. He brought his other hand up to swat mine away. We were locked in a sticky battle until I realized Jasper had crushed the delicate pastry. I let him go. His grimy paws were covered with the shrapnel of my cannoli, and he wiped them on his filthy grey sweatpants.

I don't know what came over me, I really don't. I pushed him. A little shove. Not hard, of course not hard.

He stumbled backwards and went running to his mother. My hands were covered in crushed cannoli, and I felt the room go quiet. I looked up and realized everyone was staring at me, aghast. I swear, one of the women was even clutching her necklace, a thick Mejuri chain instead of pearls.

"Your kid stole my cannoli," I said to Amelia, who was comforting her son while he buried his head in her crotch. At least he wasn't screaming and pointing at me, the wicked woman who fought a child for the last homemade Italian dessert.

"He grabbed the cannoli off my plate."

If I could reason with them, they would see my side, surely. But they just kept staring, mouths agape.

"He stole it … it was mine."

The women continued to stare. Panic rose in my chest.

"You can't teach your boys that anything they want is theirs."

My voice pitched higher, and I let out a little aggressive laugh. I caught myself and gasped. But it was too late. It was the wrong thing to say to a group of mothers.

They looked at each other, mothers giving other mothers a knowing look, and started whispering.

"Come on, I … I didn't mean …" I stammered, cannoli hands extended in front of me.

The whispers were getting louder. The mothers on the couch all rubbed their mountainous bellies in unison, as though trying to pacify the fetuses who would be shocked at the event that just took place against one of their own.

I was becoming hysterical, my chest and neck felt hot.

Evelyne heaved herself out of her plush throne and came over to me. "Okay, it's okay, let's get you cleaned up." Evelyne grabbed a tea towel and ran it under cool water. Liz came over from where she was standing back against the wall and wiped up pieces of cannoli off the floor. The other women started mobilizing too, but most of them walked over to Amelia and Jasper. Those bitches, they were my friends first.

I was crying so hard I couldn't breathe in enough air. I threw my hands down and splattered all the remaining crumbs and cream that were in my grasp on the floor, making even more of a mess for Evelyne and Liz.

My eyes were puffy and my face was covered with tears, but I couldn't wipe them away. I had too much cream melted on my hands, plus whatever germs I'd picked up from Jasper. So I just stood there, crying and hyperventilating and sniffling. Nat came over and took the towel from Evelyne. They exchanged low words I couldn't hear. Nat walked up to me and grabbed my shoulders.

"What in the fuck is going on with you? Are you okay?"

I couldn't speak, my mouth opened and closed, catching salty tears and bits of sweet. I must have had cannoli on my face. Nat wiped cannoli off of my hands and arms. That little fucker Jasper. None of this would have happened if he hadn't stolen my dessert.

Evelyne attempted to take control of the situation. She put Chappell Roan on the speaker and clapped her hands to get everyone's attention: "Let's do the photo shoot outside!"

The women walked past the scene of my crime, avoiding eye contact with me, through the patio door to the floral balloon arch beyond the deck. Through my tears, I watched my friends sing along to a song about waking up realizing they were nothing more than a wife, while they took their shirts off and painted mountains and flowers on their bellies. They were dancing headfirst into motherhood together, eyes toward the sun, its rays so bright they couldn't see what I could see, while I stayed behind in the shadow of their past lives, grieving my losses.

BRENNA WARD is a writer living in Golden, B.C. She has an academic background in gender studies and media Studies. Brenna writes about women's lives and experiences, and has an interest in narratives that explore abject femininity. While she has published academically, this is her first fiction publication. You can find her discussing post-apocalyptic novels and films as a co-host on the *Brave Girls New Worlds* podcast. Instagram @BraveGirlsNewWorlds.

CHRISTOPHER MACKIE

Couching with the Fox

An excerpt from the first chapter of a novel set in Scotland during the civil war of 1689

Gunn could kill the man who sat across from him. But, he decided, it wouldn't be easy.

Gunn had no *moral* hesitation about killing the man. But the man was wily, and this could make it tricky to take his life. Something about the way he cocked his head to the side and leered at Gunn while he spoke, let him know that the man was accustomed to slipping away from danger.

"The writers call it a letter of horning, Mister Gunn. Read aloud across the river at the market cross in town." He spoke like a Lowland man. Gunn was glad to be back on Scottish soil after so long abroad, but this southern tongue grated.

"And what of the market cross, Mister …?"

"Donaldson. I'm called Donaldson." The leer creased his face again, before he paused to take a sip from his jack-stowp, a tall leathern mug. "They read aloud this letter of horning at the market cross. Now let me see …" As he sought to recall, he gazed up to the vaulted stone of the ceiling in this nook of the inn.

Gunn had chosen to sit on a crate in this rear chamber of the Sandy Velle, as the inn was called. He preferred the low, windowless vault: He could see who might approach him from the common room. Though the vault was lit only by a lamp, the common room beyond was bright with the fireplace and other lamps.

But now Gunn realised that, with Donaldson sitting across the tiny table from him, his escape route from the vault was blocked.

Donaldson nodded confidently. "Aye. Something akin tae, 'I … somebody Cameron, Messenger at Arms … by virtue of letters horning, in His Majesty's name and authority, lawfully warn and charge you, David Roy Gunn, to make payment to the … complainer of the sum of one hundred and twenty pounds Scots'!"

He seemed pleased with the accuracy of his memory. His small, pointed beard disappeared for a moment behind his stowp as he took a celebratory gulp of ale.

Gunn glanced over the man's shoulder: To the left was a pile of firewood stacked on the floor, but the right side was clear. If Gunn needed to flee, he would go right, fast, with his shoulder low.

"Mister Donaldson, you'll no doubt be agreeing with me when I tell you that it is not a sound practice to pay monies—especially in such large sums—to nameless creditors and without any paper accounting for the same. How is it that I am to pay a debt for which ye have no proof?"

"Are you forsaying the debt?" Donaldson frowned and tilted his head to the side again.

"I am telling you that without this letter of horning before myself to consider, I'm not of a mind to pay over a year's wages to you, or to leave this place in the hands of a thief-taker." Gunn reached for the sheath of his dirk at his waist, out of view of Donaldson.

Donaldson scowled. Was it for naming him a thief-taker? Or to convey his disdain for paper? Perhaps he spied Gunn's dirk. It was a long knife of the Highlands, fashioned from the fragment of a broken sword blade.

"What need hae ye for the letter itself? It's only the writers and magistrates and the like who can read such things. I've told ye what it said. Dinnae ruffle me by saying I'm lying."

Gunn grunted. He again looked over Donaldson's shoulder, catching a glimpse of a dog dashing across the floor of the common room, snarling with a bone in his jaws.

"It's not a liar I'm calling you, to be sure. But is it not wise to be careful in matters of money? Surely it's wise, for one like me who *can* read, to be wanting proof of a claim for money."

"Wise, is it?" Donaldson raised his voice noticeably. "Was it wise to borrow one hundred pounds frae Sir William Forbes for arms and gear and passage to fight awa' over the water but with no means to repay the debt?"

The dog barked sharply, and Gunn blinked. This man had more knowledge than he anticipated. "So it's Sir William who is your employer, is it?"

"I did not say that, Mister Gunn."

Gunn took a long draw on his stowp. He finished the ale and wiped his wet beard. "No, I suppose you did not." His cheeks were even warmer now. He could feel his desire for the drink growing. "If it's after talking of money we are, Mister Donaldson, be kindly, won't you, and buy us another quaff?"

The man smiled with only a corner of his mouth. There were black bits in his teeth that, in the flickering lamplight, melded with the black of his pointed beard. He leaned in his chair, which creaked like a gibbet.

"Hostilar!" he shouted into the common room and raised his stowp.

Gunn used the moment to push his crate back from the table, creating some space for him to move, if need be. His dirk was now easier to grasp.

A boy came to collect the men's mugs. Gunn stole another glance past Donaldson at the room beyond. A fiddle had started up. Gunn could see a man stretched out along the length of a bench, face down and besotted. Then the boy returned with full stowps.

"The complainer claims one hundred and twenty pounds. But if ye were tae place, say, seventy pounds on the table between us, I'd gang away into the night and it's me wha'd be surprised if we ever saw each other again."

Donaldson winked, but Gunn sighed. "I'll not be deceiving you and telling you that I have any money to speak of. I've only enough to pay my room this night." And he was honest: Gunn had had to sell his sword in Rotterdam to buy passage back to Britain. His purse had only grown lighter since as he voyaged on fishing vessels up the coast to Aberdeen.

Donaldson leaned back in his chair again, and his voice changed. "Ye caterans are alike: liars all. No man goes tae fight for the Dutch and the Germans without gang for gold." His scowl curled into a sneer. "And if ye think tae skelp away in the night, I'll be wakin' ye. And yer blunt blade will be nae help in the dark." He gestured with his stowp at Gunn's dirk.

Gunn flashed a smile. Then he placed his own stowp down carefully on the table and withdrew his hand silently to his thigh.

"Now let's be sure we understand each other, Mister Donaldson. It's you who is the clever thief-taker, clever at finding and taking men and clapping them in chains. No doubt you've had many a man oppose you. It's dangerous work, to be sure."

Donaldson smirked at him and nodded. But he watched Gunn very carefully.

"But it's me who is the soldier. Clever is not the word for me. I kill. Killing is not clever. It's the work of a savage. And savage is me, Mister Donaldson."

A thrill passed through Gunn. He thought to reach for his cup to take a drink, but his hand trembled on his leg.

Donaldson's smirk was still in place. But it was tight.

Gunn continued. "Savage is me, and that means my work is taking a man's life fast, bleeding him so his blood turns the earth at his feet to mud." He exhaled slowly, his eyes locked on Donaldson. The sounds of the common room had faded to nothing. "And so if it's after taking me you are, then be sure the risk is worth the price."

Gunn's tremor was gone. And so was the vault: Donaldson was all there was to be seen. But his smirk was no more …

CHRISTOPHER MACKIE (Gillecrìosd Mac Aoidh na Carraige Bhreatannach) is a writer and actor based in Victoria, B.C., in the traditional territories of the W̱SÁNEĆ people. His focus in his creative writing is on historical fiction that incorporates folklore from Indigenous communities. Follow him on instagram: @carrickbraith.

NEESHA RAO

Hurricane Season

The announcement that we were arriving in Quebec City startled me. As the train pulled into the station, I closed my eyes and hoped that no one would take the empty seat next to mine. A family piled in. Children pushing their small suitcases. The mother carrying a folded-up stroller. The father lifting a larger bag into the overhead compartment. Water dripped off their coats.

The man behind the family was short and well dressed. He wore a black wool overcoat unsuitable for the rain. Under his jacket, I noticed a brown zip-up sweater that matched the reddish flecks in his beard and amplified his brown eyes. He nodded as he sat next to me. I nodded back, averting my gaze away from his and out the window. I heard my sister's voice in my head telling me how avoidant I can be when I find someone attractive.

"How can you see anything in all this rain?" His accent was less subtle than Mat's, but his voice was deeper. "You must have really good eyesight." He smiled as I turned to face him.

"I do, actually," I replied, hating myself for bragging.

"What are you writing?" He pointed at my notebook. "Don't worry. I can't see anything without my glasses."

"Oh, it's nothing," I said. "I'm sorry. I really don't feel like talking."

"I get it." His eyes creased gently. He opened a portfolio bag and pulled out a folder full of paper.

I examined the pages, but I couldn't read anything. Self-conscious of my own hypocrisy, I abandoned my seat and hurried toward the back of the train, where I hoped to sit alone in the viewing car.

The train pulled away from the station, and I clutched the walls for balance as it sped up. I crossed between cars, stepped into the gangway. I remembered being a child and taking the train with my mother and Anita in the reverse direction, from Halifax to Montreal. I had been scared of these connecting spaces. My mother held my hand and told me it was impossible for a train to fall apart. In India, she said, she had taken trains crammed with people. Children piled onto laps, windows with no glass, and women in separate compartments from the men. "Were there monkeys on the train?" I had asked. She smiled in that way that made her lips seem so big and red and said, "The only monkey I see is right here."

The rain seemed louder than before, and as I crossed into the next car I saw a branch smash against the window. It was late and dark and the observation lounge was empty. Rain tumbled over the car, and the wind battered the sides and the windows. Occasional track lights revealed the trees dancing in the storm.

The lightning strike was fast and illuminated the domed windows. I saw sparks on the metal exterior of the train. The electricity flickered and then, slowly, the train came to a halt. I searched in my bag for my phone, but I didn't have any service. The last message was a follow-up from Mat, a simple "hello?"

I expected an announcement, something in both official languages to tell us what had happened, but instead there was silence. Silence except for the thunderous roar of the hurricane growing wilder outside the train.

"What's your name?" I recognized his voice before I saw him. The man in the black overcoat was standing next to me in the aisle.

"Excuse me?"

"Your name," he persisted. "I'm Isak."

"Ruby. Did you follow me here?"

"I'm pretty sure you don't own this car. And it's nice to see someone who isn't on her phone. I love trains. It's romantic how they make the journey more important than the destination. The chance to feel space as you move through it."

"You think it's romantic to corner a woman alone in a train stuck somewhere along the St. Lawrence River in the middle of a hurricane? I don't know if you're allowed to do that anymore." My eyes flickered toward his.

His eyes held mine for too long.

"Can I sit next to you?" He smiled gently. All the nervousness I had been carrying since I boarded the train softened when his arm brushed against mine. "Where are you headed?"

"My mom is sick. I'm going to Halifax because she had a stroke."

"I'm sorry. My dad died last year," he said. "A bike accident. What are you writing about? I've been trying to write about my dad, but I bore myself. It's so typical. Taking childhood memories, your own personal experience and trying to spin it into something bigger than yourself. Here's a question: In a different life, a counterlife, where you get to be some other kind of person, what would you do? Who would you be?"

I laughed at the spontaneity of his question. "I'd be in a band," I said. "I'd play electric guitar. I could never do that now. In this body. In this life. Never. Even when I'm alone, and I imagine myself playing the guitar and a song I really like, I hold myself back, even in private. I'm sorry about your dad. What was he like?"

"Difficult." Isak smiled sadly. He pulled out his phone. "But wait, let's try something." Then he asked me to pick a song.

Like magic, he had everything: Radiohead, Roxy Music, Dire Straits, Stevie Nicks, New Order—a list only of music I liked. The storm was louder now. Wild drum beats on a metal can. His overcoat was off. Resting on the back of a chair.

The tinny sound of music from his iPhone speaker echoed throughout the car, barely audible over the hurricane. Isak was standing, sort of swaying, in the frozen train. He reached for my hand. I let him hold it, and then we were both laughing. I was dancing in a way I had never let myself dance before. That sticky spot in my stomach didn't feel sticky, and then somehow we were dancing. Not touching. Just jumping and lunging between the seats. Climbing over them. Running back and forth from the front to the back of the car. When the song was over we sat next to each other in the best seats, watching the rain.

"Show me your writing," I said.

He handed me the soft leather case and I opened it, but it was filled with empty pages. He shrugged and put his head on my shoulder, his overcoat a blanket placed softly over our laps.

||

I woke up to the sun breaking through the clouds. The conductor announced that we were just outside Moncton. Only two hours to Halifax. There were people in the viewing car now, drinking coffee and eating pastries and a child running down the aisles the way Isak and I had the night before. Isak. Where was Isak? His coat was gone and so was he. On the tray table I saw a note, written in clear black letters. *Maybe play guitar in this life?*

When I arrived in Halifax the sky was blue and clear. A seagull dragged half a chocolate donut across the parking lot. A maple tree outside the station was adorned in deep red leaves. I walked outside into the damp, cold air.

NEESHA RAO is a writer living in Vancouver on the traditional Territories of the Musqueam (xʷməθkʷəy̓əm), Squamish (Sḵwx̱wú7mesh), and Tsleil-Waututh (səl̓ilw̓ət) Nations. She was born in Newfoundland and spent the longest period of her life in Yellowknife. She writes fiction and non-fiction.

MATTHEW STUCKEY

The Wait

It was 8:32 a.m., and I was on hold with my dental-insurance company again. Because of a pillow. More specifically, a Smart Pillow that ratted me out. I had purchased the pillow one month prior and apparently, over the past few weeks, it had been sending my insurance company data about my teeth grinding at night without my knowledge. So, the company now knew that I hadn't been wearing the mouth guard they prescribed. I used to wear it, but I always ended up yanking it out of my mouth sometime in the night while I was asleep. I'd wake up to it jabbing me in the eye or stuck in my nose when I rolled over. So, I had finally given up on it.

The pillow was supposed to help me sleep. It was designed to cool off your head if you got too hot, soften or harden based on inflammatory markers it sensed in your neck. It connected via bluetooth to your phone for things like long-distance pillow talk. It could even play alarm tones like my favourite: "Elephants Playing Volleyball."

But now I was stuck with a narc for a pillow and a payment plan to boot.

The letter from the insurance company told me that I needed to contact them within ten business days, and this was the final day. I had been on hold for three hours the day before but finally gave up. So, on this day, I was in it till the end of time.

I dialed them before breakfast and was hopeful that I'd be through to a real person by the time I was done eating. Maybe it was just unusually busy last time I called. I finished eating and did the dishes. Two hours had already slipped by.

By midday, I had memorized the hold music and would catch myself accidentally singing along to the chorus:

"... and when I look at you I am blinded by your bright white smile ..."

It was a kind of upbeat pseudo-rock, but instead of being about, say, heartbreak, it was stain-free teeth and the endless virtues of fluoride rinsing.

By three o'clock in the afternoon, I found myself in the closet with the door closed crying into a pair of childhood Batman underwear.

"I hate your teeth and your dumb smile!" I cried into the phone.

After the closet incident, I took to scrubbing the shower with powdered bleach. Then I vacuumed the house, then vacuumed it again. Next, I found myself alphabetizing the spice rack and scrubbing the walls with Lysol to prevent the hold music from lingering on them like cigarette smoke. The house started to smell like a hospital and feel like one too: sparkling clean and full of misery.

By five in the evening, I decided that I had to leave the house and began heading toward the cemetery, which was on a hill and had a good view of the sunset.

Eight p.m. The hold music stopped. I held my breath and was careful not to press anything on the screen in case I would accidentally hang up.

"We appreciate your patience. Someone will be with you shortly," the calm voice said. They hadn't said that all day. Clearly this was a sign that I was close. Soon, it will be soon.

It was a clear night, and I lay on my back in the damp grass and tried not to be angry while looking at the stars. It didn't work.

Then a green light appeared on the horizon, dim at first, but growing brighter and brighter as it moved closer to me. Before I knew it, it was hovering right above me, the grass and gravestones all glowing green. Then the light dimmed, and I could see that it was a ship, shiny metallic green like a giant scarab beetle.

And what does one do when a gigantic beetle-shaped UFO stops directly above them?

Nothing. You do absolutely nothing because your brain does not understand what is real anymore.

So I just lay there, mouth open, phone in the grass somewhere playing its stupid song for the five hundredth time as the ship took me away.

First, there was a bright green light, then complete darkness inside of the ship.

Yellow lights started to flicker all around me. Then I realized that they weren't lights but eyes, huge ones, the size of basketballs, with the slit of a pupil running vertically in the middle.

"Kitty cats?" I asked.

"Umm … no. Definitely not," one of them said.

I still couldn't see their bodies in the darkness.

"But—"

"And we're using telepathy so don't ask about that either. They always ask us that. So many questions. Blah blah blah, who cares. Look, we don't have much time, and we have plans for you. I suggest looking out that window behind you."

So I turned to the circular window to see that the Earth, my little planet Earth, was getting smaller and smaller by the second. I pressed my face to the glass. "My God."

"No, that's next," one of the pairs of eyes said. This was followed by snickering before they hushed each other.

"Next up, God!"

I could feel us accelerate as the view out of the window began to swirl. The stars looked like they were being flushed down the toilet.

"We're going back!" the eyes said in unison. "Back to the beginning of time!"

The blurring lights spun faster and faster before slowing down all at once.

Then I saw something. A massive glowing object. Pink, with the solidity of a planet. We started to circle the object, and its form became more clear. It was more like two planets, sandwiched together.

"Is that …?" I stammered

"Yes!" the eyes said with what seemed like forced composure. "A giant ass!"

And, perfectly on cue, an enormous cloud of yellow-green gas erupted from the middle of the sandwiched spheres, the butt crack, billowing and sparkling with light.

"You are witnessing the birth of galaxies!" the eyes said. "That is how your planet was born. The origin of rocks and trees, people and pillows …" I heard a snort from the back of the room and more suppressed giggles.

"No!" I yelled. "Too much!" I staggered back from the window, feeling lightheaded.

And that was my last memory before blacking out.

When I finally regained consciousness, I found myself lying face down in the grass of the cemetery, naked. Of course I was naked, the bastards. It's like you can't do an abduction without stealing the poor fool's clothes. Somewhere there's a UFO floating around with a bunch of dirty old clothes like a thrift store—what the hell?

Then fuzzy memories started to come back to me. Must have been from when I blacked out. Conversations from the definitely-not-cats.

"That never gets old," one had said

And I think, I hope, the word hologram.

I propped myself up on one elbow and looked around. By the light in the sky, I could tell that it was almost daybreak. I had been gone all night.

Then I saw the gravestone that they had deposited me next to. It had the name "Whiskers" on it and an epitaph that read, "you had me at meow."

Then I heard it, the hold music, still playing in the grass nearby. I turned my head to one side and threw up.

Not only had I just been abducted by giant space-cats and (possibly) shown the origin of the universe, but it all played out to the worst soundtrack in the world. This hold music, worse than even elevator music. And how much more of my life would be reduced to this waiting, this music?

I reached for my phone in the grass.

We were about to hit the chorus.

MATTHEW STUCKEY is a poet and short-story fiction writer who lives in Tucson, Arizona. As a humorist, he finds his way into some neglected part of your brain and tickles it with a feather.

SUZANNE CHIASSON

Last of the *Rémouleurs*

Madame Chardon leaned into the heavy green door and stepped out onto the sidewalk, carrying her knives rolled up in a tea towel. She looked left and right but could not spot the knife grinder's cart. Maybe he was at the bistro. She hurried to the corner and caught the eye of the waiter, Antoine, clearing a table on the terrace.

"He is where? He is where?" she called out.

"Madame Chardon, *who* is where?" Antoine replied.

"But the *rémouleur*."

"But Madame, the *rémouleur* retired long ago."

"But no! I heard his bell."

"My god," Antoine said, slapping his forehead with his free hand. "Did we miss him?"

"Yes, I believe we did." Madame Chardon dropped her roll of knives onto an empty table and plonked her large self onto a chair. She rested her elbows on the table, and let her head fall into her hands.

"Don't worry, Madame. Here, give me your knives. I will have them sharpened in the kitchen."

After her husband died from smoking too many cigarettes, close to twenty years ago, Madame Chardon moved into a *chambre de bonne*, which turned out to be on the route of the last Parisian knife grinder. The clang of his bell became a balm to her grief, and every time he passed in the street, bell clanging, cart rattling, she would scuttle to the tiny elevator and descend from the sixth floor, throw her hip into the heavy green door, and line up behind the barber with his steel blades flashing in the sunlight and the junior cook from the bistro with his leather roll of precious tools. She was but a widow who needed to butcher a small hen and chop the vegetables for the pot, but they loved her.

The knife grinder loved her.

"Ma belle Madame, where is your sword? Have you not come from

Orléans?" he would say. "Or perhaps you've come from Reims, risen from the tomb. Where is your sword? I will sharpen your sword so that you may fight another day!"

Madame Chardon would laugh and blush and hand him her modest packet of knives.

"And what will you cook this evening, Madame?"

"A little beef stew."

"Thank you for the kind invitation." The knife grinder winked. "But sadly, I have to get home to my wife."

And they would laugh.

Her husband had never made her laugh. Maybe in the early years, but not later after they'd worn each other down with mundanity.

Madame Chardon took the roll of knives back from Antoine.

"We didn't miss the *rémouleur*, did we?" she said.

"No, Madame, we did not."

She felt the coarse linen under her thumbs and the weight of the knives wrapped inside. In these moments when she realized she'd been mistaken—that there was no bell, no cart, no knife grinder—it was like there was a curtain closing in front of her.

"I want a job," she whispered.

"Pardon?"

"I want a job," she repeated. "In the kitchen."

"But Madame …"

She looked up at Antoine. His eyebrows were raised so high she thought they might fly off his face.

"I want a job in the kitchen."

The proprietor and the chef could not understand. "All day on your feet," they said. "The kitchen is cramped and hot. It's no place for you. You are lucky. You don't have to work. And we have no spot. We could barely pay you."

Nothing the two men said could sway her. Antoine brought a round of espressos. The chef stirred in some sugar. The proprietor folded his hands on the table and leaned in.

"Madame Chardon, ma chère Madame Chardon, have you ever held a job?"

"Of course I've held a job."

"What kind of job?"

"Cranial research. In newborns."

The proprietor and the chef looked sideways at each other, their own eyebrows ready to take flight.

"I helped with the studies," she explained. "How babies' heads are shaped."

"Why? Why would you do that?" the chef asked.

"To help the research."

"Are you a doctor?"

"No, I was an assistant. I liked science. And then I got married."

The two men shared another sideways glance.

"And now?" the proprietor asked. "Why, now, after all these years, do you want so badly to work?"

How could she explain it to these men who got up every day and went to their job, to the same place year after year, decade after decade, to this place that was like a second home? They said that she was lucky not to work, that she could rest all day. But what would they do if they did not go to work? Would they rest? Would they relish their retirement? Or would they grow mad chasing some impossible dream?

Madame Chardon heard the distant clang of the knife grinder's bell and turned her head even though this time she knew the bell wasn't real. Sometimes she'd remember what was real. Sometimes she'd forget. It didn't really matter. She would never catch him.

What if she had invited him for dinner one of those times? Would he have accepted? Would he have come up to her modest apartment and sat at the table while she chopped onions with a knife that glistened? Would he have told her about his wife? Would she have told him about her late husband? Would she have cooked a stew? Or would that have taken too long? Would she have made a salad instead? Or eggs?

Madame Chardon took a sip of her espresso. It was already cold.

"I would like to cook for someone other than myself," she said.

Fiction writer SUZANNE CHIASSON lives in Vancouver, B.C. Her debut novel *Tacet* was published by Guernica Editions in 2019. She has a background in theatre and an affinity for underdog stories.

ALEXIS JACKLIN

The Wedding

A short story

I have a love-hate relationship with airports. On one hand, they're the best place to people-watch. But then, that's also kind of the problem. Too many people, all exhausted, irritable, and crammed together.

Some guy bumps into me and rolls over my toe with his suitcase, and Nick doesn't even notice. Not that he's noticed *much* lately anyway. I shoot the guy a dirty look which I soon regret. I want to come across as a good person, but sleep deprivation is not for the weak.

"So, your sister's picking us up?" I shield my eyes from the blazing sun. How the heavy rock on my finger shimmers in the sunlight is pretty though. It's the small stuff. I scan the crowd at the airport arrivals section for Nick's oldest sister, Paula, but she's nowhere to be seen. Or she could be right in front of me, and I'm failing to recognize her since I've been awake for over 24 hours.

Nick nods with a grunt. Like it's such an annoying question from his fiancée. He's busy texting someone. Who knows. Forbid he tell me anything important. And he's been oddly secretive about his phone these last few weeks. Not like I just flew for an entire day and night because he insisted on an earlier celebration with his family or anything.

I brush it off. He's probably exhausted too. That's what I tell myself at least. He's having second thoughts. Maybe I am too. But it's too late. Too much on the line. I need the stability for my future. A little pain in exchange for security seems a fair trade. That's what everyone does to a certain extent, right?

"Ah, there you two are!" Paula cheers. "Welcome to Melbourne, hope your flight was alright!"

At the parking lot, she pushes her designer sunglasses on top of her head and helps me climb into the backseat of her brand-new Jeep. The doors are all off and random shoes and clothes are scattered inside the car. Still better than an Uber.

I enjoy the salty air whipping through my hair and the scorching sun against my cheeks. It's a much-needed reprieve from the miserable, relentless iciness and darkness plaguing Canadian winters.

Paula tosses a fresh energy drink back to each of us. I'm ecstatic—I desperately need something to jolt me awake and cure my inevitable jet lag. That makes me like her a lot more. Maybe Paula and I could get along. Maybe she's not as snooty and privileged as I thought.

"So, are you two both excited for the big day tomorrow?" Paula glances in the rearview mirror at us. Her passenger seat is piled so high with clutter that no one could sit there, even if one wanted to.

"Yep, happy it will be a nice small engagement party at home, looking forward to the cake." I peer outside at the rolling grassy hills and crystal blue waters as we drive through the winding roads of Melbourne.

Paula's emerald-green eyes dart from side to side, and her shoulders creep up to her ears.

"What is it?" Nick glances up from his phone for half a second. Paula's managed to get more of his attention than I have in the last three months.

"Mom's planning got a bit out of control then."

"Of course it did," Nick scoffs. He shoots me a look, but I'm not sure what he's trying to imply.

"It's not an engagement party, it's a whole wedding tomorrow, ceremony and everything ..." Paula says.

My head spins. My heart races so hard I worry it might burst out of my chest. There is no escape in this dreadful speeding vehicle. Everything closes in around me, and it's hard to breathe.

"Over a hundred people are coming," Paula continues. "We're taking Margot dress shopping right after we get back. I thought you guys knew." Paula frowns at us through the rearview mirror.

I can't believe what I'm hearing. I've only met Nick's mother twice, and she doesn't approve of me. That much is clear. She is an intense woman. She has a presence. One I don't particularly enjoy, yet I desperately long for her approval. I was raised by a single mother and had two jobs in my teens. I worked my butt off to get to where I am. No matter how many pleasantries, smiles, or compliments I force, or how well I treat her son, I'll never be enough for Nick's mother. His family won't make it to the wedding in Canada. The engagement party was meant to be a compromise.

"I can't get married tomorrow. The wedding is all planned. Are you sure? I thought this was an engagement party at the house. I'm not prepared for a wedding. This is a huge overstep on her part," I say. Nick and Paula are tight lipped. I'm sick of this. When it comes to his side of the family, even a shred of disagreement or discomfort is never accommodated.

"You should appreciate the time and money that went into this," Paula scoffs.

I say nothing the rest of the drive. It's easier that way.

||

"Nick, I can't go through with this. The dress is too tight, and your mom got mad at me at the dress shop and said it would fit if I laid off the fast food." I sit on the hotel bed in the restrictive wedding gown before throwing on the veil, fighting back tears. I've always been the most insecure about my weight, and his mom throws that in my face any chance she gets.

"Look I know she's overbearing, and this is far too much. But it's already been paid for, guests are here, and there is nothing we can do now but enjoy it. Please do this for me." Nick looks at me pleadingly with his bright blue eyes I once fell in love with. I think I still love them and him. But that blissful feeling is so far away from me now. Nick joins me on the bed and rubs my back.

Then his Mom burst through the hotel door. How she convinced the front desk to give her a key, I'm not sure.

"Out with you, Nickolas James, bad luck to see the bride before the ceremony!" She clasps her hands together and shoos him out of the room. My stomach sinks as Nick leaves. How could he leave me here with her?

"You need this." My future mother-in-law eyes me coldly. Then she orders, "Stand up."

I stand up and she shoves the sparkly over-the-top belt I hate with a vengeance around me. She motions for me to follow her, and I head out into the hallway and down the elevator.

An attendant of the venue shoves a bouquet of daffodils in my hand. If Nick's mother had given me a chance to help plan, I would have been able to tell her I'm allergic to real flowers and will be using fake ones, but she'd probably tell me I'm making that up for attention, so I don't bother. My body doesn't even feel like mine anymore.

"See you up there!" She chirps before the crowd swallows her. I rush down the aisle with my head down. I want this to be over, but somehow, I still love Nick and am willing to do anything to make him happy. We have the rest of our lives to bury this with happier memories.

"Do you take Margot Verrington to be your beloved wife?" the officiant asks, turning to Nick.

"I do," Nick says with a huge grin and takes my hands in his. I do the same and we dance back through the aisle hand in hand as all the guests cheer.

In the hotel lobby, Nick picks me up and twirls me around. The familiar flutters in my belly swirl as Nick sets me down on the ground.

"Ah! I'm so happy this all worked out!" he exclaims.

A pit settles in my gut. *What?*

"Nick," I exhale. It's hard to get the words out.

"Were you a part of this?" my voice breaks. "Did you know about this?" I drop the bouquet and put distance between us.

His refusal to answer the question is all I need to know exactly what Nick and his mother did.

ALEXIS JACKLIN lives in Ottawa, Ontario. She writes commercial fiction, primarily in romance but is also a fan of genre blends. You can find her on Bluesky @alexisjacklin.bsky.social or send her an email at alexisjacklin.author@gmail.com.

CLARIS FIGUEIRA

The Messenger

Flash fiction

There are no windows in the hallway, only doors concealing secret worlds of dreaming and waking, of drunken arguments, of lovemaking, or of waiting, as I am, for something or someone to arrive.

There is little to see besides a faded carpet of uncertain inheritance, without pattern, without even a precise colour (is it blue? grey?), cross-lit by the fluorescent bars overhead. Instead, I listen to the thrumming of recirculated air, the sporadic retchings of the ice machine down the hall, the mysterious bell-like sound which plays at irregular intervals. But mostly I listen to the elevators, which rush and clatter by with the rasp of pulleys and the whoosh of displaced air.

I am highly attentive to the elevators because I am awaiting a message which must arrive between midnight and 02:00 hours. It may never arrive; so much depends on chance, on the actions or inactions of strangers who might, at any moment, summon from their incessantly shifting positions one of the four elevators. I must remain optimistic. My task is not difficult, yet it requires persistent attention; if the doors open I shall have but a moment, lest the elevator be called away before I reach it and the message lost in a hotel of strangers. They may not comprehend its secrets (naturally, the message is enciphered), but they are therefore all the more likely to toss it aside, and I shall never know if my original message was received, nor hope to read the response.

So much can go wrong in such communications, reliant as they are on the movements of machinery and the attention of strangers, and the ever-present possibility (if not eventuality) of interference, by innocents or more nefarious interceptors alike. In fact it is possible that such an interception has already occurred, that the message I wait for is a counterfeit, sent as a trick or a trap—or, more innocently, that it has been stumbled upon by a child who mistook it for a frivolous game and, by some stroke of luck, succeeded at decoding it. Or succeeded in interpreting *a* message, though who can say for certain whether it was correct?

And such a message, inexpertly untangled, might have been dispatched in the incorrect elevator, at an incorrect hour, to be received not by the intended operative but someone else—a bored businessman, let's say, on his way to the tenth floor with a paper-bagged bottle tucked discreetly into his overcoat.

And such a man, having little else to do on yet another infernal business trip, wearied by the barrage of empty discourse that has dominated his life, phrases batted across boardroom tables like a deflated squash ball in which the only measure of meaning is the half-hearted return of that limp rubber, the choreographed serve and rally in which nothing is ever really risked or gained, the smile, the handshake, the glass of scotch … such a man would stoop to pick up the little folded paper, dropping his spectacles in the process, dizzied by the sips he had already taken of the sherry in his overcoat. Such a man would stay up until dawn interpreting a note of unknown origin and intent, a message which simultaneously unveils a secret and obscures any context that might permit its interpretation.

I know this because I am precisely such a man. And once I had drunk all of the sherry and buried the long hours of the night flipping through the tattered codex I have, for years, brought along on the endless train and plane journeys I have endured in my long, dull, successful career (during which my business dealings have resulted in profit and disaster in equal measure, though not equally distributed) I was faced with an enigmatic message, to which I replied:

XENAPSZ 874 – M27 ATLED 3

Thus I find myself waiting at the Delta Hotel, having dispatched this message to an unknown adversary or ally, confirming a deal I do not comprehend, awaiting instructions from the unknown—or at least confirmation that the message has been received, that amidst the messy traffic of human enterprise and discourse there is hope of a response.

It is true that I have been waiting here for some time, that I was expected in Hong Kong three days ago, and that the message is overdue. Perhaps it will never appear. But I am, if nothing else, an optimistic man: Having hurled this message with the last of my strength down an elevator shaft, I am determined to wait as I have waited all my life, indefatigably hoping for a devastating overhand return.

The Fool's Circus

Flash fiction

Well, I'd been on the streets of Lisbon long enough, living on spilled wine and suturing time together with old cigarette butts, and one late night, I was thirsty, walking down Avenida da Liberdade when I saw the fire-breathers. They were standing in the plaza yawning fire at the sky, and I stood for a while getting dizzier and thirstier, watching the flames pour out of their throats until a clown came toward me through the crowd, holding a hat out for change. I turned to walk away, but he called out, "Brother! It's me, Carlos!"

We used to busk on the same strip down the Bairro Alto, no better place to score change or a half-drunk bottle. It was really him, though I had to touch his face to make sure under all that paint.

"What the hell happened to you?" I asked.

He said he'd joined something called the fool's circus. The gig was they'd feed you and give you a place to stay if you learned a circus act to make a living on the street.

"Teach a man to juggle," I joked, and when Carlos laughed his makeup cracked.

"Come with us. Think of it as a holiday," he said, and I figured I could use one, so I climbed onto the bus with Carlos and the rest of the jugglers and fire-breathers, and we drove to an apartment complex outside the city. It was a nice spot, a fountain in the courtyard, real pillows, and fried fish for supper, even.

"You're no acrobat," the ringmaster said when he saw me stumble in, "but you'll make a good clown."

They put me in the frills and painted me up white-faced and red-lipped until I looked like Carlos, but when they held up the mirror, I didn't like what I saw. Washed my face clear in the fountain and said I'm no clown. I'll spit fire or nothing.

At first they said I'd light myself up—Leo, that bastard Italian tightrope walker, said I wouldn't even need the kerosene, that my breath would do—but I was good after a week or two, everyone said so. It was like playing the trumpet the way I used to before I pawned my horn, except for the fire, of course. I'd forgotten how it felt—like standing onstage at Club Étoile, the crowd flickering, all those eyes wide and waiting, whispering and laughing and pressing closer and closer until Carlos played his drumroll—*rat-a-tat-a-tat*—and the flames burst out of us, the whole crowd breathed in at once, and I couldn't see their faces, but I could imagine their eyes wide open like mine, blinded by flames against the black sky like mine, and I wasn't supposed to look, but I wanted to hold all that gold burning my eyelids, and we spun and spat and the crowd roared and everything danced faster and louder, and the coins rattled on the stones and sweat ran down my jaws and I felt like a dragon, like a god, and I thought, hell, maybe I could get that horn back, sure I could, it was still sitting there at Desi's pawn shop, I went by sometimes, to check—

And then it was over. The light and applause faded away, and all those eyes wandered home down the sleeping streets, their little lights bobbing into the distance, filled with fire.

But I was still thirsty. I was even thirstier than before, and the kerosene warmed the back of my throat like whiskey on a cold night, and the truth is once I start on a bottle, I'm hard-pressed to stop. No matter how it burns.

CLARIS FIGUEIRA was raised in Vancouver on the unceded territories of the səlilwətaɬ (Tsleil-Waututh), xʷməθkʷəy̓əm (Musqueam), and Sḵwx̱wú7mesh (Squamish) peoples, and currently resides in Montreal. She writes short fiction and is interested in exploring the absurdity of existence through various narrators. Claris is also a songwriter and musician who performs under the stage name Phantom: Instagram: @iheardaphantom.

JW SONG

When the Sly Rabbit Dies

The second time Porphyria calls, Charlotte answers.

"Hello." Charlotte stares at the stained ceiling of the hotel room.

"Charlotte," Porphyria's voice is fuzzy and distant through her cell phone speakers. "Listen. I want to talk to you."

Charlotte is struck by the voice, distorted and static through a machine. "Now is not a great time," she starts.

"No, now is a great time," Porphyria says. "Listen, you asshole, okay? I'm sorry I reacted that way when you brought your parents up."

"Oh, jeez." Charlotte rubs her forehead, tired. "Listen, Porphyria. Bunny. Rabbit."

"Why do you sound so fuzzy?" Porphyria asks.

"Hm?" Charlotte takes her cell phone away from her face, looks at it, and then puts it back against her ear. "This is an international call," she admits.

Porphyria takes a second. "Where are you?" She sounds suspicious.

"I'm in London."

"Why are you in London?" Porphyria asks after a long pause, in a tone that says she's asking because she has to.

"I may have lost my head," Charlotte admits, after an equally long pause.

There is a long exhale on the other side of the call, and Charlotte is absurdly glad of it, the first real sound she's heard all day.

"Okay," Porphyria says, sounding anything but. "Okay. Whatever. Listen. I'm sorry I lost *my* head when you brought up your parents. I know how important that is to you, and I shouldn't have just reacted that way. Problem is, Charlie, I get in too deep. I keep thinking, any day now, this will end, she will be gone, and I'll be left on my own. And I have to know how to be okay on my own. And then I realized, I'm terrified of it because I don't think I will be. I won't be okay without you."

"Rabbit," Charlotte says.

"And Christ, I can't believe I'm doing this over the phone when you've fucked off to another continent, you asshole. But what I'm saying is that none of that matters anymore, because I—"

"Porphyria," Charlotte says, helplessly, and the word sounds a lot like something else. She takes a deep breath.

"Did you get started with me?" a woman's voice asks, from the other side of the hotel room, flirtatious, loud. Everything, including time, pauses. Speed of time is not absolute; right now, there is a black hole hanging in front of Charlotte's face, in the middle of the room, slowing down time to an eternity.

"*Wait,*" she speaks into the phone; perhaps it takes an eon to say. "Wait, Rabbit, wait, it's not what you—" Then, hand over the receiver of her phone, she says, "Sweetheart, no, just wait there, I promise." Back to the phone, she adds, "Just a sec, it's not what you think, Rabbit."

"For fuck's sake." Porphyria hangs up.

||

Three months later, Charlotte sits in front of her friend, stirring a glass of iced latte, and her friend watches with fascination and horror.

"And then did you immediately book a flight out of there?"

"No," Charlotte says. "I mean, yes, I did book the next flight, but it left in the morning. Horrible connections it had, too, I think the whole trip back took me thirty-one hours."

Her friend gives her a look. "Charlotte, please don't tell me you finished sleeping with the other person."

"The flight didn't leave until the morning," Charlotte repeats. "I didn't—I mean, what else was I supposed to do?"

||

Nearly three months ago, thirty-one hours after that fateful phone call, Charlotte walks into the patio of a coffee shop. She spots Porphyria right away, sitting and reading a book in a corner, a cup of something on the table in front of her. Her yellow hair glints in the sunlight, even through the pastel parasols. Her hair drapes long behind her back, despite her best efforts to tie it up.

Porphyria is the most beautiful woman Charlotte has ever seen. If asked to describe her beauty, Charlotte would always bring up her phone, frowning as she scrolled through the photos, wondering why none of them seemed to capture how beautiful she truly looked in real life.

Charlotte sits in the chair in front of Porphyria, who doesn't look up.

"Rapunzel," Charlotte says, "let down your hair."

Porphyria twitches, much the way a cat twitches its ears when it hears its name, but doesn't respond.

"Ra-pun-zel," Charlotte says. "Rapunzel, Rapunzel. Look at me." She catches a strand of yellow hair in the air and curls it around her finger. "I'm here to grovel."

"You'd better look very pretty when you beg." Porphyria doesn't look up from her book.

Charlotte somehow doubts this. "Porphyria. Nothing happened that night."

"One fight and two minutes later you're off to a different continent."

"Okay, that happened," Charlotte acknowledges.

Charlotte wishes there was a robbery happening right now, the world falling apart in a blaze of fire and a bullet for her to take, bravely stepping in front of Porphyria. If Porphyria were to get terminally ill, Charlotte would devote all her life to taking care of her—for surely, Charlotte wouldn't last very long without Porphyria. Yes, perhaps a chance to end her life, to prove her love.

"Say thank you," Porphyria says.

"For what?"

Porphyria turns over a page. "For letting you apologize."

"All right then," Charlotte says. "Thank you."

"You're welcome."

The thing is, they both mean it.

II

Two years before, Charlotte looked across the club floor and saw the most beautiful woman she had ever seen.

"Did you fall from Heaven?" Charlotte said, just to see those lips twitch.

"I don't believe you," the pretty girl said, laughing, and Charlotte would probably have killed, to keep her smiling like that. The club lights flashed neon red in her eyes.

"Rabbit," Charlotte said, because it was the first word that came into her mind.

"Excuse me?" She leaned forward.

"Rapunzel," Charlotte said instead, because that somehow seemed less offensive. She reached out and slowly took a strand of that yellow hair, and when the girl just watched her, she pressed her lips to the hair. "Rapunzel, Rapunzel, let down your hair. Anyone call you that before?"

"You're the first," the girl said, and Charlotte doesn't believe her.

Rapunzel said her name was Porphyria, and Charlotte asked if she could call her Pore, or Filly, or Ria, and Porphyria turned down all of them.

"This is your first time at this bar, isn't it?" Porphyria asked.

"Yes," Charlotte said, because there are other lesbian bars in the city, aren't there? She just hadn't been to them.

"Have you ever slept with a woman?" Porphyria asked, and for years after, Charlotte doesn't know why she didn't lie. Time does not move linearly, and the moment hangs for eons, before Charlotte shook her head.

"Hm," Porphyria said, and Charlotte saw a glimpse of something. She leaned forward, her hair shielding them from the rest of the bar. She looked up at Charlotte. "Do you see that girl, over there?"

"Yeah," Charlotte said.

"Go sleep with her," Porphyria said. "Or somebody else, before you come to me. I'm not going to be anybody's first. I'm not going to be an experiment, either." Her blue eyes flashed.

What a crazy notion, is what Charlotte should have said. *Who hurt you, Rabbit?* is what she could have said. Be dismissive, be kind. Trauma could be the start of a beautiful friendship. A stranger or a friend would be perfectly adequate. She did neither. She could have said, *One night stand is a one night stand is a one night stand.* None of it had to matter. But she did.

She calls Porphyria, after the first time. The next time she sees Porphyria, those rabbit-like eyes widen, caught. "Hey," Charlotte says, and she sees the tiniest smile. Rapunzel's hair comes down. Understanding moves in the darkness, like a predator ignorant of its fate.

JW SONG writes speculative and literary romance in Vancouver, B.C. She earned her Bachelor's in Creative Writing and previously volunteered as editorial staff in various literary magazines. After more than ten years in a faraway career, JW is back and hungry to jump back into the literary world.

CYNTHIA C. FARLEY

Along Comes Jane

I might be the reason she's not here.

Someone finds me lying face down on the ground, my mouth open and barely able to speak. Fellow passengers help me back onto the ship, where a doctor checks my temperature, hooks me up to a saline drip, and orders rest. A few days later, my fever is gone, and my brain fog begins to lift. I greet other passengers with a smile and remember the name of my cabin steward, Ali. As the cruise nears its end, I make my way to the buffet stations aboard the *Imperial Majesty*, loading my plate high with hash browns, bacon, and eggs sunny-side up. It's been an incredible trip—pyramids, ruins, ancient wonders—but I hadn't travelled alone. I came aboard with my old classmate, Mavis Tapley. Now, as I prepare to go home, she's not with me. And I can't quite remember why. Or maybe ... I do. But I don't want to. Because I'm starting to think I might be the reason she's not here.

||

Almost two weeks ago, I received a message from my wealthy friend, Mavis, who asked me if I was interested in going on an Egyptian cruise. I imagine she flicked through her rolodex of friends first. How did I know? "Mavis, you can't believe how many people can't take this vacation. Can you go?" I told her of course I would go, and would it be much money? "Don't worry about the money, Jane," she messaged.

While packing my things the day before the embarkation, I picked up a call from her. In her loud breathy voice, she said, "Jane, Jane, don't forget to bring something fancy to wear. There are two fancy evenings during the cruise. You don't want to look like a washed-up housewife." Mavis and I go back a long way, ever since I met her in Catholic high school. She befriended me after I did most of her homework in hopes of joining her circle of friends. Over the years, I graduated high school and worked as a government clerk, while Mavis took a medical office assistant course, eventually landed a job at a clinic, then married the young doctor who ran the place. Thirty years ago, her husband divorced her for a younger woman, and I, too, decided to separate from my lawyer husband, Bob Landings, because he'd become addicted to his work. Five months later, I got a message that Mavis and Bob took their marriage vows at a drive-through chapel in Las Vegas.

I have always believed Mavis stole my first husband.

I remarried five years after Mavis's marriage to Bob. I fell for a fellow government worker, Alex, who happily provided me with the proper work-life balance to raise our only child, Fred, who grew up to become a popular dentist with 200 five-star Google reviews. Now and then, usually before drifting off to sleep, I wondered how Mavis managed to put a wedge between me and my first husband. My psychiatrist told me to talk to her to resolve my unanswered questions. Due to my work schedule, an opportunity never came. Until now.

But the next day, during the cruise, Mavis started sneezing and coughing. As she lay recovering in bed, she ordered me to get her cold medicine and tend to her hand and foot. Two days later, she felt well enough to ask for her coral lipstick and mirror. She was also ready to go on an excursion to the great Karnak temple complex, where we'd explore the vast network of ancient pillars, statues, chapels, and other buildings.

As we walked down the winding courtyard that led to more structures, I marveled and tried to decipher the inscriptions on the ancient tablets. Mavis exuded confidence and energy, transforming into her chatty, confident self.

"When can I meet Alex?" she asked. "I know you've been married for twenty-five years, but we've never met."

"Some day," I told her, thinking that day could never come, because Mavis already had everything, so why was she so interested in things that I had? She took a long time in the bathroom that morning, making me wait, while she coiled her blond hair up into a bun and tried on various shades of blush.

"How did I look this morning? Do you think there are any single doctors or other rich tourists on the ship? Why don't you ask the steward to see if I can meet the captain? Do you think he's single?"

"Sure, Mavis. You look wonderful."

"Compared to someone like you, who only dresses in simple tops and long shorts. You know I am just joking, my dear."

I assured her that my skin was thicker than it looked. Now, with our excursion underway, she walked down a trail that led to more temples, passing through a roped-off area with a sign that warned, "Excavation in Progress—Enter at your Own Risk."

I followed her, turning around to see that the southern entrance now looked like a pinhole, unrecognizable from a distance. When we arrived, the sun beat down hard on the pillars, and all the ancient columns shimmered in the dusty light. It had been several hours since the private cab we hailed dropped us off, and now my ankles began feeling numb and tingling. With every step taken, the imposing brown structures grew darker, because the sun was sinking beyond the horizon. I couldn't help feeling my heart beating hard. "We should head back, Mavis. I don't think we should be here. See the yellow rope over there?"

"Don't be a big sissy, my little mouse," Mavis said, fanning herself with a paper fan because the air was thick and heavy with humidity. Somehow, we became separated, and I could hear only the light clicks of her open-toed sandals against the dry soil as she strode ahead. Her voice sounded distant too, until suddenly, I heard a scream. It was the loudest, most plaintive sound that I had ever heard in my senior years.

I looked around. The sky, now a shimmering orange and red, stretched endlessly above and faded into the vast desert landscape. I couldn't see a single tourist. Everyone had gone back to the buses by now. Shadows from the ancient pillars stretched and blended with the dying light, forming eerie, dangerous monster shapes.

Then I heard it, faint and sharp.

"Help me, dear! I'm down here. Please, I'm stuck!"

I ran toward the voice. After thirty more steps, I found one of Mavis's sandals strewn about, the straps broken and twisted. I peered into a narrow crevice, which was nearly five metres deep. She stood down there, waiting, hoping. Her designer hat lay beside her, fear etched in her eyes.

"Mavis, are you all right?"

With her dyed blond hair wild and undone and mascara streaking down her cheeks, she looked anything but a glamorous, older widow on the hunt for her third husband. But when she spoke, the old familiar Mavis channeled through her words.

"Of course not! Find help, you stupid ox!"

I turned and ran, battling back the dust and sand which stung my eyes, causing temporary blindness. The skyline was invisible behind a cloud of rising wind and swirling sand. I thought I heard a sob behind me, but it was only a vulture's cry bouncing off the pillars. Mavis was now over a kilometre behind me—or maybe more. The further I ran, the more I stumbled. And as I continued down the dirt path, I found a fallen hair pin and realized with horror that I'd been going around the giant grounds in a huge circle for hours. Oh, stupid, stupid, me.

When someone found me lying in the sand, parched and disoriented, I could barely speak, or even say my name. They asked if I'd been with a friend—if someone else was lost out there too, in this unforgiving, ancient land. I took a long drink of water from someone's bottle, feeling satisfied because it felt like the kind of liquid gold that refreshes and slides easily down your throat, like the first lick of an ice cream cone on a sweltering day. After a pause, I whisper, "It was just me." I travelled alone like a stupid ox that didn't bring enough water. I sobbed before everything went black.

Born in New Westminster, B.C., CYNTHIA C. FARLEY is a third-generation Chinese Canadian who writes both fiction and non-fiction. Her work has been curated on Medium.com and was named a "Top Story" on Vocal Media. She has completed short films that premiered at Toronto's Commffest. Cynthia enjoys exploring themes of aging, friendship, AI, and spirituality. She is currently working on several thriller novels.

ZHENNI WU

The White Lioness

To A. F. with my blessing and respect

It was November third. On the ground floor in his place, Anderson had been playing *Street Fighter* the whole night. The heat was on, and the window was closed so the room was supposed to be warm; but just past three o'clock, Anderson noticed goosebumps on his forearms. He heard something moving outside the window even though his ears were muffled by noise-cancelling headphones. Anderson rose, carefully pressed himself against the window, peering out. It was dark and frigid in the garden. Under the black lamppost, a layer of thick ice shone on the paved path leading to the garden gate. A sharp glare, like an icicle, glinted in the frost. Someone was beside the gate. Anderson's gaze fell on a pair of eyes floating in the dark.

Whose irises could glisten with such a wild shade of amber? Anderson thought for a second, flinched, grasped his throat, tried to stop his heart from jumping. The white lioness! She was back.

The lioness sat there, in the shadow of the fir tree, not moving. She knew Anderson had recognized her. She rapidly blinked at him. "Am I dreaming?" Anderson harshly rubbed his eyes. The shining white feline body started to expand like a balloon.

"No, no, no, no, no."

Anderson shrank back, peering from behind the curtain. The animal grew aggressively; the gate, the fir tree, and the stone fences shrank and disappeared behind her. She knocked over the frosty bushes, the lamps, cracked the ice and the concrete path. She approached the window. "Holy, Godzilla!" Anderson exclaimed horrified and closed the curtain.

It started to snow. White flakes billowed in the air, melting on the growing lioness. Anderson hid under the window sill, hardly able to breathe." Calm down, calm down, calm down." He kneeled on the ground, covering his ears.

On the other side of the room, a bedside lamp shone on a woman's sleeping face. "You don't wanna see this, Kelly-bird," Anderson whispered. She didn't wake up. She might have taken too much melatonin. Anderson crawled toward the bottom drawer of his desk. The shadow on the curtain was gigantic and dark. Wind howled madly.

A year ago, Anderson abruptly quit using cocaine, but he kept a small stash for emergencies. He took some out and snorted. Sitting on the carpet, he closed his eyes and let out a long exhale. All of a sudden, things felt better.

Opening his eyes, Anderson noticed the window was clear. "She's gone?" He listened for a while, then turned back, moved closer to the window. The yard was quiet as usual; the animal had disappeared.

II

Anderson was in high school when he first met the white lioness.

He joined a local gang after he turned seventeen. Friends at school gave him the nickname "Jungle King" because he always knew where to get drugs, handguns. No one dared to steal anything from him. He had a reputation of being harsh to people he disliked. Only once, there was an incident.

It should have been a normal weekday, but during lunch break a fire alarm was triggered for no reason. People panicked and ran outside to the designated evacuation spot at the soccer field. The alarm screamed endlessly. Worried, Anderson rushed to his car in the underground parkade to grab his precious bag of drugs. In the passenger's seat, digging to the bottom of the glove compartment, Anderson realized the bag was missing, as well as the pistol that he always kept there. He was about to get mad, but in a second, an unusual scent snuck into his nose. It was so intense that it entirely distracted his attention from the missing stuff.

Where did the smell come from?

It was from a long, long time ago. Somewhere he had visited as a child. A zoo, in which for the first time, Anderson saw a lion.

He couldn't recall too much about that experience, but he remembered his father leaning on the rusty iron bar which protected the visitors from the animals. His father mentioned lions were the kings of the jungle. A lion and a lioness lay on a small square of shade, lazily gazing at the blistering sunshine. The lion didn't look like the king of the jungle at all. And it was one of the very few memories Anderson still had about his father. He left Anderson's life soon after that visit to the zoo.

Anderson attempted to search for the source of the scent. Getting out of the car and turning around, he saw a white lioness sitting on her hind legs about five metres behind his car. How did she get here? She pricked up her furry ears and kept a long gaze at Anderson. The gaze was so warm, as if she was there to welcome a long lost friend. Anderson's pistol was hanging like a pendant at the bottom of a thick silver chain around the lioness's neck.

Anderson didn't realize he was transfixed until he heard a voice in his head. "Run now! But how?" He robotically shifted his steps backwards. The lioness watched him, not moving. She was stoned. Anderson thought she had taken all his drugs.They stared at each other for a few seconds, before he suddenly sprinted toward the exit of the parkade and didn't stop until he began vomiting on the curb right by the soccer field. On the field, people stood, chatted, and watched a fire truck creeping out of the parking lot. Anderson stood up, and took off his jacket, which was covered by the muck of his undigested ham sandwich. He folded the jacket, hid it under his arm, and walked off the campus, heading home.

||

Anderson thought he had made real friends in his gang. They worked together in the same business for more than ten years, hardly taking any losses. Until two years ago, after three of his friends were murdered by a rival gang. A rumble between the two groups attracted the RCMP's attention. Anderson was told that the RCMP had blacklisted all of them. He had to glance over his shoulder all the time when he was out on the streets.

Anderson worried about his life with Kelly. They had lived together for three years. Kelly didn't mind Anderson's business as long as he was passionate about her. Sometimes they dreamt of their future. They wanted to walk hand in hand in the sunshine without worry or fear. Kelly wanted to open her own hair salon, and Anderson promised her one. For that, Anderson had to quit the business. He thought about turning himself in thousands of times, but when?

||

The room turned cold as if it was filled with ice water, yet the wallpaper glittered amber. Anderson realized that the white lioness had actually appeared in this room. He heard the animal growling behind his desk. "Let's go, gooo, gooooo." Maybe it was time to go. He was surprised how calm he was now. If the lioness needed him, then he had to give himself up to her. The room started to rock like at the beginning of an earthquake. Anderson took a deep breath, stood up; sadness entangled him.

He pulled a chestnut hoodie out of the closet, put it on, zipped it up to the top, edged toward the bed. Kelly still slept. "How much melatonin has she taken?" Anderson thought. He noticed her eyes rapidly moving under the eyelids. "What are you dreaming about now?" he thought, laying a hand on the tattoo of his initials on Kelly's forearm. She responded with a subtle, peaceful smile from her dream. Anderson watched her for a moment, thinking they would never see each other again. He had made up his mind.

A frigid wind blew in as Anderson opened the door and walked outside. Once the door closed, Anderson thought, the white lioness would be gone and his past would be blown away.

November 3rd, 2003, 3:33 a.m.
Anderson Fox, 29, male, voluntarily surrendered to RCMP
Offences: illegal drug trade and arms trafficking

ZHENNI WU is originally from mainland China, where she earned a Bachelor of Arts in Chinese Literature. She writes in both English and Chinese. Her Chinese short stories have been published in *SanMingZhi*, where she also serves as an editor. Zhenni is a licensed acupuncturist in British Columbia and currently practises in North Vancouver.

LAURA-LEE DESAUTELS

Kids in Love

Jack and Maisie met for the first time in an unusual place: the sunlit courtyard of Pinecrest Home for the Aged. There to visit his granddad, Jack was immediately drawn to the thick auburn braid that curled around Maisie's shoulder, glowing like fire. She was focused on the sketchbook in her lap, head tilted forward like a sunflower.

"Is this seat taken?" Jack gestured to the spot beside her on the wooden bench.

She shook her head, a small smile tugging at her lips.

"I'm Jack."

"Maisie." Her voice was soft, like wind chimes in a gentle breeze. She held out a graphite-smudged hand toward him. From that first touch he knew his life had changed.

||

"Granddad, I met someone!" Jack pushed the door open to his grandfather's room, a small but cozy space with mint-green walls. The room was empty, and Jack glanced at his watch. It was already past two thirty; his conversation with Maisie lasted longer than he thought. Granddad was probably out for his appointment with the cognitive therapist, a daily occurrence since the dementia had gotten severe enough to warrant moving him out of his house. It hadn't been safe for him to live on his own anymore, especially after Grandma passed away.

While he waited, Jack gazed at the photos that dotted the wall. One of his favourite things was looking at old pictures while Granddad told the stories that went along with them. He paused on one of himself and his girlfriend, Olivia, taken at Christmas when she was home on school break. The snowflakes decorated her hair like confetti at a wedding, and she gazed adoringly up at him. He hadn't seen her in such a long time. His chest tightened. He loved Olivia; how could he be feeling this instant connection with someone else?

"*Pssst.*"

Jack whirled around. Maisie's face peeked around the doorway, her blue eyes shining with mischief.

"Want to raid the kitchen? I'm starving."

Jack only hesitated for a moment before following Maisie's flicking braid down the hall and around the corner.

||

"Here, try this." Maisie offered him a bite of her shortbread cookie with a thick layer of peanut butter and a smear of strawberry jam on the flattest side. She held it up, and Jack took a giant bite, nearly getting her finger in the process.

Maisie giggled, and he marveled at the way her freckles danced, like moving constellations against a pale peach sky.

"I hate this place," Maisie confided in him as they sat side by side on the counter, their feet dangling above the gleaming floor. "It's so depressing."

"It's not so bad," Jack offered. "There's lots to do, and the nurses are great with the old folks. I don't mind hanging out here."

Maisie's laugh washed over him like warm spring rain, refreshing his very soul. "I should get back." She slid down from the counter, landed with a less-than-graceful thump. "They'll wonder where I am."

Before Jack could ask who she was visiting, Maisie was gone. He stared off into the distance, questioning if she was real or just a beautiful figment of his imagination.

||

Much to Jack's delight, every time he visited the courtyard that fall, Maisie was there. Sometimes they talked non-stop. Other times he slid on his headphones and closed his eyes, letting his favourite music fill his head while she sketched.

He confided in Maisie that he felt guilty about Olivia, and she rested a gentle hand on his.

"Oh, Jack. I understand. I'm sure Olivia would want you to be happy."

||

One day, Maisie asked Jack if she could draw him. He agreed reluctantly, sitting as still as he could for the better part of an hour before curiosity got the best of him. He craned his neck to try and take a peek. When she caught him looking, Maisie flipped the sketchbook closed and slid it into a crocheted granny-square bag.

Another afternoon, Maisie talked him into crashing a ballroom dancing session. Jack was sure the instructor would chase them out, but she was surprisingly welcoming when she noticed them at the back of the common room.

"The more the merrier!" she chirped, placing Jack's hand on Maisie's slender waist. He could feel his pulse in his fingertips. Warmth flooded his body as his heart tripped over a stray beat. He hadn't been this close to anyone since Olivia. The subtle scent of rose petals wafted from Maisie's hair, and he relished the feel of her hand in his.

They danced together for the entire hour. The elderly participants couldn't help but smile when they looked at them, so oblivious to the world around them, focused only on each other. While everyone else doddled back to their rooms, Maisie pulled Jack behind the projector screen, already set up in the corner for movie night and kissed him.

Jack floated down the hall to Granddad's room, yanked the door open, ready to tell him all about Maisie.

A stack of linen stared back at him and Jack faltered, stepped backward. He glanced around uncertainly until Laurie, Granddad's favourite nurse, noticed him.

"Alright, Jack?" she asked. "Were you going to give us a hand changing the linens?"

Jack laughed. "I just got turned around."

Laurie smiled and took his arm. "These hallways all look the same. Come on, I'll walk there with you."

Of course, that was all it was, but Jack threw one last dubious glance over his shoulder.

||

Autumn faded into winter, and the courtyard grew too cold for visits on their bench. Maisie and Jack turned to the common room, with its gas fireplace and never-ending supply of tea and coffee. If the nurses were bothered by their presence, they never let on. The residents looked at them with undisguised envy, and Jack knew they were remembering what it was like to be young and in love.

They watched as a team of nurses wrestled up a fake Christmas tree, "Winter Wonderland" playing in the background.

"Do you know what I'd like for Christmas?" Jack asked.

Maisie raised an eyebrow.

"One of your drawings of me." He had a sudden desire to see himself through her eyes.

"Oh, I'm not that good," Maisie protested, even as she flushed with pleasure. "But I'll see what I can do."

||

In the days leading up to Christmas she was never without her sketchbook. Jack pretended to try to peek, and she swatted him away playfully. Finally, the day arrived, and they sat in front of the Christmas tree before the family luncheon. She handed him the sketchbook.

Jack sat with it on his lap, prolonging the suspense. He was just about to open it when a nurse paused by them. She rested a hand on Maisie's shoulder.

"Mrs. Lambert? Your family is waiting for you."

"Of course. I'll see you later, Jack."

Jack stared as Maisie shuffled her way over to the table of smiling strangers, her thick white braid glistening like snow. A teenaged girl with shining auburn hair stood up to embrace her. With trembling fingers, he opened the cover of the sketchbook and gazed at the drawing.

It could have been a photo. The craggy lines of his face were heavily shaded, but in his smile and his eyes he saw the young man he was seventy years ago. Maisie captured him perfectly. Jack closed the book, a single tear sliding down his weathered cheek.

||

In the spring, Jack and Maisie resumed courtyard visits to their bench. As the cherry blossoms burst into frothy pink, Maisie sketched, and Jack listened to his favourite Frank Sinatra songs. Other times, they sat hand in hand, lost in their memories, and content to be together.

Jack's daughter, Ava, stood in the doorway with Laurie and gazed out at her father, hugging herself against the cool spring air.

"The cognitive therapist says his decline is getting worse, but that he still has moments of extreme clarity," Ava said. "Today he told me that he thinks Mom would be happy that he met Maisie. I think he's right."

Laurie nodded. "Sweet, isn't it? Their connection was unexpected, but it's done wonders for his quality of life. You could almost imagine they were two kids in love."

LAURA-LEE DESAUTELS lives in Dryden, Ontario. She writes while gazing out at the rocky shores of Wabigoon Lake, on the traditional lands of the Anishinaabe people. Laura-Lee's heart lies with well-crafted, often nostalgic Young Adult novels, and she does her best to reflect her home setting in the stories that she writes. You can find Laura-Lee on Instagram: @rockyshorewritingandediting.

STEPHANIE DURÁN CASTILLO

The Late Death of Mauricio Montes

In a very small forgotten town, a marriage struggles with infertility

Valentina, on the other hand, began to decline and her husband did not know how to solve the problem (because these are women's issues); he only knew that her fire could consume her. It was at this time of blind desperation that Valentina fell into a series of adventures, as her sister Prudencia decided to take her to a dubious warlock who read in the guts of a black hen that her uterus had been extinguished. They sold her a regimen of fasts and ceremonies that did not yield any results. Shortly after, her illusions were captured by the parish priest, who spoke delicately to Valentina about the sins of the flesh and the miracles of the Lord toward his most determined penitents. It worked. Valentina came back home feeling guilty and terrified, and she convinced Mauricio that the absence of children was due to the many, many years that they had been copulating without being married. So it was logical that they had to apologize, together. He wanted to make her happy, so they started to go to church on Sunday and to work on pious labour in the afternoon. To work harder on the religious festivities and to pass alms punctually. But the Christ nailed to the colonial altar still looked down on them, just like the wealthiest townspeople. Valentina, the teacher in the public school, had become a fervent Catholic. When she was not with her husband or mother, she avoided parties and commitments. And even when it came to love, she only allowed a few kisses and the quick dismissal of her husband.

Mauricio did not desire to spend his days between incense and candles, but he also did not want to offend the superior forces that rule us all. He was a man who wanted his wife back, because ultimately Valentina did not even complain about her students. It was as if the air had run out, for her as well as for him, and the room began to darken at the corners. Mauricio had a faith that was as simple as water; he went to the Supe River and there, in front of the talking river, he asked for a solution to ease his wife's pain. Like in an old biblical story, he found what he needed on his way home. Or rather, he found someone who needed him: a pregnant stray dog. He took her home as a good omen without knowing that Valentina was already looking sadly at every pregnant girl in the town. As soon as he entered the house, the innocent went into labor. His wife began to moan along with the dog, both whimpering in pain for opposite reasons. Mauricio sat between them, pulling each puppy out. After the six puppies had come out, the mother licked them and checked to see if they were alive. Mauricio took his wife and lay down on the bed next to her. Valentina cried all night. And those plans, made so innocently by her child-self, died. Her husband felt the desolation and offered himself to her like a faithful dog to a little girl. That night, after crying, Valentina's body closed. The next morning the mother dog was gone, leaving her puppies behind.

II

The couple lived in limbo for some time, with the house closed and feeding six puppies with cow's milk. Mauricio would lose his job due to a change of owners. He mostly sat home, except on rare days when there were odd jobs available. He sold sweets outside Valentina's school, helped his uncle with his rice harvest, carried sacks of potatoes with his nephew and, little by little, he became wider, like his father. His short-sleeved shirts and well-kept pants were set aside, making way for threadbare polo shirts and labourer pants his parents and grandparents had worn. It was then when his wife (who always wore impeccable white blouses with simple lace) suggested that he study something, like she herself had done with his help. He ignored her. Soon enough, he hurt his back carrying a sack of flour, and with that he lost his most secure jobs. The teacher was left in charge of the house for three long years, during which they fought a lot. Valentina became strict and increasingly impatient with her students and her husband. Mauricio became an evasive and absent teenager; he lost interest in the house and began to wander. In his mindless walks he would find dogs, friends, cigarettes, and women. He already knew the foul smell of those places and didn't want to lose Valentina, but he didn't want to be close to her either. He started smoking with a legless man named Jeremias. The melancholic philosopher loved him, but not enough, not to make him himself. After a year of intermittent meetings, Mauricio began to think that he himself was crippled.

That's how he met Rosaura.

Jeremias knew her before he lost his legs in a bus accident. Rosaura was a thin and small woman who had come to town from the city of Chimbote. She worked as an assistant in a market stand and had had a man and a child a long time ago. She was affectionate with Jeremias and occasionally let him have sex with her. In an unspoken agreement, Jeremias gave her money "for her expenses" whenever he had some. In a way that made him feel better, more of a man. Having a woman was not just about sleeping with her, but also maintaining her. Rosaura treated him with affection and practicality, accepting his money and his cigarettes. Her man, who had promised her a new life if she ran away with him, had abandoned her after arriving in that town. Her child had died of cholera a few years ago, and she could not return to her cruel aunt.

They met on a cold winter night, when the chilled winds of the mountains took over the town. As soon as she saw him sharing a few cigarettes with Jeremias, Rosaura liked that dark-skinned man who talked slowly, and when she learned that he owned a house in Los Geranios, she became convinced of her choice.

II

Behind Jeremias's back, she began intercepting Mauricio in other places in town until she managed to take him to her room, on the outskirts of Supe. It took Mauricio a while to understand the situation. Confused, he accepted Rosaura's advances until he ended up in her bed. He knew she was Jeremias's woman, but he didn't care about anything, not even his friend. He undressed her in a hurry and unleashed his animal desperation. Rosaura's body was small and bony but ripe for illicit love. As expected, it was she who understood and capitalized on Mauricio's frustration, teaching him that it was okay to make love with anger. They began to see each other in the mornings in that little room without a bed. At night they still smoked with Jeremias. They underestimated the crippled intellectual. Jeremias knew well that Rosaura did not love him, but his heart broke when he knew that she could feel love for another man. It was everywhere, in her smile, her smell, her new way of walking. Rosaura began to make excuses not to see him, and this proof of attachment to her new man was what humiliated him the most, because he was willing to share her with Mauricio. It wasn't necessary for them to discuss and settle anything, Rosaura simply slipped away from Jeremias's arms, and he cursed the hypocrite Mauricio to hell, who snuck away like a rat.

STEPHANIE DURÁN CASTILLO (b, Lima 1987) is a Vancouver-based media artist, writer, and art administrator. She is interested in the intersection of colonial paradoxes, mythology, and ecology. She has exhibited her media work in Canada, Mexico, and Peru. Her poetry has been previously published in Vancouver and Ottawa. Find her at Instagram: @tefatrufa.

L. PRINCE

Off/White

Chapter one: My Birthday

I was born one minute past midnight on August 29, 1963. The day before my arrival, Hurricane Cleo tore through the Southeast, flooding streets, shredding trees, and stripping the roofs off of seventeen homes in our small Florida community. Hours before Cleo and I landed, my parents, drenched in sweat, sat in their 700-square-foot track home listening to a speech about dreams.

One month before Dr. Martin Luther King gathered a united people at the Lincoln Memorial, my mother announced that she would join the march. "This is bigger than us, Willy," she cooed, stroking my father's brow. "This surely will be bigger than anything we have ever seen." On the day of her resolve, she packed a small, brown, monogrammed leather suitcase with a green and white smock, the last "respectable" item in her wardrobe that still fit her swelling body. She placed the bag to the right of their front door, signalling to my father her imminent departure.

Grace wanted to witness the uniting of a people who believed in a world she needed to believe in, a world in which she could raise a child. She threatened my father daily, telling him that if he didn't drive her, she would take a bus. Every morning for nearly three weeks, wet-eyed, she'd plead, "We *need* to be there." She'd urge, "This isn't just about *a* people, Willy." And every morning, my father sat cross-legged in their mint-green kitchenette, sipping black coffee and smoking Camel non-filters, listening to her entreaties and watching her belly grow.

He did consider the trip. He even bought AAA route maps. He huddled with her daily at the kitchen table, running his finger along the I-95 through Georgia and the Carolinas, always pausing when his fingertip hit Chapel Hill. He'd grin and ask if she remembered how they met. "I knew in an instant," he beamed, wrapping his smile around her, "and, you knew, too." He'd typically suggest a stop at King's BBQ. "We could get a load of sauce to bring home," he'd muse. "Enough to last us the year." But with each day, with her bulging and hardening belly, they both knew that there would be no trip.

The afternoon before my arrival brought a tarmac-melting heat. Humidity hung in the swollen air. Grace settled with William on their small, blue linen loveseat facing an eleven-inch black-and-white television screen. The images were blurred and broken. Squinting, she asked William to turn the volume up. "I don't have to see him, Willy," she said, teasing, "but I would like to hear him!" William walked over to the teak television console and rotated the brass button two digits to the left.

Dr. King's voice, rhythmic and elegiac, drifted through the room. Grace began to struggle, her breath shortening. She lifted herself off the couch and slipped onto the floor. William leaned forward, touching her shoulder. "Let's get you to the bed, Gracie," he spoke, casting a worried gaze at her womb. "I don't like you on the floor like this." Raising her hand gently to his face, Grace whispered, "Shhhh," then, "I'm all right, Willy, I'm just going to lie here and listen a little while longer." Her face contorted as she heaved her body onto its side, resting her cheek on the brown linoleum. She gazed up at the ceiling fan and watched as the blades rotated to the beat of King's voice.

"… but we refuse to believe that the bank of justice is bankrupt …"

Grace closed her eyes and wiggled out of her orange and yellow floral tunic, letting her stomach rest naked against the cool, hard floor. She looked out the kitchen door, past the screened porch, past the clothesline where the blue and white table linens hang lifeless in the still summer air. The afternoon sky was taking on the copper hue that comes with a summer storm. Mountains of grey blooming on the horizon began tumbling forward. *It's coming,* she thought. *She's coming.*

William walked over to the icebox, opened the freezer door, and stood motionless, bathing in the cool air, washing the heat away. He leaned over, took out an ice cube, and returned to Grace. Tenderly, he touched the back of her neck, running the cube along her spine. He watched as it melted between his fingers, watched as the silver droplets zigzagged their way down her glistening alabaster back and onto the floor.

"In the process of gaining our rightful place, we must not be guilty of wrongful deeds ..."

A tear slid down Grace's cheek. Her passion was infectious, William thought. But he worried about her passion. He knew that they would have to keep their heads low. They were outsiders, and worse, they were liberal white folk who had not learned the ways of white folk in this town. He knew that they'd have to fit in if he was to have any chance at building a practice, any chance of putting food in their baby's mouth. Could this child settle her? William wondered.

His eyes wandered across the expanse of Grace's body, at the stretch marks around her breasts, at the sweat across her brow. His mind drifted to the day they first met. He'd been assigned to watch a group of second-years attend their first autopsy. As he checked off names, he instructed each student to take a tissue. "Keep it close to your eyes, if nothing else," he hinted. "The formaldehyde will bring you to tears." The last name he called was for a G. A. Hicks.

A petite blond woman, and the only woman among the students, stepped forward, extending her hand, which Wiliam attempted to shake. "Excuse me," she demurred, withdrawing her hand and gesturing to the tissues. "Do I get one? Or is it just men who cry?"

"Why the initials then?" He rallied back, grinning. "Woman of mystery?" She looked at him soberly, her smile evaporating, her grey eyes flat. "No mystery," she replied, examining the resident's pin on his lapel, "It's just easier in this world to function as an initial than as a woman." And, in that instant, William knew.

A flash of light followed by a slow, moaning rumble shook William from his reverie.

Grace slid her hand across the landscape of her enormous stomach.

"... I have a dream that my four little children will someday live in a nation where they will not be judged by the color of their skin but by the content of their character ..."

At 11:30 p.m., Grace woke, a spasm clutching her back. She needed to vomit, to sit up, to scream. The ceiling fan was static, the street lamps black. The power was out. The storm was tearing across the sky, rain pushing its way in through the screened porch. Cradling her belly, Grace lumbered upright, adjusting her eyes to the darkness. She searched the room for William, who slept motionless, his long torso sloped over the gold La-Z-Boy chair.

"Willy," Grace whispered, "William, it's time to go." She gripped the chair, spasms choking her. Her knees buckled as she stumbled forward. "Willy," she stammered and with a gasp, shouted, "William Ambrose!"

In the car, Grace held her breath. Adrenaline pulsed through her. She began to tremble uncontrollably. "Breathe and count to ten." William soothed. "We're almost there."

They arrived at the hospital at 11:49 p.m. When I came, twelve minutes later, on a gurney in the hallway lit by a generator, an older nurse strolled across the room where I lay swaddled in day-old headlines. She picked me up, her face gleaming with sweat, and brought me to my father. "More sanitary," she smiled, winking at my father, "than any linens we have lying around here tonight. Isn't that right, Dr. Thomas?" She placed me gently into my father's arms. He stared down at my beet-red, ink-speckled face. He looked at my mother, whose face was beaded with sweat, brow knitted and eyes fixed on the bundle in his arms, and then he smiled down at me. "Martin," he said, looking back up at my mother. "I think we should name her Martin."

L. PRINCE grew up writing in a land where alligators cast lazy glances at children playing in nearby tall, sweet grasses; where prehistoric water oaks spill moss into green sulphur lakes; where boys with chew-packed cheeks drive pickup trucks bejewelled in Confederate flags and shotguns down dirt-packed roads looking for "fun." Still writing, though now residing in Vancouver, it seems that Florida will never let her go.

ANNE-MARIE LANDRY

What She Saw

Prologue

The awning over the paint-chipped door to the travel agency dips precariously close to the entrance. Faded red stripes frayed at the ends flap in the humid air. Posters ripped at the edges and bleached by the sun are half-plastered to the inside windows. Years of dirt and soot cake the inner edges of the window display. Poppy peers at the much-wrinkled ad in her sweaty palm and back to the travel agency. "This must be the place," she mutters, taking a deep breath. With a mixture of excitement and trepidation, she grasps the door handle. To her surprise, it comes off in her hand.

She jimmies the door, glancing furtively around. With a sudden jolt, Poppy is propelled inside. A smell of decay and far-off places tickles her nose. Stepping further into the main room, she calls out a tentative "Hello, is anyone here?" Silence, except for the ticking of the mantle clock atop a fake fireplace. Along one wall are bookshelves displaying a disorderly stack of outdated airline guides, train schedules, and maps. Interspersed among these are dog-eared brochures and pamphlets depicting exotic destinations. To her right is a trio of old wooden desks with accompanying swivel chairs in a hideous green shade, stuffing spilling out from their cracked leather. Seeing a door at the rear, Poppy calls out again, to no avail. She peers down at the ad she's been carrying around for days:

> *Bustling travel business, prime location, $3M gross sales annually, all furnishings included, MUST SELL. Price: negotiable.*

"Right," Poppy whispers under her breath. The place is beyond repair. Disappointment and despair wash over her. She turns to leave but stops abruptly in her stride at the sight of the art deco poster on the wall displaying the Venice-Simplon Orient Express.

As if in trance, Poppy steps closer to the poster. Memories come flooding back, images racing across her eyes. The trembling begins in her feet, quickly moving up her legs, and travelling down her arms. Her eyes widen, her breath coming in ragged gasps. She grabs the back of one swivel chair, only to be sent crashing to the floor while it spins uncontrollably. Sobs rack her as she moans and whimpers. Thirty years. Thirty years since she and her mother took that fateful trip to celebrate Poppy's eighteenth birthday and graduation. A trip that should have been the beginning of something wonderful but instead had turned into tragedy.

The poster mocks her. Luxury travel and exotic cities filled with romance and intrigue, but in her case, betrayal and death. Poppy thinks she's done well with her life. She's managed to fool everyone, including herself, for so long.

Slowly, she rises to her knees, the trembling not fully abated. Her gaze never leaves the poster. She has regained some equilibrium in her life after that fateful train ride. After several years filled with low-paying jobs and instability, Poppy settled down into a career in the travel industry. The aftermath of what transpired on that trip has been a life built on lies, and more lies, which piled on until she has begun to believe them herself. Now here was a reminder of memories best left forgotten.

She releases the now crumpled ad, gazing as it slowly floats to rest at the foot of the poster. She silently retreats to the front door, grasping the absent handle and cries out. She presses her forehead against the cool glass pane, panting slightly as her breath returns to normal. Her cotton shirt sticks to her clammy skin. She slowly unclenches her hands and turns around to face the interior of the travel agency once again. She listens to the voices of past demons beckoning to her softly. With leaden legs, Poppy rights the overturned swivel chair, its wheels still spinning wildly, placing it in front of the poster. With resignation, she settles into the cracked leather, willing herself to keep her eyes fixed on the poster, allowing herself to remember.

The gentle rocking of the train throughout the night, sliding her into slumber under the comfort of the duvet. Feeling herself unfurl like the petals of a summer peony under Adam's tender gaze. The sight of her mother and Adam, limbs intertwined amongst the tangled sheets, blood pooling on the floor beside the bed. Her blood-soaked white eyelet night-gown. Her shock and disbelief at the tableau before her. The doubt and fear that she might have been responsible.

In a daze, Poppy forces herself back to the present. She steels herself against the uneasiness which always threatens to overtake her whenever the memories visit. They come less and less frequently now since that fateful day. But there were always triggers, and Poppy prides herself on avoiding them as much as possible. Except for today. She could not have prepared herself for today, seeing the poster so blatantly taunting her. Remember me? At eighteen, Poppy was as romantic and fanciful as any other girl her age. She fantasized about tall, dark European strangers falling madly in love with her, but Poppy felt invisible around her mother, Althea. When Althea was around, Poppy slipped into the background. Althea commanded the scene wherever she went. Poppy was realistic about her looks and the effect she had on boys. This is why Adam's attraction to her was so unexpected. Reluctantly, Poppy's mind returns to that day when Adam entered their lives.

ANNE-MARIE LANDRY is an emerging writer living in Vancouver, currently working on a mystery novel and a travel memoir. After working in tourism, public relations and healthcare, she now devotes her time to writing, reading, volunteering and travel. She is a member of the Federation of B.C. Writers and a volunteer with the Vancouver Writers Fest. You can find her on Instagram: @amlandry_writes.

AMY KELLY

Book Snub

An excerpt from "Are you there, Mr. Cube? It's me, Karen."

The minimalist design of Bridget's house gave it a clinical feel, like she could murder her family there and have little to dispose of. Oh, except for the jute rug, Karen thought. Blood stains were a bitch to get out of jute.

The book club ladies were sprawled across two sectionals, each with minimal back support, so the women were forced to sit on the edge to support their bodies with their feet on the floor or sink back like some absurdly modern homage to Zatzka, with faces more sour than demure.

More drunk than sober, Karen thought.

In the ocean of pastels and beiges, Karen wore an orange jumpsuit. She found her spot on a modern armchair that was the shape of a lazy *Z* if the corners were not rounded in grey linen upholstery. Linen and grass. It was a prairie motif, from the cement floors, the linen couches, and the single plume of dried miscanthus shooting from a narrow clay vase.

A group of woven seagrass circles was the only wall art, other than a few family portraits in white frames. Bridget's family inside, all in white, with white smiles, bright light illuminating their happy moment in a field.

Karen hoped they got stung by bees.

"How did we all enjoy the book?' Bridget asked the room as she poured another glass of wine from her cart of full bottles.

"Which book was it again?" Jill piped in, shoving another jalapeño popper into her mouth. "I didn't read it."

Jill was fit, but the grip on her rigid diet loosened with every sip of wine. She was a triathlete and a doctor. Karen would have admired her, except she felt inadequate by proxy. When Jill admitted she hadn't read the book and had unhooked her jaws to devour every toothpicked, minied, and fingerfied offering at the snack table, Karen felt a fleeting superiority.

"Life-changing. A master class in finding your authentic self … I was changed by it." Misty was tall and languid. She wore layers of silks and sold her beaded bangles for much more than her workers in Bangladesh were paid. She had a wisping presence much like her thoughts and opinions. She seemed unaffected by most things, shrugging them off with bumper sticker platitudes. She made the same comments every time.

Karen was ruffled. Book club just descended into vapid comments about themselves and then tangential wine-fueled comments about their friends.

She had kept quiet since the cold grasp of mistrust had held her. How did you measure friends you couldn't trust with your inner self? The pressure was building, her true feelings threatening to erupt at any moment.

"So, I was at the farmers market today and came home and made the most *amaaazing* smoothies to give to my girls," Misty went on.

Who knew *amazing* had so many fuckin' *A*'s? Karen thought.

"Do you ladies manage to get there?" Misty, in a rare turn of semi-self-awareness, acknowledged her audience.

A quiet hush fell over the women. Each suddenly feeling called out.

"Oh, it's the only place I buy produce. It must be local and organic." Misty drifted like a cloud of gaseous smug across the room.

"Oh well, you know, I am just too busy, but I send my housekeeper every now and then," Jill said between bites of baked brie.

"Well, we all do what we can, I guess," Misty said, condescendingly. Somehow, they all felt like abandoned kittens in her tone.

Ash, gas emissions, and steam were building up in Karen's head.

"For fuck's sake," she vented, quietly to herself, or so she thought. The organic elitism churned her stomach. She was about to hurl unearthly comments all over the carefully chosen earth tones.

"Sorry, did you say something?" Bridget asked crisply.

"I, uh …" Karen was suddenly self-conscious.

"Book club is a safe space, Karen," Bridget began.

"Yes, we can speak our truth here," Misty added, reclining over one of the sectionals.

"Mrmph," Jill added enthusiastically through a mouthful of charcuterie.

"We need to respect each other's journeys," Bridget topped up her glass.

Many nods and laser eyes boring holes into Karen's head.

"Right. Your truths. Your truths …" Karen seethed.

"Yeah, this space is sacred." Misty had righted her posture only to melt into the upholstery again.

Karen bolted to the wine trolley and chugged a bottle of chardonnay, tasting the textures, legs, and hints of wood and berry as she drained it down her throat.

"Karen!" Bridget snapped.

Karen slammed the empty bottle down.

"My truth! My truth! What about my truth? You know what? I can't do this anymore … I shop at Superstore." There was a gasp in the room. "And the kids, I mean, they were so little, and now … now it's like living with a group of monkeys—"

"Troop," Jill blurted. "It's called a troop." Bits of cream cheese spewed from her mouth onto the floor.

"Please Jill, so not the point. And watch the rug!" Bridget admonished. "You were saying, Karen, about how terrible your kids are?" Horns poked through her perfectly coiffed side part, and malicious glee spread over her face.

"Is it just my kids?" Karen was starting to stagger. "Misty, you would bubble wrap your daughter if you could find some that came in organic material." She had switched to complete assassination.

"Karen. Karen. Stop it," Bridget scolded, her grin reaching Bond-villain levels of self-satisfaction.

"So, truth telling is just for the truths we like or the versions of truth we like? Well, how is this for a version? Bridget, you live in a pretend land where your daughter has not grown up to be the neighborhood's biggest pothead."

The force of the stunned silence hit her chest.

"Well, I guess that explains a lot then." Bridget smoothed her skirt and her hair.

"What? Explains what? What does it explain, Bridget?" Karen was swaying now.

"Why your husband and troop of monkeys can't stand you," Bridget spoke knowing her words got through Karen, drilling the crust of her insecurities to release the magma trapped beneath.

Karen lunged at Bridget, whose face and hair she managed to claw, before falling to the floor. Four even lines of blood seeped across Bridget's cheeks, and her hair was askew. The red wine in Bridget's glass sprayed all over the jute rug as she struggled to regain her balance.

"Get out!" Bridget spit-screamed, her red face and throbbing neck veins grotesque against her pretty pink sweater.

By the power of Zumba, barre, and yoga, Karen was hoisted out the front door. The mob had almost closed the door by the time she reached in with her hands.

"Wait! My boots!" They all understood the universal value of fashion.

Karen did the awkward creep back in, searched for her boots in the pile, and stumbled back to the door.

"Oh, and your book choice was a ridiculously self-indulgent piece of crap! And jute. Jute is bullshit!" Karen threw one last dagger through the door as she exited.

Zipping her boots back on, Karen felt that she had been swimming underwater and had finally surfaced. Wait, was the neighbourhood always spinning?

Between the friendly faces of the gerbera daisies, Karen bent over and spewed every fruity, floral, and earthy note. She stood to straighten her orange jumpsuit and scarf, only to make direct eye contact with the entire book club, who were gawking out the window of Bridget's great room.

Regaining her composure and sense of indignation, Karen turned around, unbuttoned her jumpsuit, slipped her arms out, and bent over. Through her legs, Karen was certain she saw an upside-down choir of open mouths sucking air and pinot. Bridget hit the button on a remote to lower the blinds. The blinds lowered at a glacial speed. Gleefully, Karen watched Bridget hit the button like a rat looking for a heroin pellet, then finally threw the remote as the blinds' slow descent provided the book club with maximum exposure to Karen's milky white moon. Karen swore she heard one of them say:

"Wow, her Pilates have really been paying off."

The force of her expulsive efforts brought Karen to her knees. Her position locked, face down in the daisies, was where she was when she saw the red and blue lights flashing beside her.

AMY KELLY writes fiction, non-fiction, and poetry, and lives on a Vancouver Island hobby farm with her neurodivergent teens. Her fiction appears in *As the Snow Drifts*, *Recipes for Romance*, and *805 Lit+Art*, with non-fiction in *Yummy Mummy Club* and poetry in *Tiger Leaping Review*. Find Amy on Instagram: @amykellywrites or on TikTok:@amy.writes3.

JESSICA MCNEICE

Howling

There is toothpaste on the mirror. There's a crack in the ceramic from when I dropped the hammer while hanging it up myself. My landlord never noticed—I blamed it on the contractor who comes to fix the drain every month or so. It's late, and the bathroom light is unflattering in an honest way. The light paints yellow streaks on my slightly blue skin, reflecting something greenish outward. I look at the sea creature looking back at me. Her face is slightly crooked. One brow raised in surprise, while the other stays still. Hair that was clean in the morning is now slick and has crawled to the top of her head. The eyes that look at me don't startle me, but they don't comfort me either.

I woke today at 28 and realized I bypassed the age where I was supposed to become incredibly sexy. The time of metamorphosis came and went. I went from ugly duckling to duck and missed the swan variation. At first I wasn't worried. Twenty, twenty-one, twenty-two came and went. I waddled with a clunky calm while the swans glided past me making figure eights. That my late bloom would be worth the wait. That all my awkwardness and asymmetry would eventually alchemize into elegance.

As I worked, my shoulders hunched inwards. As I grew tired, the blue-black rings under my eyes went from visitors to permanent residents. Spiderweb veins protrude outwards instead of dissipating in the rain. Twenty-three, twenty-four, twenty-five, I didn't think to mourn the loss. The girl in the mirror hadn't changed in the ways I'd hoped, but she kept showing up, and I assumed that one day, she'd reveal something else. Something better.

I press a finger to the mirror, just to see if she's real.

The girl in the mirror. The sea creature. The duck.

I blink. The creature blinks back at me. We watch each other, eyes darting around.

I lift my shirt to show small pieces of broken flesh. I uncap the needle and push the needle against the skin to break it open again, over and over. The smell is clinical. Alcohol, plastic, the medicine does its job. I close the lid.

The phone buzzes in my pocket. I answer it.

"Happy Birthday, buddy." It's my sister.

"Thanks."

"You doing anything tonight?"

"Just got home. Gonna take a bath or something."

"Nice. Self-care, right?"

"Sure."

A pause.

"Okay well ... just wanted to say hey."

"Thanks."

The line goes dead.

I turn on the tap. I wait for the water to go from cold to slightly less cold. I wet my hands and reach for the cleanser on the shelf to my left. I squeeze too much into my palm. It flows out through the gaps between my fingers as I lather it into suds, spreading it gently across my face. Circles on the cheeks. Down the bridge of the nose. Across the forehead, over the brow bone. I press between my eyebrows, trying to smooth the crease. For a moment, they soften, then snap back into place. Some of the suds settle gently into the lines in my face. Micro bubbles percolate and pop gently in the craters of my skin.

I watch them burst, one by one, and think about the passage of time. About all the things that bloomed and withered without ceremony. And then, I think about time with you—the small infinity we spent together.

"You're not the type of person I would ever notice in a bar, but you grow on people."

The memory comes to my mind. We were sitting on a pebbled beach watching the waves come back to kiss our toes over and over. No beach blanket needed because I was a cool girl and didn't care about getting my jeans dirty. I was looking at his beautiful face and laughing. The words echoed inside of me and I wondered. Like mould? Like regret?

He said it like a compliment.

It lingered in my gut and started to rot.

I lifted my head and stared at the ceiling of my very old building. The panels had been recently painted a crisp white, probably to cover whatever was festering behind them. I could smell it, that faint, sour mustiness.

I imagined pressing my fingers into them and feeling the truth: mushy, waterlogged, soft with neglect.

The same give as pressing into the flesh of my own thighs. Some bounce. Some resistance. But not too much.

I looked again in the mirror at the sea creature.

Her skin was bloated, waterlogged—swollen with salt that couldn't be rinsed away with tap water.

But beneath the flesh, in the bones, there was something … prettyish. Not delicate. Not radiant. But structural.

I wondered what might have happened if I'd layered something different on top of those bones.

Frosting. Swirling and delicate on top. Overly sweet.

Soft enough to be bitten into. I wouldn't bite back.

Could I have been her?

Spatula in hand, smoothing batter into neat little paper cups. Swirling frosting into pink and white peaks. Batter under fingernails, scraping the sides. Licking frosting from each of my palms.

I wondered if that version would have been easier to love.

With the sink full I plunged my face underwater to wash the frosting off my skin.

Cupcakes did not seem the likely answer.

I grab the floss and wind it tight around each pointer finger—too tightly—until the skin puffs and purples beneath the pressure. I pull the string outward, taut like a wire, and begin the ritual. Between each tooth, I drag it down hard, digging into the gums like I'm searching for something buried. Blood rises in thin lines. When I reach the canine—the sharp one, slightly longer than the rest—I angle the string and slide it along the edge. It catches. Snaps. The floss breaks in two. I stare at the frayed thread, still wrapped around my fingers like evidence.

Somewhere along the way, I became the woman who gets things done. Who is chosen for reliability. For performance. For emotional labour. And I cannot remember the moment I agreed to that trade.

But I feel its cost.

I whimper slightly and watch the face in the mirror contort into something entirely different.

Then, something in the mirror shifts. My lips curve—not into a smile, but something sharper. It doesn't show my teeth. I have transformed.

The tears start to roll so I smile and show fangs.

Not into the swan, but the wolf. I prowl. I lunge. I bare my teeth. Then I lean back from the mirror, settle onto my hind legs, lift my jaw to the ceiling, and howl.

JESSICA MCNEICE is a writer and creative strategist based in Denver. Her work explores memory, perception, and the emotional residue of relationships with a focus on narrative precision. She's currently writing personal essays. Follow her on Medium:@jessicamcneice.writing for essays, and Instagram: @jessicamcneice/ for photography.

VICTOR TEMPRANO

For When I Am Far From Myself

Does the house have a soul, Grandma? Now that you're gone, I can't feel it anymore.

Today I started scanning all the photos you left behind. Some are sewn together where creasing broke them; others seem as fresh as the day they were developed. They stretch back a hundred years at least. There are so many people I don't recognize, probably all dead by now. Groups of schoolgirls and you're there among them, younger than I ever knew you, pretty in a white dress in fields of corn. I can almost hear you laughing.

But I'm not there. No, I'm in an office next door to the house, in a room with cracked yellow walls, in front of the scanner. I have the rhythm down to a solid beat. First put in the photo, then close the lid, then press a checkbox, then the green button. The machine hums, beeps, talks. I lift the lid, flip the picture.

I have some music on, all sad songs. Melodies that sting like an old scar, to bring back a past I never lived, to bring to life the death of people who smile in black and white. Even with the music playing, everything feels quiet.

The muscles at the base of my neck eventually start to ache, so I pack it up, head back to the house.

Outside, slopes rise up from the bottom of the valley, where the road winds through the village. The oldest houses, like ours, push out into the street, and back onto yards that grow to dark forest. Big oaks jostle with the pines there, defending against the eucalyptus creeping over the hilltops. Streams run down to meet the river that passes beside the road. There's so much green: on the stones, on the road, on the roofs. I can tell from the air that rain is coming.

I'm all alone, the street empty, the world somewhere else for a while. I tarry by the front door, holding the wooden box of photos, imagining things as they once were. Instead of new apartments, I see fields and mud houses and herds of sheep. I take a deep breath, blink, and they're gone.

In these moments, I see time the way it really is: a thing liquid and enormous and soft, the whispers of my ancestors floating on it like mist. But that understanding only comes when things are long dead. That's the only time I see clearly.

I go into the house and, for just a moment, I catch a smell from long ago. It's like you're there, waiting in the kitchen for me. But everything looks different now. I put the box of photos down, take off my shoes, and stare at the floor.

I had to fix the house. I'm sorry, but I had to. I found the newspapers that you were using to stop the leak in the roof, in that hidden passage near the chimney. The plumbing that you never updated. The electrical system that was a fire hazard. The rotten floorboards, the mould, the wood-eating bugs …

I had two choices. Renovate or tear it all down and build apartments. I was afraid I'd lose you, and I didn't want to change a thing. So I renovated. I tried my best, used all my power to repair the house in a way that held on to everything, to you.

Before, every wall was alive. The house breathed my memories, exhaling through the tiny holes that the bugs made. It was cold and the windows didn't close.

Now everything seals up tight, and I spray poison to keep the bugs out. I can hang up the old pictures, I can drag around the old furniture, but everything I cared about has disappeared. I did all I could to hold on, but it's all gone.

You weren't in the wallpaper, nor the old linoleum, not in the mouldy smell, nor the scary basement. You were in between all those and not, and yet, with everything new and livable, you're no longer here. And so I sit on the old wooden stairs alone and grieve, crying until my eyes are sore.

I should have just let everything rot.

II

Thousands of years ago, before you were or I am, other people lived where the house is now. They crept down the hillsides and explored this forested valley. They slept under the long rain, they danced, they spoke languages we don't know anymore. That was all a very long time ago, but I wonder if there are traces left of them too, just like the photos you left behind.

As far as I've heard, those people, our ancestors, believed that everything has a soul: every leaf, tree, raindrop, person, river. Every house, too. Theirs was a world filled with giving and taking, with transformation and letting go. When I walk in the woods and see the ivy spiraling around the old oak trees, when I stand at the base of a waterfall, eyes closed and consumed in the roar, I sense their fingerprints, like trails of blood on the granite.

They say those ancient people buried the dead right underneath their houses. They dug pits in the floor, put the corpses in, covered them back up, and lived on top of them. They celebrated, ate, cried, loved above them. And deeper, deeper, down went the generations.

In the end, everything comes and goes. I can let go when I think about my own soul.

But yours? I don't want to forget.

My soul may now be far away, drifting, waiting for me to remember the right way to look at things. One day, maybe, when I'm ready to listen, it will descend the valley, come out of the dark oak forest, and crawl into bed with me again.

||

I notice, from the sound on the roof, that it's raining, just like I knew it would. I get off the stairs and stand in front of the window. It's so new and clean and big. The raindrops on the glass seem to collect all the world: my face, the forest, the dark sky, the white walls.

Your soul never left, did it? It's still in the forest, in those oak trees, in the granite rocks.

My soul, your soul, the house's soul … how could we be different? All along the years, we've spent so much time like this, watching the rain through the back window and trying to hold on to the past.

Stay, stay just a little longer. But nothing stays.

My last memory of you is your weeping, you trying to hide your tears as I left the house, saying, as you always did, that we might never see each other again. Maybe you're right.

Breathe in deep, breathe out. The window fogs. The rain keeps coming.

I watch the dark forest, and I can almost hear it: the footsteps of this soul walking back home again, to its own house, to our house. And I close my eyes, and I listen.

Bit by bit, I listen.

VICTOR TEMPRANO lives between Galicia, Spain and British Columbia, Canada. As the creator of Native-Land.ca and a YouTube channel exploring fictional maps, he's drawn to the stories land can tell. Blending magical realism with Galician folklore, Victor writes evocative tales of loss, grief, and hope, rooted in ancestry, place, and a longing for home.

| poetry

LAURA FUKUMOTO
Poetry Editor

Introduction

A while ago I had this coworker I disliked. We'll call her Nora, after my niece, because I am training my heart towards love these days. But fucking Nora got under my skin. She talked about herself constantly, which I found annoying in an already stressful job, and being one of the longest-serving employees, she took on the air of Dwight Schrute, Assistant to the Regional Manager. From 8:00 a.m. to 6:30 p.m. we worked side-by-side as a team, and I did my dang best to find some alignment between us. What food do you like? Where have you travelled? Where is your favourite place in the city? Finally, one morning, it happened: It turned out Nora and I had the same favourite podcast. We never had to speak again, because the sultry voice of our favourite podcaster finally shut Nora up.

These poems are a lot like coworkers who, on the surface, have nothing in common with each other. These fourteen poets take us across the world: from Barkerville, to Fujian, to Port Said, to a tropical night watching moonlit petals unfurl. These poets walk through the chaos of an unseelie war, to a photo of rubble and displacement in 1956; follow Kerouac's long road through the '60s, to children playing in a graveyard, 1978; through the decade-deep layers of peeling paint, revealing secrets only a girl-now-woman's childhood bedroom could know.

As I read, I made a colour-coded spreadsheet to track themes, and finally started seeing where the seams of these pages would stitch themselves together. Here are the names of some of my spreadsheet columns: addiction; womanhood & dissociation; (be)longing; rebuilding & reframing. The most common theme I saw in these poems was a confrontation of failure in all its varieties: a mother tongue that never roots; an embryo that might not stick; a life spent in front of a screen; the pen slipping outside the line; the human body, glitching. I started wondering if the wars mentioned in these poems were also a kind of failure, but then again, that kind of violence is incredibly on purpose, and not a failure at all. These poets ask us to linger a little longer on what our eyes can see while we're still here and able to write elegies to lives lived.

Often, when we don't like someone it's because we are recognizing something we struggle with in ourselves. We have more in common than we think, so it's important to have a sense of humour about these things. My last two columns were: playful and reframe/reclaim. Thank goodness for cheeky poets. Thank goodness for rhymes and silly word associations. These poets imagine worlds where the earth gifts us food like freckles on her scorched face. They dream dragons will fall, and also of the dragons who protect us. They dream of our ancestors. They dream that our homes can talk, and love us. There are worlds of words in these poets' eyes.

LAURA FUKUMOTO is a poet and theatre artist, and has been committed to loving her neighbours in Vancouver for more than fifteen years. Laura's writing explores her family's displacement during World War II, queerness, the climate reckoning, and mycology. Sometimes you'll see her around town yapping into a microphone and wearing a flowy dress. Land Back and Free Palestine!

AIDAN REDWING

A Murder of Elves

This poem is part of a longer collection still in development.

Burned by sapphire flames,
clouds of black smoke
rain ash on a forest
glowing in sunset embers.

Poisonous night air
dims the failing stars
reflected in an acid lake.
Its surface ripples,
buckling beneath the blows
of battering wings.

Fruitless trees drink deep.
Leaves crumble into dust.
Shades of red and yellow
rot to brittle brown.
Roots curl.
Bark peels,
as dry and flaking
as an unshed scale.

Ghostly moonlight dazzles
slit serpent eyes.
The forest shudders.
The wyrm shifts,
settling into slumber
on its bed of burning coals.

Elves, ashen-haired
with sallow skin of mottled hues
breathe putrid morning air.
A rasping gasp,

passing through lips,
as cracked as leather.

What in Spring grew fair and green
is fouled and falls from grace.
Charcoal lines the corvid masks
clasping unseelie faces.

Gathering behind the hunter's blind
rifle-cannons braced to shoulders,
their blackened beaks glisten.
The murder gathers in the dark
to watch the dreadful shadow fly.

In the pause between breaths
gunfire, smoke, and lead
erupt like sorcerous flames.
A rolling drum roar spits deadly hail
from the shelter of quivering trees.

Dragon scales shatter like glass.
Wings curl like torn parchment.
The beast comes down
crashing like a zeppelin,
breathing its final breath
in a cloud of deadly gas.

In the exhale of tension
and the inhale of filtered fumes,
rifle muzzles are slowly lowered,
smoking in dawn's fetid light.

AIDAN REDWING writes speculative fiction and poetry. He often haunts the woods of Nova Scotia, the traditional territory of the Mi'kmaq. Aidan loves all things fantasy and will tell tales of adventure to anyone willing to lend an ear. He can be reached at a.redwing.writing@gmail.com or at Facebook.com/aidan.redwing.

ANGELA REBREC

In the wreckage of Port Said

After Chim (David Seymour), Inhabitants in the wreckage of Port Said after the Franco-British air attack during the Suez War, Egypt, 1956. Photo.

A mother in a threadbare coat
one child half slung over her shoulder
another trails like a ghost
through the gutted geometry of war
a silhouette against the blasted facades
a quiet anthem of survival

And there, another woman
veiled in grief and cloth
balances a chair
as if carrying her vanished home
on the crown of her head

She walks upright through
dust and ruin
each footstep spelling
I remain

Woman and chair

After Chim (David Seymour), A woman in the ruins of Port Said after its destruction by Israeli bombing. Egypt. October 29, 1956. Photo.

His lens is candle flame
catching the breath
of children too frightened to scream
of mothers too proud to beg

He saw the woman in her burqa
dignity undimmed in the ash-light
her sorrow
not other but familiar
aiming not for spectacle but truth—
raw, unbeautiful, necessary

And perhaps he believed
in the marrow of the shutter's click
that the world might change
if only it looked

So he kept looking
until crossfire found him
not for his politics nor his name
but because bearing witness
is like walking into a fire
to hold a mirror up
to what we've done

For Chim, who bore witness

In the end it was not the bullet
but his gaze that killed him—
a gaze too soft for war
too tender
for the jagged arithmetic
of empire

He walked into Port Said
not with a weapon
but with the eye of a man
who believed that even
in the smoke-swallowed streets
and the rubble of people's anguish
possibility remained

While the air vomited shrapnel
he cradled his camera like an infant
to document how silence turned feral
to frame not soldiers
but the tremble
of those fleeing them

ANGELA REBREC is an artist, filmmaker, and writerly raccoon who amasses creative projects from trash-treasures discarded by unsuspecting humans. Her writing has appeared in places like *EVENT* and *PRISM* international, and her films have been recognized by the Barcelona International Film Festival and FilmmakerLife Awards. Winner of *Pulp Literature*'s 2024 Magpie Award for Poetry, Angela also leads the Delta Literary Arts Society by rummaging through the creative dumpsters of the community and dragging out overlooked, gleaming doohickeys.

LESLIE ROBERTS

Antecedent

Didn't buy maternity clothes
wintered in big sweaters, too exhausted
too nauseous, mostly slept, struggled
to believe it was real
would stick.
Hovered over
chances of miscarriage by week
searing statistics, still—

didn't know what to call this:
weeks progressed, movements began
hiccups jostled every evening,
foot forever forced in my liver
gradual transition from "it" to "they"
hated every name.

Disbelief of it all
the way through labour
until the baby settled
on my chest
and with nothing
prepared, said:
"Hi."

Now conversations revolve
around "him"—antecedent unneeded
as though he
is the only one
in the world.

LESLIE ROBERTS is a new poet in Vancouver, B.C. She holds a Master of Arts and her writing explores themes of identity, faith, friendship, presence and absence, and matrescence. She is married to Luke, and together they have one son. Leslie enjoys hiking, running, biking, hammocking in the sun, and petting dogs. You can follow Leslie at LRoberts.substack.com.

SABRINA SHABANA VELLANI

Sestina of the Nebula

I approach a nebula
float beside its wings for a decade,
encircle the universal iris,
search for answers in her retina.
When do we get to find starlight?
When does our light appear?

So many pulsars appear
far away, far from the nebula
weave and spin fiery starlight,
fabricating the next decade
without the vision of woman's retina
nor the bulb of an iris.

On earth, they unroot the rhizomes of iris,
so that the men can appear,
on stage, in a circle, in a retina,
in suits, calling themselves a nebula.
The women spend the decade
in wilted flower meadows looking for starlight.

Perhaps, art is starlight.
I conjure my own iris
to dilate to the decade,
hoping imagination to appear
in the heart of the nebula.
But nothing colours my retina,

except news articles through the smartphone retina.
Administrations call themselves the starlight,
wanting to regulate a woman's nebula.
Many colours come from the plant of an iris:
blue, pink, violet appear.
One would never know in this decade.

This decade,
awaits my retina
for the silver glint to appear:
our reclamation of starlight
in the buds of the iris,
in the beards from our nebula.

In this decade, we wait for starlight
even when lies from afar inflame. We wait in a field of iris
for the petals to appear within the cold, wanting nebula.

Kadupul

Kadupul flowers
dress in ivory petal
and bloom only in
the night, underneath
a full moon for mere
hours.

Delicate, alive
for an evening, they
wilt before a day
can touch them—
before the sun can
believe them.

And in those short
stretches, they
paint willful portraits
of themselves, thick
and sweet. Fragrant
and bold.

It is worth knowing
of them. Past
and absent. The universe
plans for their demise.
It is worth knowing what they grow into.

Ink Bottles

Ink bottle with the blooded waxen stopper
sits unbothered on the bottom shelf.

Its feather and badge prescribe art in a
French box with brown paper backing.

The words I never wrote stashed beneath
stacks of tax papers, academic

magazines, and voiceover microphones. I
publish and broadcast the only sentences

that reach the bouncers at the barrier. An artist,
in this world, obtains employment when she

abandons her tools. But an artist
finds life when she abandons the gates.

SABRINA SHABANA VELLANI is an Indo-Canadian actress and poet from Vancouver, B.C., the unceded territories of the Musqueam, Squamish and Tsleil-Waututh First Nations. Her poetry has been published in *The Literary Review of Canada*, *New York Quarterly* magazine, *PRISM international*, and others.

JERRY MURPHY

Jack

Jack, I have been there with you
writing down the cries
of the lonely waves
at Big Sur.
A Dharma bum riding the boxcar of life
singin' the haiku blues
seeking the scripture of the golden eternity
living in a subterranean San Fran-New York world
with Allen Ginsberg and William S. Burroughs
eating a naked lunch
watching everyone watching you with your Black girlfriend,
    Alene Lee
wondering if you are too self-conscious about it
too manly a star football player to howl.
A poet as novelist
singing the French-Canadian Catholic spiritual blues with jazz
    overtones
moving to the syncopated black beat
one of the angel-headed hipsters worshipping at the altar
of the Goddesses of sex and drugs
trapped between the non-conforming self-indulgent spontaneity of
    the trip
and the rigid rules of small-town life and Catholicism
where the drab grey-brown tenements of Franco-Canuck textile mill
    town Lowell Massachusetts
with its shrouds, deaths and funerals
and the horrors of Jesus Christ passion plays
and the shadow of the caped, leering, evil Doctor Sax, hat slouched
    down over his face
and visions of Gerard, your nine-year older dead brother
haunt the back alleys of your childhood memories.

Always looking for the next trip
on any road or
any pill
frantically searching for the meaninglessness of the loneliness of life.
Finding oneness
in the Friday night literary salon
of Kenneth Rexroth
and like Gary Snyder
you never work in the office
or mow the lawn
because you have to climb that goddamn mountain
to the watchtower to
look for fires of the soul.
Learning how to meditate
so you don't have to think anymore
like a shot of heroin
you are a Bodhisattva achieving nirvana
oh, so briefly
like me in '78, awaking
among a SoHo Greenwich Village Brighton Beach band
of poets, painters, and musicians.
You write *On the Road*
in spontaneous prose flowing continuously
onto a 120-foot-long single roll of teletype paper
so you never have to stop to change sheets
in a frenzied three-week bender of
benzedrine and alcohol.
Improvising a novel
like a bebopping symbolistic impressionistic jazz musician
in a way I could never do.
So shy, too shy, you answer questions
in a monosyllabic low-voice head-down TV interview
tapping your fingers while gulping a bottle of muscatel

until asked to read *On the Road.*
Then the words flow in a mad ecstasy from the page
into your voice, slowly at first,
accelerating west with Dean across Colorado and Arizona
racing to see visions of America
with its drive-in wedding chapels
and dismal divorce bars
seeing visions of God as Pooh Bear.
On the road, again,
with Neal Cassady
an Irish skid row kid, falling meteor, racing through your life
never stopping at red lights.
You, like me,
not quite able to keep up.
Neal tells you to stop farting out on that mean mountain
and abandon your self-consciousness to capture instead
his hyper-manic rapid-fire spontaneous mad quixotic confessional
    actions and letters
with words that move across the page at the speed of thought.
If only I'd had my own Neal.
But then Neal is found
on a Mexican railway track chasing after a train
high on speed, never able to stop
until his heart gave out.
You're on the road again, searching
between the town and the city
finding satori in Paris,
like me,
for a night.
On the road
again,
like me,
tired of it all,

heading home to Mom's,
sitting in the living room
feet up
watching TV
waiting to die.
I understand, brother,
but   I   cannot   do   the   same

JERRY MURPHY lives in New Westminster but has travelled globally. This has contributed to a diverse range of topics in his writing, including Beat poetry, science fiction, haikus, as well as Canadian and Irish history with his writing focusing on social issues. His poetry has appeared in the RCLAS E-zine. He has also won a New Westminster Story Slam and a haiku contest. His email address is Jerrym1@shaw.ca.

GIGI LE FLUFY

Ship to Shore

Here we are, adrift so far,
lost within the fray

A sinking ship, a tap—*drip-drip*—
the shore far-far away.

No stage to bow, no time to row,
no suitcase filled with sun.

Shoes sink deeper, costumes steeper,
waters blur who's won.

Before our ship began this trip
I dreamed of open seas

But at the helm I'm overwhelmed
a flag lost in the breeze.

Grab an oar! I beg once more,
Row us back to shore!

You row us dear, you got us here
is all you say once more.

I never thought our ship would rot
while we stood proud and tall.

Too proud to row, too scared to grow
too lost to see it all.

Early morn I hear you call
but wake to see you're gone.

The waves turn black, you don't wave back
Alone I face the dawn.

Daylight sweeping, all my dreaming
banished to the caves.

Sirens calling, ship mast falling,
I weep, I weep in waves.

Drag me down, but I won't drown,
no seabed made for me.

I'll swim, I'll ache, within your wake,
I'll rise, I'll grow, I'll be.

I'll make it through without a clue,
the shore will feel my feet,

I'll walk right by you on the dock
where, as lovers, we used to meet.

Twinkle, Twinkle

little star,
little star—
oh, there you are!

Up above the trampoline,
I dare to dream, I am a Queen.

Bouncing, twirling, jumping high,
whisking wishes to the sky.

Mum shouts, Stop! Dad stomps down,
tips my crown into the ground.

Tumble, jumble, can't stop now,
down, down, and out of town.

City-struck, smothered spark.
Foreign signs, alleys dark.

Chasing crowds, blow to blow,
searching nightclubs for your glow.

Tried to wish when I was high:
apartments rise to block the sky.

Dancing, spinning, words a-slur,
tripping out—outside a blur.

Sweating, shaking, face to floor,
barely breathe, to wish once more.

But in the corner of the night,
through a crack, shining bright,

’twas your safe and guiding light—
beyond my reach, within my sight.

Strung out, struck out, sick in shame,
twinkle, twinkle—still you came.

Though I know not what you are,
I know you’re there
        my little star.

GIGI LE FLUFY writes from the unceded, traditional territories of the hən̓q̓əmin̓əm̓-speaking xʷməθkʷəy̓əm Musqueam people. She is an early childhood educator, children’s author, and poet, with forthcoming publications with Orca Books. You can find out more at GigiLeFlufy.com or connect with her on Instagram @gigi.le.flufy.

HOWARD SMITH

fost & lound

in my terrible thirties, nobody knows what they are doing yet
I'm living the way I want with no regrets
I'll stand back up, just taking some "me" time
but months turn into a decade, is finding myself a crime?
I don't remember a time that I was "found"
screaming internally so no one hears a sound

the walls are closing in–I'm losing everything
been lost at sea so long the search party stopped looking
spent my last change to crawl back into the bottom of a bottle
I'm a natural-born leader who's just happy to follow

I'm living with one of the four, try to guess which
fortunate and fame, pleasure or the pain

house keys in hand, I will still pass out on the lawn
but I'm on my way back, hoping I'm not too far gone

    drinking with my dark thoughts...
    when he pours, he reigns

wait, hold up
    wasn't... wasn't I just writing a poem?

like I was saying, you can't just a book by its stereotype

eye don't need help, eye know what I'm doing–
    doing or going?

I been drunking a lil so droving is a bad idea
    but I'm getting dangerously low
        so eye have no other choice

glad it's dark so no one will see my doubts
    soon as I start the car
        I hit the nights blackout

HOWARD SMITH a.k.a. The Texas Tornado a.k.a. The Naughty Native a.k.a. Sasha if you nasty is a middle-aged Haisla writer from where the land meets the sky, where the eagle & the raven fly free, under the sun and the moon… he's a Virgo, likes long walks on the beach, and is looking for that special someone…sorry, wrong bio. He's a Haisla writer / beatbox champion / sandwich artist.

PINDER JHAJ

Dear Beeji

This beautiful temple is no longer your home.
The home you kept so exquisitely embellished
The one that felt your bliss and your burdens
that housed your spirit
your home
        that will soon be reduced to ashes

This beautiful temple is no longer your home.
The soulful melodies that once permeated your walls
are replaced with silence
the steady flame that always burned
is no longer alight

This beautiful temple is no longer your home.
Now adorned in soft pink silk
with delicate white lilies hand-embroidered throughout
If the shades were not drawn
if the windows not closed
        your chunni surely would have danced with the breeze of
            September

I ache for your Olay-scented embrace and too-wet kisses
but you're not coming back
You are no longer confined by this vessel.
Maybe
        you are right here
                watching me
                        watching you

The Gossip's Brew

Chitter chatter
        tittle tattle
They stand in a corner, sipping their tea
A look to the left
A giggle to the right
That's when they catch
        the sight of me

The Queen steps forward
wearing an innocent mask
She gives half a smile
        extends a warm loving hand
Come hither, my friend, for a taste of this tea

I take a hesitant step towards the sweet honey scent
How lovely of them to invite me to tea!
They hand me a cup
I feel I belong
Maybe one small sip of their delicious tea

Oh, so sweet it is! An intoxicating elixir
One sip
        leads to two
            leads to three
                leads to four
I drink, I devour, I crave
I need more, more, more

Soon the syrupy sweetness suffocates my senses
This tea's a little toxic
ingredients are amiss
my stomach starts to churn
        with growing unease
I'm afraid I must spill this cloying sweet tea

That's when I see her, standing off to the side:
A lost young girl, with longing in her eyes
I take a step forward
        extend a warm loving hand
Come hither, my friend, for a taste of this tea

PINDER JHAJ is the wife of a really cool guy and the mother of cool guy's two little minions. They currently reside in Coquitlam, B.C. She is a bookkeeper by day and aspiring writer by night. She ponders life through poetry. You can find her on Instagram: @pinderponders.

JANET POLLOCK MILLAR

Barkerville, 1978

Schoolkids,
we wander the hard-packed streets
of this mausoleum town
its preservation a deep ache
felt in the musk of dark brown buildings
in bright slick peppermint sticks in their glass jars
on the wooden counter with its sting of shellac
where we jostle with our pocket money
then suckle the sharp sweet.

The long-dead are offered up for our edification:
we squat in the cemetery
scratch charcoal over paper on their headstones
under the quiet roar of the pines
and a bright pearl sky, unchanged for a century.
We condemn them to immortality
with our incessant probing
our remembering.

Let us sleep, for the love of God.

JANET POLLOCK MILLAR is a writer, editor, and educator living on lək̓ʷəŋən territory in Victoria, British Columbia. Her fiction, poetry, essays, creative non-fiction, and book reviews have appeared in various publications. Exploring topics such as the natural world, grief and loss, relationships, and human rights, Janet writes to render the world as it is and to nudge it toward what it could be. JanetPollock.ca.

EDEN HOEY

Please Don't Feed the Birds

Do not give them this day their daily bread. Or some change if they ask nicely for it. Even if you have some in your pocket. For once. Do remember, it's not part of their natural diet. It may alter their foraging behaviours. And migration patterns. They'll come to depend on us. Teach a man to fish instead.

If you feed them, they will come. An overpopulation of certain species. Increased competition for food. And aggressive behaviour. Bodes badly for property values. You've seen them pile near park benches. Swarming the sidewalks. Watched them take running dives toward finger-clutched sandwiches. Tell me—do you want that in your neighbourhood?

If food-conditioned, they may become bolder toward people. Bold enough to lie in wait under ATMs. In case a doughnut falls into an open beak. Potentially causing nuisance or damage to property. No one needs a nest on their roof. Best remove the makings before best plans are laid. Spare your sanctuary from the swooping. If you don't preserve your perfect home, who will?

But who carries change anymore? Or breadcrumbs. In San Francisco, there are billboards with numbers you can text. If blessed with spare bills for spare bills, do not approach a broken bird. Don't worry. You can donate $5 by texting the word 'share' to 80077.

Caretaking

I

My father begins his retirement years back at school.
Weekday mornings he trudges next door, adjoining lands
hard-worn by small feet. Rain or shine, he opens the gates,
unlocks the doors. Caretaking
more hours than due, his iPhone timer still counting.
Another way of clocking in and out until you die. Telling me:

Christ, school has changed so much!
Trampoline in the basketball court, special walkway
for laps and necessary breaks. One wonders how children
learn anything these days. One child in particular,
a livewire child, sparking louder and LOUDER
to be heard, before being labelled
a disruption! Get out now!
Go to the principal's office. Again.
Wait for your mum to arrive. Again.
And ignore our silent acknowledgment
that you're twelve. And we've all given up.

II

My father left school at seventeen, breaking free
from Christian Brothers beating the life out of young boys.
A handful of discontinued coins glued to a belt,

the ring of it still on your arse. Even when you're sitting down
in the driver's seat of the car you bought. And local radio telling you
the man who swung it hard against your bare skin
has died. The fucker is dead. At last!

He'll never live to strike another. The hazards are on
and he's raced off the side of the road to scream at the sky

to wish the dead man an eternity of fire. As the sun's fire falls
over neat rows of council houses.
Three kids in the backseat, silent for once.

III

You know how people sometimes say:
'This teacher changed my life?'
Filing into Tony Eaton's funeral, I knew him as the closest thing, that.
The first to say, 'You can do it.'
If you have a seven-stranded cable, rather than a solid cable,
Take one strand round, wrap it back into three strands,
Then twist it clockwise, cut off the excess, make sure the screw turns in the hoop.
That I still call a Tony Eaton Hoop.
Every time I go to do it.

'You can do it.' Said casually and off-hand, not
'You better do this or else!' Or 'If you don't do it this way, you're stupid!'
Which was the teacher's way, the Hierarchy's way.
'And if you don't get it right at first, just try again. You'll get it next time.'
He was right. Funeral full of former apprentices
attesting to that. Lads from a bygone generation,
once told what to say and do and
believe about ourselves.

IV

Talking to my father now,
watching him string an Eaton Hoop,
back through hard lands, hard-worn by small feet
back to the school
no belts or bollockings.
But children running laps to similar sentiment:
Live up to someone's expectations
or live down to them.

Blossom Cherries

(& other slightly disrupted word associations)

Blink and you'll miss it!
The cherry blossoms at the end of my road. Killed
by the wind just after they bloomed. Fully
naked branches already, left bare while their brothers are barely
  attired. Proper
spring weather might've helped keep their clothes on. Off
with their heads! says the rain, spilling petals to nearby car bonnets.
  Easter
is coming. Going, going, gone! says the tree, barking,
beckoning passers-by to come see us, quick! Fix
your eyes upon us while you still can. Can't go to Florida for a
  fortnight in late March. Death
shall become us come April. Shower
yourself in pink while we are here to blow you kisses. And tell
yourself that life is worth living. Dying
in Spring—would be a shame. On you.

EDEN HOEY is a writer, poet, and proud Irish immigrant based in Vancouver, B.C. Her work primarily explores the human condition, drawing on a diverse practice including poetry and fiction. She studied at the Irish Writers Centre, Curtis Brown Creative, and was longlisted for the FBCW Literary Contest for Short Fiction. She is completing her debut poetry collection and her first novel, set during the Irish Abortion Referendum campaign. Read more at Substack.com/@EdenHoey and on Instagram @thepagefright.

MEGAN POLIQUIN

//Chorus

the music box of my mind
has glitched

needle skips
chorus plays

chosen song:
"Rootless Tree"

needle skips
chorus plays

Damien's voice
aiming right for my pain

needle skips
chorus plays

pinning it to the peg board
a remnant of a time I still dreamed

needle skips
chorus plays
needle skips
chorus plays

now my mind occupied by faulty wiring
putting out fires along pathways laid long ago

needle
needle
needle skips
chorus plays
plays
plays
plays

"fuck you"

//Changes

I try my best to hide the signs of aging. I inspect corners where stucco meets dusky lavender, checking for anything that doesn't belong. To ensure the colour that covers over the layers of red, blue, and remnants of floral wallpaper are pristine and presentable. Even I can no longer recall what exactly adorned these walls in the beginning. Time creates overcoats and change, so I keep the layers to strengthen my resolve; to hold onto these memories. The slatted maple boards with the large gaps, the most recent flooring, is polished, as if that would remove the years of feet and furniture that danced upon it. Even I am not full of enough magic to create a palace of this place.

So, here we are. Breathing deeper in an allusion of expanse. Allowing moments to hang for a beat longer than the average. For today is a special day, and I of course am privy to it. Sitting on the vanity bench that did not originate in this room, or decade, I can see her eyes shine. There are not enough pages to share all that can be seen within. Excitement and the nervous energy that comes along with it play joyfully at the forefront. Those surrounding her know this look, yet have not seen it on this level before. There is also that which may go unnoticed by those who did not watch her grow and experience the life she has had thus far.

I was here when her arrival was anticipated. I feel the chorus of surprised laughter rumble throughout the other rooms with the news that a fifth child would be joining the family. I saw the changes to these floors, walls, and lives, as each new chapter of this girl was revealed. I watched over her when she could not sleep, rocked about, her tossing and turning causing the water underneath to become more animated with every frustrated wiggle. I see her roll to the edge of the dark-stained twin bed frame, grasp the edge and slowly lower herself to the awaiting carpet. Her small feet cradled by the lush olive-green shag carpet, she tiptoes to the door, careful to not run into the mirrored version of her bed two feet across from her. She knows not to turn on the overhanging lamp between the beds. For its light may be hidden by the large dome of pink fabric and tassels but it is still powerful and will most certainly wake her elder sister.

I smile as the walls slowly change to a blue the colour of a sunny day, then begin to be covered with band photos, movie posters and blue tacked pictures of smiling faces I've seen lounging on the wooden floor or the soft mattress that has replaced the waterbed. Colours explode everywhere: a hollowed-out TV holds a fishbowl with one chunky goldfish. An inflatable blue chair with large white daisies is brought in, sat on, then taken out, deflated, as the months pass. Laughter, secrets, and inside jokes are tossed out to every surface in this teenager's room, even spilling outside the window as she climbs through to sit on the roof. Either alone, or with confidants. To laugh, or to cry. Her voice carries; it has lost the softened edges but keeps the joyfulness.

There are late night remodels and sleepless nights. Red paint replaces blue, and once more, the layers of experiences begin to be covered. Faith is found, joy adorned, hurt experienced, and loss encountered: when she is struck with her role as peacekeeper, it leaves heavy welts upon her heart. I record the echoes of words spoken to her, for future listening: "You are too sensitive, you are too big, you are not enough, you are too much." She colours over the hurt, as she does my walls, with things that bring her joy. These memories are important, too. As I give her safety in this space I tuck them amongst the others. Even when the other rooms held tension or became unsafe, I was a refuge. A place where this young woman could store her thoughts, experiences and memories without being suffocated or lost in them. I created room for her community, courage, and boldness to grow, along with her perception of the spiritual. It's as if each breath lent her a glimpse into who she was created to be. Room is all this girl needs.

So now as she sits here, I see it all reflected in those eyes. The past, with all that it holds, the present, and the future. She is looking around taking it all in. Every part of who she is and will be. As she glides over my aging bones, I know she is grateful. Grateful to see me again and to relive even a few short moments of all that she has experienced with me. For I have held onto them all her life. And now I will hold one more for her: The one in which she is sitting in the dress she will be married in, surrounded by her nearest and dearest. Her mother slips on the blue garter that her closest aunt, whom she has recently lost, wore on her wedding day. She is dreaming of what her future may hold. Although her dancing eyes do not know it, she will say goodbye to me in a few years' time, unable to open my door and feel the safety of home. She will continue to think of me often, envisioning my colours, textures and memories that I have kept safe for her. When she thinks of home she will remember our kaleidoscope of humanity that was untethered amongst the space I offered, forever thankful. She will remember me–always–when she thinks of home.

This is MEGAN POLIQUIN's first publication! Poetry has been an effective and cathartic way to process and share her experience with chronic nerve pain. Megan currently resides in Maple Ridge, B.C., on the traditional and unceded territories of the Katzie and Kwantlen First Nations. She lives with her husband Brandon and Winston the dog, who are as silly as she is. Instagram: @MegPoliquin.

LEJLA PEKARIC

A Soul's Soliloquy

There was an earthly moment years ago when I lent my soul
to an older woman. Hers was preoccupied with the space
where ideas go to die. She thought it was some barren parking lot
and not this technicolour wasteland brimming with the sum
of disparate parts, of equations never computed nor made
into their embodied forms to be deliciously admired.

Until that day, I was enamoured with striking men who admired
me for my worldly achievements. One dared to look for my soul
in the most predictable places. He revealed this skeleton key made
of my bones, but I outran his fingers. I hopped and hid in spaces
anyone would suspect. Still, he couldn't detect any element of the sum
of my selves. He comforted himself knowing I did this a lot.

He lived happily ever after in his comfort. Of course, that's what his lot
worshiped. Comfort. Not harlots like me. My kind desired and admired
this slippery subsistence serenely sandwiched among a sensual sum of
enigmatic parts.
Comfort amuses the flesh but not much the soul
of the creature who sings in riddles and pens sestinas to nurture the space
where the abstract roams and connections among the disparate are made.

It turned out he wasn't wrong. I did do that a lot. With every step he made
I waltzed in exemplary opposition. He wasn't the first nor last of the lot
I twirled and spiralled with, until our bellies ached and the lustful space
between hopes and reality subdued. With preposterous irony, he admired
the inimitability of the tableaux we performed night after night as two sole souls,
a hunted and a hunter, delivering a spectacle for the ages and then some.

Ha! Ironically preposterous, that the prey might forfeit more than the sum
of its flesh and bones. Oh, how droll that this soul was nourished and made

for anything but gargantuan glory. And note that this particular shape of soul
is not to be frivolously endowed to just any bag of bones, particularly not the lot
who grip the world through achromatic tendrils, and have only truly admired
those whose essence floods exactly no more than negligible amounts of space.

Well, this harlot wasn't built for trifling but rather for gorging on the space
where ideas are caressed with a piercing tenderness. It regrettably took some
vigour to waltz and twirl convincingly, so as to be less feared than admired.
With enough repetitions, even the most loathsome dreads risk being made
a reality. Heartbreak and frustration, in their most ravaging, for this lot
are survivable. Less so, a lustrous veneer imprisoning a frustratingly broken soul.

As I grazed this woman, who admired the essence with which I shielded the space
for ideas to bloom, her soul twitched with a memory weighed down by her sum
of waltzes danced, of tableaux made. At first a mere bit, and soon, a whole
damn lot.

An Ordinary Failure

When I dreamt of failing, it was spectacular.

It was so impressive,
I could hardly wait.

The ruckus,
the hubbub,
the explosion
of shock and awe
at just how
awesomely
one can flop.
I would sit in math class
and doodle my misfires.
I used markers
and crayons to
shade in the details
so that it was
unmistakable
how marvellously
I floundered.

Seriously.

I didn't know then of these ordinary failures.
The kind no
one talks about.
No headlines.
No whispers.
No comfort held
in tales of exploits,
divulged valiantly.

Now I pencil in quiet details.

I dream
of failing eve
so subtly,
so invisibly,
so silently,
only the shadows stir.

Every now and then
my pen slips
outside of the lines.

And I wonder
if this time it will be
extraordinary.
If this time,
my failure just might be spectacular.

LEJLA PEKARIC writes poetry and short stories shaped by her enigmatic journey as a first-generation Bosniak-Canadian, businesswoman, mother, world explorer, artist, podcaster, and farmer. Living between Vancouver and Salt Spring Island, she draws from the richness of her layered identities and roles. Her work explores the shifting terrain of identity, ambition, soulfulness and belonging—marked by the nuanced ways stories connect disparate worlds. Lejla.ca.

STERLING

Doll Parts

I used to be
your favourite,
tiny fingers untangling
dark hair—fit in your fist,
painted lips. You would pinch
the back of Ken's head, press his face
into mine, satisfy those unspeakable urges.
Twelve and curious: what does it feel like to
be kissed? Now, I've passed through
many hands, felt their foreign
fingers fumbling my
figure.

Most did not play
as gently, smashing
their bodies into mine, a collision
of hard and soft—bruises peppered all
over pristine plastic before tossing me aside.
I have gotten used to this game, comfortable with wear
and tear, at least I know how to play. Unceremoniously
stuffed faced down in a drawer, limbs bent at odd angles,
he picks me up. Tenderly, he smooths my hair back, looks
at me like I am more than doll parts, presses a kiss to the
throat of my wrist and tells me I belong with him.
"We can play house," he says. Towering over
me, bent eyebrow of expectation.

The rules:
I am to shapeshift—
use my body as a vessel,
to house, feed and deprive myself
for a stranger. Then, I will be filled with golden
glue—kintsugi kink. The residue seeps inside and reacts,

effectively piecing me together and tearing me apart. I let
the creature live inside of me—shove the purple and blue
inanimate organs aside to make themselves at home.
How do I say no to the person who plucked me
from the drawer and showed me
something real?

It is the only game he asks me to participate in, the only one he cannot
play himself.

So, I sacrifice this body, though I have spent the last decade manufacturing it
and the alien arrives through the pulsing, pink portal with grabbing hands,
desperate to suck the sweetness from my perky pearls.

I was once your favourite.

Now I am hollow, I am husk—operating a foreign body with no warranty.
One third of a family, matriarch, stay-at-home, life-giver, former doll,
woman, wife—
do you want to play
mother?

The Reckoning

I

Every winter, we go searching for snow—
miners seeking those sweet spots where strings of diamonds
fall from the sky—withered branches gemmed
with frost. Each year, the veins are trickier

to tap. It used to be a sure thing—
not anymore. Different from when I was small,
growing up in the heart of the country, squeezed
into a snowsuit—rouged cheeks & runny nose, immune,
as kids are, to the cruelty

of cold. Now, the ground is bare. It is the time of year
when Canada is ugly—confined to a colour
scheme of grey & brown. It is the melt,
the shed before her formidable wings unfurl,
and we are left to reconcile the dead.

II

I think about this shift while being served yam soup
& homemade bread by cult members. Fifties cottagecore,
ambient clatter, flute & fiddle, yellow gingham curtains
frame a wood window. The skin of a cow patches an imperfection

on the sill. They are kind and were, perhaps, in the beginning,
well-intentioned. Yashua and his Twelve Tribes, their reputation and religion eroded
under the deluge of discourse, lustre and sheen lost to labour exploitation
and abuse allegations. It is stifling—both these heady thoughts, and the room.
If I close my eyes, I could be somewhere else, somewhen else.
A Coca-Cola truck rattles by, bottles babbling—
wet peelings of cars crescendo and the reverie evaporates. My gaze shoved

out the window to see factories where forests should be—solid
carpets
of concrete to replace the cushion of moss. I wonder what places
look like
absent of infrastructure—if we let nature cycle without
interruption, let it engage
in its restorative loop—for all that we take, with time, would it
reclaim?

III

The morels would sprout first, freckles on scorched earth.
Then, of course, the weeds. The ivy will wrap around
telephone poles,
smother buildings, animals will occupy our homes,
insects will burrow under the tattered remnants of a once
proud nation,
eagles will roost in rusted satellite dishes, elk will travel in
herds along open highways, bees would repopulate
building hives worthy
of their queens in the armpits of monuments, the quality of
the air
would improve, hard-worn steps of ancient sites would
finally rest,
the temperature of the ocean will revert,
the water will stop rising and, maybe,
we won't have to go searching for snow.

STERLING didn't set out to write poetry, but here we are—and frankly, it's been a fruitful excavation. These poems are part of a chapbook-in-progress that dives into gender, sexuality, body image, climate dread, female rage, and the cultural silence around women's bodies—plus a dash of love, because why not. These are the remnants discovered after digging around in the dusty corners of her mind.

ALYSSA SY DE JESUS

I Say Fujian in English

Fujian,
home province of my grandparents
has tones and sounds
unknown to me

Fujian
flashes in my mind in English letters
rattles from my
teeth, tongue, lips, lungs, and breath
in broken Chinese.

no matter how hard I try
the proper sound for Fujian never
seems to root.
my tones, always messed up
like an amateur melody stumbling,
clumsily on the bars.

when my ancestors crossed that ocean, facing Luzon
did my great-grandmotherland curse me?
did Fujian say:
"turn your back on me and your daughters
will never be able to say my name again"?
Ancestors lose things when they cross oceans
they drop things like accents to lighten their load
make it easier for their arrival.
If I dive backwards, deep enough
into that salty water, route between
Fujian and Luzon,
will I retrieve that lost sound?

twenty-five years since my last visit.
I look out from our hotel window:
A green Minnan mountain range,

like a dragon's body, enclaving the wires and cement of Xiamen
watches its city sleep.
it watches me, its great-granddaughter, dream of her ancestors
in English.

ALYSSA SY DE JESUS is a poet of Chinese heritage in search of the words and artifacts of her family's settlement in the Philippines and migration to Canada. She is based on the unceded territories of the Musqueam, Squamish and Tsleil-Waututh people. Previous publications: *Chinatown Stories* and *Living Hyphen*. Forthcoming: *Ginger & Smoke Magazine*. She was co-editor of *decomp journal*'s "Translate Me Not" issue.

Acknowledgements

We would like to thank our mentors, guest instructors, program facilitators, and apprentices for their guidance and support in the creation of these works.

Thanks to the TWS alumni who bolster this community of writers through their contributions to *emerge*, including our editors Laura Fukumoto, Janet Homeniuk, Dayna Mahannah, Leah Ranada, Emily Stringer, and KT Wagner. Thanks to Blaine Kyllo for teaching the students about the publication process. Thanks to Lynn Duncan and Kilmeny Jane Denny at Tidewater Press for believing in, and uplifting emerging writers, for making this book so beautiful, and for getting it into the hands of readers.

Thanks to Joanne Betzler and Grant Smith for their years of generous, unwavering support. Special thanks to Stephanie Shack. Thanks to Container Brewing, for providing the venue for our monthly reading series, and to Janet Homeniuk and Maggie Derrick for running it with such warmth. Thanks to our Lunch Poems organizing team: Renee Saklikar, Kim Gilker and Kiran Dhanoa, who each month bring together two brilliant poets, and get them talking in unexpected and insightful ways.

Thanks to those who came before, and who helped shape our program and this publication, including: Andrew Chesham, Laura Farina and Jonína Kirton; former managing editors of *emerge*, Leanne Dunic, Janet Fretter, Emily Stringer; and so many others. Thanks, as well, to former directors of the Writer's Studio, Betsy Warland and Wayde Compton. We see their work in large and small ways on every page of this publication.

Thanks to the *emerge 25* production team of Stevi Valentine, Jennifer Greenhorn, and Maya Miller, and the production editor, Janet Homeniuk.

Thanks for our copy editors: Gordon Cornwall, Alexis Jacklin, Amy Kelly, Justin Ancheta, Raluca Sanders, Stephanie Coelho, Anne Hamilton, Kelly Nice, Angela Rebrec, Sophia Kooy, Sally Rudolf, Sylvia Tran, and Christopher Mackie.

Thanks to all the friends and family who support the student's writing journeys, and to the writers we turn to for influence and inspiration.

If all writing is a conversation between ourselves, our influences and our readers, we're glad to be talking with all of you.